Praise for
JOANNE PENCE's
ANGIE AMALFI MYSTERIES

"Joanne Pence provides laughter, love, and cold chills."
Carolyn Hart

"If you love books by Diane Mott Davidson or Denise Dietz, you will love this series. It's as refreshing as lemon sherbert and just as delicious."
Under the Covers

"A rollicking good time . . . murder, mayhem, food, and fashion . . . Joanne Pence serves it all up."
Butler County Post

"A winner . . . Angie is a character unlike any other found in the genre."
Santa Rosa Press Democrat

"[A] great series . . . [Pence] titillates the senses, provides a satisfying read."
Crescent Blues Reviews

"Joanne Pence just gets better and better."
Mystery News

Angie Amalfi Mysteries by
Joanne Pence

RED HOT MURDER

AN ANGIE AMALFI MYSTERY

JOANNE PENCE

AVON BOOKS
An Imprint of HarperCollinsPublishers

This is a work of fiction. Names, characters, places, and incidents are products of the author's imagination or are used fictitiously and are not to be construed as real. Any resemblance to actual events, locales, organizations, or persons, living or dead, is entirely coincidental.

AVON BOOKS
An Imprint of HarperCollins*Publishers*
10 East 53rd Street
New York, New York 10022-5299

Copyright © 2006 by Joanne Pence
Excerpts copyright © 1993, 1994, 1995, 1996, 1998, 1998, 1999, 2000, 2002, 2003, 2003, 2004 by Joanne Pence
ISBN-13: 978-0-06-075805-9
ISBN-10: 0-06-075805-8
www.avonmystery.com

First Avon Books paperback printing: February 2006

Avon Trademark Reg. U.S. Pat. Off. and in Other Countries, Marca Registrada, Hecho en U.S.A.
HarperCollins® is a registered trademark of HarperCollins Publishers Inc.

Printed in the U.S.A.

10 9 8 7 6 5 4 3 2 1

To my mother, Rose, with admiration for her courage, optimism, and constant good spirits; to my beautiful and talented niece, Vittoria Barra, who is already (gasp!) Angie's age; and to David for all his help, love, and support, as always

RED HOT
MURDER

Chapter 1

On a bridge midway over the Colorado River, Angie Amalfi read the WELCOME TO ARIZONA sign. Her heart palpitated, her breathing quickened, and her feet tingled as a feeling of warmth, well-being, and certainty filled her. Above her head like a bubble in a cartoon strip, she was sure the words "Destination Wedding Locale" danced in red neon letters.

Not only was this going to be the perfect place for the perfect wedding, but that she'd found it on her very first try was nothing short of remarkable. Something told her Jackpot, Arizona, would be a memorable spot—from the moment her fiancé, San Francisco Homicide Inspector Paavo Smith, suddenly announced that he planned to spend a week there.

Before then, she'd never even heard of Jackpot, so when Paavo mentioned that he had spent time there as a boy, she was stunned. Paavo was close-mouthed, true, but to have kept an entire chunk of his childhood from her was maddening. She was doing all she could to get him to open up, and usu-

1

ally she thought she'd succeeded. But every so often he threw her a curve that left her gasping.

This was one of those times.

While he claimed to be a "private person," she
was someone who believed that it was necessary
for people to share their feelings. As a matter of
fact, she'd speak her thoughts to anyone who'd
listen, always interested to hear the response. If
not, what was the difference between being with a
real live person and being with a statue in a dark,
stuffy museum?

That was why, as soon as she learned about Jackpot, wild horses couldn't keep her from joining
Paavo to see it for herself. And the more she
learned about the area, she realized wild horses—
bucking broncos, mustangs, stallions—and plenty
of other large, intimidating four-legged beasts
might well be in her future.

No matter. The trip was a way to learn more
about her taciturn fiancé. And if she just happened
to find an interesting and unique wedding locale
at the same time . . . well, who ever said killing
two birds with one stone was a bad thing?

Just getting there had been an adventure. They'd
flown from SFO to Palm Springs, California, and
rented a car. Paavo had wanted a four-wheel-drive
truck, she wanted a Beemer. When they found a
four-wheel-drive Mercedes SUV, they'd compro-
mised. The drive to Jackpot took over three hours.

Angie had to admit, though, to being impressed. The sky was a brilliant turquoise and the
desert stretched out like a butternut sea of rolling
sand and gravel, dotted with saguaro, barrel cac-

tus, sage, and scrub. Precariously balanced red and granite rock piles, high crags, and jagged ridges of low-lying hills touched the horizon.

She'd never been deep into the desert before and found the land harsh in its emptiness, yet it held a quiet, naked beauty that intrigued and mystified her.

Turning off the interstate, they'd edged the river, driving along a two-lane road until a small, dusty town appeared in the flatness.

"There it is," Paavo said, and Angie felt anticipation bubble up inside.

Paavo had explained that Jackpot, Arizona, a town of 912 permanent residents, quadrupled in size in winter when the "snow birds" arrived to get away from harsh northern climates. Each spring they'd leave, complaining that the land was too hot and dry and spindly, and Jackpot would once again become as lonely as the desert surrounding it.

Now that the warm days of spring were rapidly hurtling toward a fiery summer, the town should be quiet.

She knew that going back to a place he'd spent time in as a child was bringing back lots of memories to Paavo. Some happy, others not.

She reached over and grasped his arm, giving him a smile of support. He lightly patted her hand, glancing at her briefly before his eyes returned to the road, letting her know he appreciated her understanding.

When Paavo was very young, his father had died, and for reasons he'd only recently came to

understand, his mother had abandoned him. A
Finnish friend of his parents, Aulis Kokkonen,
raised him.

Years ago Aulis became good friends with a Dr.
Loomis Griggs who was in San Francisco studying at the University of California Medical Center. Now Doc Griggs lived just outside Jackpot,
where, prior to his retirement, he'd been the
town's doctor as well as the doctor at the nearby
Colorado River Indian Reservation. When Paavo
was young, Doc invited Aulis and Paavo to spend
time with him on his ranch. Paavo had gone there
three times, at ages seven, nine, and twelve. They
were three of his most memorable summers. After that, being a teenager in a big city, he thought
himself much too "cool" to go on a vacation to a
small town and ranch with his guardian. And, as
Aulis grew older and Doc busier, their visits also
stopped.

Still, the two men kept in touch. Last week,
Aulis received a phone call from him. Doc said
some troubling things had happened in the town
surrounding the death of a former patient, a man
in his seventies, named Hal Edwards. But Doc
wasn't one to fret unnecessarily.

Still, Aulis had sensed some real worry beneath
Doc's jovial and garrulous manner. Sensing Aulis's
concern after speaking with him, Paavo phoned
Dr. Griggs. Just hearing the familiar gravelly voice
brought back many fond memories. Doc tried to
blow off Paavo's and Aulis's concerns, declaring
he was just a foolish retiree with too much time on
his hands. But he protested too much, and the

more Doc said nothing was wrong, the more Paavo sensed just the opposite.

He also realized how much he'd loved that old man as a boy, and how much he'd missed seeing him. It was time to remedy that. Paavo's workdays were spent investigating suspicious deaths. He'd make sure nothing was amiss or if something was, that the perpetrator got caught. He could surely spend a week's vacation doing the same thing for a dear old friend.

He told Angie all this, and they decided to go to Jackpot as tourists, to nose around and ask questions. Most likely, a simple explanation would be found for whatever was troubling Doc.

Angie knew this trip was important to Paavo for a variety of reasons, and was glad he'd asked her to be a part of it.

As she prepared for her week in Jackpot, the realization that it might make a perfect "destination wedding locale" was simply an added bonus.

Merritt's Café was an established institution in Jackpot. LaVerne Merritt had run the coffee shop for twenty-four years. "Chief cook and bottle washer," she called herself. Although she employed a cook, she did much of the "special" cooking—sauces, gravies, roasts, stews and the like—and nearly all the baking. But most of all, she enjoyed being with her customers. She knew everyone in town and every bit of gossip about each of them. Heaven forbid she miss out on a good story because she was standing over a hot stove.

With the shop being dead center in the middle of Main Street—all five blocks of it—while working the counter and waiting tables, she had a perfect view of everyone's comings and goings. Or, at least, those few who came or went anywhere during this time of year. Tourist season was over. For the most part, the only ones who came to town now were either lost or illegals who had snuck across the border, and there weren't that many these days.

LaVerne was pouring coffee when she spotted a strange-looking vehicle approaching. She would have poured the cup to overflowing if Junior Whitney hadn't cried out.

Pot in hand, she stepped closer to an apple-and-grape café-curtained window. Her small, sharp face was scrunched into a scowl, her mouth forming an upside-down *U* as she adjusted thick bifocals. One eyelid drooped lazily. Her short dyed blond hair was faded and showed too much gray, and was so brittle it stood on end like miniature lightning bolts.

For the car not to be a pickup was odd enough, but that it wasn't even an American sedan or a "normal" SUV like a Jeep Cherokee or Ford Explorer, made it stick out like a hammered thumb. The glare from the bright desert sun bounced off the dust-covered windshield and prevented her from making out who was inside. The car slowed nearly to a stop, and she leaned so close to the window that her nose flattened against it as the scowl on her lined face deepened.

The thought struck that it might have been some out-of-state reporter, or maybe some officious

alphabet-soup-named law enforcement officer—
the FBI, Arizona State Police, or possibly someone
who came all the way from Phoenix. As word of
Hal Edwards's death got out, she'd been expecting more of them to come snooping around—
either conducting an investigation, or at least
fishing for a lurid story. They wouldn't have to
fish too deeply in these waters.

The silver car parked vertically in front of the
diner and she was able to clearly see the hood or-
nament. She gawked. It was a Mercedes. A Mercedes SUV here in Jackpot, Arizona? It had to be
some lost Californians, she thought, shaking her
head dismissively. Still, she watched.

A tall, trim, and fit man got out from the driver's
side. He was very good-looking, LaVerne noted,
with dark brown hair and aviator-style sunglasses. He wore jeans and a green plaid shirt, and
was probably in his mid-thirties or so.

He walked around to the passenger door and
opened it. The door blocked most of LaVerne's
view.

High-heeled yellow sandals, with only a thin
strap holding them on the toes, touched the street.
The driver held out his hand.

LaVerne's eyebrows twitched as a slim, petite
woman got out of the car and stood by the man.
She wore a yellow-and-white dress, and wrap-
around lavender-tinted sunglasses. Her thick,
wavy hair was brown with gold highlights, chin-
length and worn loosely swept back like some
Hollywood starlet.

LaVerne grimaced as she watched the too-
stylish-for-words woman run her fingers through

shiny hair, then smooth her outfit while teetering on those ridiculous high-heeled shoes.

The two looked up and down the street, then began to approach the café. As the woman stepped onto the wooden sidewalk, however, her skinny heel wedged between the slats.

LaVerne chuckled to herself. Definitely a lost Californian. They'd be on their way soon. Nothing for them in this town, that was for sure.

She scurried behind the counter, leaving an imprint of the tip of her nose on the window.

Angie balanced against Paavo's arm as she pulled her Prada mule heel free. She didn't know any real towns still had boards for sidewalks, but thought they were only used in ghost towns refurbished as tourist traps.

"This is all so authentic!" she cried, wriggling her toes back in place.

"It's the real thing," Paavo agreed.

"It reminds me of Disney's Frontierland when I was a kid."

He did a double take, but didn't say a word.

The late afternoon sun was muted and cast Jackpot in a golden glow. Along the highway were various automotive, gun, hardware, and feedstores. On one end of Main Street stood a gas station and a Circle K; on the other, a Halmart Store. Angie reread the sign. It was an *H*, not a *W*. A couple of weary-looking motels flashed neon vacancy signs. Behind the stores stretched dusty streets lined with small homes.

The two walked into what appeared to be the only coffee shop in town, a small place with booths, wooden tables, and chairs, plus a long white counter. One scruffy, long-haired man sat at the counter, while two who were dressed for fishing were at a far table.

"Sit where you please," the middle-aged woman behind the counter called while grabbing mugs, menus, and a coffeepot.

As the woman poured, she glanced dismissively at Angie, but studied Paavo. "You FBI?" she asked suddenly.

He looked surprised. "No."

"You look FBI." She wrinkled her mouth. "More than some." Through the bifocals, magnified eyes darted toward the two fishermen. "Can't fool me. I know these things."

With a sniff in Angie's direction, she walked away.

"That was weird," Angie murmured, then added, "I take it Ned's not here."

"Not yet," Paavo replied.

Ned Paulson and Paavo used to play together as kids. His mother had been Doc Griggs's secretary. Ned was a little younger than Paavo, a nice kid who knew the desert well. Paavo had called Ned and told him he was coming. Ned had sounded both surprised and vaguely troubled, but added that he understood Doc's concerns. He wanted to talk to Paavo in person about it and suggested that they meet at Merritt's the afternoon Paavo arrived.

The conversation had only added to Paavo's conviction that there was good reason for Doc's uneasiness.

Now they waited.

When Angie had first heard that Ned ran a boat

rental on a marina in the middle of the desert, she'd thought it was a joke. It wasn't. As they rode along the Colorado River, she'd seen the lake. It had been formed by a dam, one of many that reduced the once rushing river to no more than a trickle.

The lake was the main draw for the area—stocked with fish, and ringed with inexpensive cabin and trailer rentals.

"This area hasn't changed much at all since I last visited nearly twenty-five years ago," Paavo said.

"If Ned has a customer, I can understand his being late." Angie looked out the window. "The town seems too small to get many visitors at all." A gas station and the small convenience store attached to it seemed to be the liveliest places in town.

There was one stoplight.

"Sorry you came?" he asked, studying her, and reaching for her hand across the table.

She smiled. "Of course not. We have a week together, just you and me." She ran her thumb over his strong knuckles. "To do nothing but enjoy being together, with neither your work nor any of my relatives here to get in our way. For a while I was feeling we were being pulled in so many different directions that you and I were forgetting why we want to marry each other. Or that you'd say the whole thing was a huge, horrible mistake."

His blue eyes studied her. "Not me, Angie. Never think that."

Her heart filled. Yes, she needed this time alone with him.

And to find her destination wedding location.

Despite her mother's wishes.

Her mother, Serefina, expected her to get married at St. Peter and Paul's Church in San Francisco's North Beach. Angie's parents, Serefina and Salvatore, as well as her four older sisters, had all been married there. How boring was that?

Earlier, Angie had agreed to let her mother handle her engagement party so that she could plan her own wedding, without any interference. But the agreement was already becoming shaky. She had to admit, though, the engagement party was a great success. It was beautifully elaborate, and San Francisco society talked about it for two weeks afterward, which was a long time in that city. Serefina had kept the location a secret from Angie until the last moment. When Angie and Paavo walked in—they were both an unsightly mess, but that's another story—Angie had burst into tears of joy at the sight of so many friends and relatives gathered together, and at how beautifully the Maritime Museum had been transformed into a setting reminiscent of the elegance of the gold barons and seafarers of San Francisco a century and a half ago.

Just the thought of the party, now, made her sigh with wonder at how lovely it had been. She and Paavo had danced the night away. . . .

The problem, of course, with having had such a unique and successful engagement party was that the wedding was going to have to top it.

She hadn't mentioned this little fact to Paavo.

But because of that, she was in full wedding-location-search mode.

And Jackpot, Arizona, was about as unique a wedding spot as she could imagine.

"You ready to order?" The annoying waitress stood over them, pad and paper in hand.

Angie pulled her thoughts away from weddings to glance at the basic American menu. She ordered a turkey-and-Swiss wrap. Paavo asked for a chiliburger.

The food came quickly, and they devoured it with equal speed. A few customers came and went, but none were Ned Paulson.

Paavo called Ned's business number, which went to messaging, as did Ned's cell phone.

"How about some dessert?" the waitress asked. Angie noticed a slight frown and could feel her scrutinizing her clothes and hair. Considering the waitress's bad peroxide job, she should have been asking for some pointers instead.

"No thanks," she said, returning the perusal. "We'll be leaving soon."

"Passing through, are you?" The woman's gaze narrowed as it leaped from one to the other.

"We're staying at the Ghost Hollow Guest Ranch," Angie replied.

"Is that so?" The waitress's brows lifted, but she quickly composed her face. "It's a nice place. Not too many guests out there lately, of course. . . ."

"Oh?" Angie said, waiting.

"My name's LaVerne Merritt, by the way," the waitress said. "I've owned this café so long that I can remember back when the Ghost Hollow Guest Ranch was Hal Edwards's home."

Angie glanced at Paavo and couldn't help but smile—Hal Edwards's death had been the reason for Doc's concern. Paavo had often told her that in his investigations, the best way to learn anything was to let others do the explaining. "His home?" she asked.

"I thought everybody knew that." LaVerne's mouth shifted sideways and pursed as she considered her customer's woeful lack of knowledge. "Hal Edwards was once the richest man in the whole state. Owned all the supermarkets from Yuma to Flagstaff. Halmart stores were the Wal-Mart of Arizona—and every bit as profitable. In fact, Hal always said Wal-Mart got their name from Halmart. His home was beautiful. Everybody in town still calls it the hacienda. You'll know why when you see it. Things have changed a bit since those days." She frowned. "And now it's all going to go to his son, Joey."

"The resort was a hacienda?" Angie asked, feeling her excitement growing about seeing the home of a man who'd once been the Sam Walton of Arizona. No wonder Doc thought there could have been something odd about his death. Excessive money and mysterious death—how often had she seen that combination since she began dating Paavo?

"You didn't know about that either?" LaVerne sounded surprised. "Just why did you come here?"

Paavo jumped in. "We're here to fish at the lake. Our contact at the boat and equipment rental suggested we stay at Ghost Hollow. He planned to meet us here, but apparently, he isn't going to make it."

"Sounds like Ned Paulson," LaVerne said. "If

you want, I can phone and see what's keeping him."

"No need," Paavo said. "I've used my cell phone. He's not answering."

"Oh. A cell phone." LaVerne's lips pressed together. "Those cell phones don't always work around here, you know. And, sometimes, folks might be somewhere besides home or work. I'm usually pretty good at tracking people down. Just trying to be helpful. How about some pie while you wait? We've got berry, rhubarb, and peach. Homemade and fresh."

Both declined. "We'll just finish our coffee," Angie said.

LaVerne shifted from one foot to the other. Her one eyelid sagged halfway over her eye as she said, "Suit yourself," then headed back to the counter.

They were about to leave when a woman entered. She stood in the doorway. Her eyes quickly scanned the customers and paused ever so slightly at the man at the counter. Then she spotted Angie and Paavo, and hurried over.

She appeared to be in her early thirties, with shoulder-length black hair, olive skin, and startlingly green almond-shaped eyes. Her dress was an umber and turquoise print, and the colorful Southwestern pattern seemed strangely at odds with her troubled demeanor.

"Are you Paavo?" she asked when she reached them, nervously tucking a lock of hair behind her ear.

He stood. "I am."

As they shook hands she said, "Ned told me all about you."

Uh-oh, Angie thought. Paavo being a homicide inspector was something he'd hoped to keep under wraps. How many others had Ned told?

She glanced toward LaVerne who was watching the encounter with blatant interest. Had the waitress no shame? No job to do? At the same time, the skinny, long-haired fellow abruptly got up from the counter and left the restaurant, his hand raised in a way that shielded his face. The gesture struck Angie as strange.

The newcomer extended a hand to Angie. "You must be Paavo's fiancée. I'm Teresa Flores."

Paavo invited her to sit, and she hunched down in the seat as if trying to hide.

Angie introduced herself, but had barely finished when Teresa asked Paavo, "Has Ned been here yet?"

"No," Paavo said. "I was going to ask you if you knew where he was. I've phoned, but there was no answer."

"I see." She rubbed her arms as if chilled. "I thought—"

"What is it?" Paavo asked.

Her eyes darted, constantly surveying the café, the street, and she clasped her hands before explaining. "We had a—a little misunderstanding. Today he's not answering my calls. I thought that if I could see him in person . . ." Her smile was tense. "It was just an idea. I should leave."

"You'll work things out," Angie said, sympathetic and remembering how dreadful she felt whenever she and Paavo fought. "Should we tell Ned you were looking for him?"

Teresa's eyes met hers, and understanding passed between the two women. "It wouldn't hurt." Her gaze fell to Angie's hand. "That's a beautiful engagement ring. It's different."

"Thank you," Angie said, holding out her hand so Teresa could better inspect the expensive pale blue Siberian diamond.

Teresa's voice turned wistful. "When is the wedding?"

That was one of the questions that gave Angie her wedding-plan blues. Until she decided where she wanted the reception to be held, she couldn't find out what dates the place would be available. And until she found out what dates it was available, she couldn't contact her church to reserve a time for the wedding, and until she did that . . .

Bottom line, she had no idea when her wedding would be held.

"The date isn't quite settled yet," she said in a strained voice.

Paavo seemed to sink lower in his chair.

"You'll work it out. You're very lucky. Both of you." She stood. "Ned is looking forward to your visit. I'm surprised he isn't here yet." A worried frown crossed her face. "I'm sure nothing's wrong. I've got to run."

Angie stilled at the sound of something odd in the woman's voice. Her whole visit struck Angie as peculiar.

"Are you sure you can't stay and wait?" Paavo asked.

"No. I'm sorry. I've got to get back to work—

Maritza's. It's a Mexican restaurant. My mother and grandmother own it." She gave a wan smile, then those exotic green eyes rested on Angie's diamond ring once more before she hurried out the door.

Chapter 2

About four miles from town, Paavo turned onto a rutted macadam road. Angling toward the northwest, the landscape slowly rose. As they neared the Colorado River, the terrain grew less arid and sandy. Although far from lush, it had scrub, cacti, a mixture of rugged grasses and weeds, and even a few cottonwood trees and tamarisk. In the distance, mountains loomed with a dark, stern air of indifferent permanence.

"This land is quite different from what we came through to get to Jackpot," Angie remarked.

"The greenery you see is because of a creek that runs through this area." Paavo pointed to the left. "It's out that way."

"You remember a lot, don't you," Angie said.

"I'm surprised at how much," he murmured. A crack of vulnerability, of the child he once was, came through as he said, "I guess I enjoyed it here more than I thought."

Even as she smiled at his words, he seemed to push away the memories, and the serious inspector

18

returned. His hands gripped the steering wheel tight as the car bounced and rocked. They made a steep ascent. At the crest, they saw spread out below them an unexpected valley. Dotting it, much like toy houses from a train set, stood one large home circled by cottages and other small buildings. They were looking at what was once Hal Edwards's personal estate, his "hacienda," as LaVerne Merritt had called it. Once they began their descent, the buildings disappeared from view.

Nearing an open gate in a barbed wire fence, Paavo slowed. As they crossed over the gate's cattle guard, the car vibrated and clamored with a loud metallic rattle. On the fence, a weathered sign announced, GHOST HOLLOW GUEST RANCH.

Determination filled Paavo's face. "Relax," Angie said. "They way you look right now, no one will talk with you. Even the coffee shop owner asked if you were with the FBI. Remember, you're a tourist, not a cop."

"Right." His expression didn't ease one iota.

The SUV stopped in front of a small building with a trailer behind it. The adobe brick-and-wood-trimmed building had a small sign that read RANCH OFFICE.

Angie stepped from the car. The sun beat down and there was no breeze. Still, as she looked around, the size and elegance of what Hal Edwards had built surprised her.

"It's beautiful," she said. "I never would have imagined such a place way out here. The Spanish architecture, the wood and adobe, is gorgeous—and the plaza looks like one in a small Mexican town."

A fountain made of reddish clay with a tall center spire stood spewing water in the middle of the plaza, and beyond it was the sprawling white adobe home, two-stories tall with wooden balconies on the second floor and a red-tile roof. The hacienda, she thought.

Beside it was a newer one-story building with similar architecture.

"It's like something out of a travel brochure." Angie headed toward the fountain. Listening to the water splash, just looking at it, felt cool and refreshing in the hot sun.

"Hal Edwards was a man of good taste," Paavo said as he examined the area.

"Definitely." She turned back toward the office. She blinked once, then again, but the image before her didn't change.

Three of the biggest, ugliest birds she'd ever seen had stepped out from behind the trailer. They stopped and gawked, as if as surprised to see her as she was to see them.

She'd seen pictures of such birds before, and maybe one or two in a zoo, but never out in the open. They must have stood seven feet tall, and Angie was only five-two. She pointed and when she found her voice cried, "Ostriches!"

At her cry, Paavo turned. His jaw dropped. So this, at least, was different from the way he remembered it.

"I was expecting cows and horses," she said. "Not gigantic birds."

Just then, a grizzled man of medium height sprang from the trailer. "Goddamn!" He waved his arms, swatting the air in the direction of the birds. "Get your mangy, ugly, smelly, soon-to-be-cowboy-boots hides out of my sight!"

The beasts took several long-legged loping steps away from him but remained near.

Ignoring them, the man approached Angie and Paavo. "Welcome to Ghost Hollow Guest Ranch." He was thin and wiry, his gray hair long and uncombed, and his pockmarked face unshaven and bristled. Red, watery eyes observed them. "The name's Lionel Edwards. I'm the manager here."

Angie and Paavo shook his hand and gave their names. Angie found the sour reek of whiskey on his breath overwhelming.

One ostrich left the others and walked toward them. Its skin was blue, its feathers gray and brown, and its eyes were enormous shiny black balls. On the top of its head, a small tuft of feathers bent forward rather than back, almost like a cowlick. It stopped behind Lionel and peered over his shoulder first at Angie, a long while at Paavo, then at Angie again. She didn't like the way the bird looked at her. Its eyes seemed to narrow and its long black lashes slowly blinked a couple of times.

"Nice birdie," she said, her voice shaky. *Are ostriches friendly?*

Lionel's head whipped back and he jumped away from it. "Dang useless beasts! Watch out that it doesn't peck at your earrings, ma'am. They like bright objects." Quickly, Angie covered her ears, but then she noticed the creature's black eyes zero in on her engagement ring.

Lionel shooed the bird away with his hat.

"Why do you have three ostriches?" Angie asked Lionel when he faced her again.

"Three? We got over a hunnert. All females, too. And if you can figure out why, please let me know."

She waited, confused, but he didn't elaborate.

Lionel then pointed across the plaza. "Anyways, that two-story house is where my Uncle Hal used to live. The new building is for guests. It's got a dining room and a common room with a pool table and a bar. We'll have a happy hour there at five, dinner after that. Behind it, you'll find stables, a cookhouse, workers' cabin, and maintenance building." His rubbery, stubbled face contorted into a grimace as he warned, "Those are off-limits to you."

Angie and Paavo nodded.

Lionel waved his arm toward the area behind them. "Those are the guest bungalows." Ten cottages in a semi-circle faced the plaza. They looked well kept up, roomy, and charming. "I'll take you to yours now."

As they walked, Paavo asked, "Are we the only guests here?"

"For now. The winter folks have gone, and I like taking a break after putting up with them. Then, I didn't do no more booking after Uncle Hal showed up dead. His ex-wife, Clarissa—Hell-on-Wheels, I call her—and his son, Joey, are here. You and your lady are the only paying customers in a while—as a special favor to Ned Paulson, you know."

"Hal showed up dead?" Paavo repeated.

"Oh, yeah. Guess as newcomers you don't know. Couple weeks ago, some Injun found Uncle

Hal's body in a cave out in the desert. Rich old guy like that, too. Just never know, do you?"

"How did he die?" Paavo asked innocently, although Angie knew he'd heard one version already from Doc.

Lionel shrugged. "Who knows? By the time he was found, the animals had gotten to him. I think the coroner decided he must have had a heart attack or stroke. Hell, the guy had been in bad health for years."

"How long was he missing?" Paavo asked.

"About three months," Lionel answered.

"Three months? Didn't you do a search?"

"Hell, no. Why should we? Everybody just figured he'd taken off again like he'd done in the past. Before that, he'd been gone for five years. Took a couple years before we knew for certain he was alive back then. Lived like a hermit down in Mexico best anyone can tell. Then he came back here, went out to the caves, and died."

Angie and Paavo glanced at each other. "I see," Paavo said. This was exactly the kind of information they were hoping to get from people in the area.

Lionel unlocked the bungalow door and gave Paavo two keys. The cabin had a comfortable living room with Mexican-style décor and furnishings, a bedroom, bath, and a fully equipped kitchen.

"This is lovely," Angie said, then faced Lionel with her eyes bright. "Everything is. And hearing about Hal Edwards is fascinating!"

"Yeah, guess so." He offered to help Paavo

carry in their luggage. Paavo headed out to the car, Lionel following, but just before he stepped from the bungalow, he turned back to Angie. "Glad to hear, ma'am, that you don't mind staying at the ranch of a man whose body weren't found till it weren't nothing but a skeleton. That's kind of rare in a woman." He hesitated. "That, along with the other stories about this area."

Angie glanced toward the door, but Paavo was already down the walk near the SUV. "What other stories?"

Rheumy eyes met hers. "This place is called Ghost Hollow, you know."

A chill rippled along her spine. "And I'll bet you're going to tell me why."

"It's because of the stagecoach." Lionel folded skinny arms as he watched her, then continued without prompting. "Years back, a stagecoach and its passengers all disappeared. The coach was carrying a shitload—I mean—a lot of money. Cash. Local folks said their ghosts could be seen out here at night, near the caves, still searching for the lost stage and their money."

"I see." A slight quiver sounded in her voice. Not that she believed in ghosts, of course.

"Uncle Hal was found not too far from where the stagecoach was last seen. Glad to hear none of that will bother you." He stepped outside the bungalow with a tip of his hat. "I'd better go help your man with the bags. Looks like he's got a lot of them there."

"What was Lionel saying to you?" Paavo asked once they were alone and he'd finished carrying his one suitcase and her three matching Louis Vuitton pieces, plus her makeup case and a hat-box, into the bedroom. As Angie explained to him before they left San Francisco, being at a desert re-sort for a week—nine days counting both weekends—she had no idea how people dressed. She had to be ready for anything.

"He was trying to scare me into leaving." Angie quickly relayed Lionel's words as she poured them glasses of ice water. "He's achieved quite the opposite."

"That's not good. We'd better be even more cau-tious than I'd imagined," Paavo said.

"I know." She didn't want to think about Li-onel's words or poor old dead Hal Edwards.

She went into the bedroom and took the box of See's chocolates from her carry-on. Life was easier with good chocolate. Between the scruffy hard-drinking manager, seven-foot-tall birds who wanted to eat her engagement ring, and talk of skeletons, ghosts, and dead stagecoach passen-gers, she was thinking she probably should have brought a two-pound box.

"The good news is that you've already had two people mention Hal Edwards to you," she said as she searched for a chocolate cream. "This town is an open book. It's going to be easy to find out what happened to him. Trust me on that."

As she lifted the chocolate morsel toward her mouth, she glanced up to see Paavo leaning against the doorframe, his sky blue eyes taking her in. The realization filled her that they were hundreds of miles from friends, relatives, co-workers and everyone else who could bother them; that she was here, alone, with the man she loved. She lowered her hand.

Their gazes met, and she began to slowly walk his way.

Forget chocolate.

Chapter 3

After testing the bed's comfort—an important thing to check out in a new hotel or motel room, or even in a cabin in the middle of the desert—then showering and changing from the wrinkled linen dress to a Marc Jacobs scoop-neck top and flared striped pants with gold high-heeled Via Spiga slides, Angie was ready to face the guest ranch's happy hour.

She and Paavo were crossing the plaza hand-in-hand when she spotted several more ostriches pecking at the rocky ground. The wind was blowing and a gamey bird smell wafted her way. Angie's nose wrinkled. She wondered why there weren't any males among them.

One of the birds—the one with the cowlick—lifted her head and stared in their direction. The ostrich waddled closer, and Angie swore that the bird's whole expression seemed to soften and her eyes turn all moony as she gazed at Paavo.

He never even noticed.

Angie kept looking over her shoulder at the

bizarre beast as she and Paavo continued toward the common room.

The room was huge with a kiva-style fireplace dominating a corner. To the left, a full-size billiards table stood before a wall filled with bookshelves, and to the right was an area with overstuffed chairs and sofas. In the corner opposite the fireplace was a modest bar. Double doors led to the dining room.

A freshly shaved and clean-shirted Lionel stood behind the bar; otherwise, the room was empty.

"Greetings!" he called, waving his half-filled glass. "Join me. It's said I pour with a heavy, generous hand."

"Do you have any white wine?" Angie asked as she reached the bar.

"I do now that Hell-on-Wheels is here," Lionel grumbled.

Ah, yes, she thought. The ex-wife.

Before she could respond, she heard voices at the door. Lionel's expression filled with disgust.

Entering were an older woman and a man who bore a slight resemblance to her. Angie watched them with interest.

The woman didn't merely walk, she swept across the room. She was probably in her seventies, yet still striking. Tall and thin, she wore simple but elegant beige linen slacks and a billowing silk top adorned with enormous pieces of turquoise and silver jewelry. What demanded attention, however, was her angular but perfectly proportioned face. Swept-back, stiffly lacquered pale blond hair emphasized a full and determined mouth, a long and slightly sharp nose, and most of all, cold but incisive sapphire eyes.

That's trouble, thought Angie before turning her gaze toward the man as he reached the bar and sat.

He was also tall and thin, but where the woman stood straight and commanding, he was stoop-shouldered. He wore a white long-sleeved shirt and brown slacks. To Angie's surprise, he also wore fancy, albeit scuffed, cowboy boots with intricately tooled patterns and silver tips protecting the leather on the toes and one heel. The second heel tip was missing.

Unlike the woman, his chin was lowered rather than proudly raised, his mouth a sullen mass, his brown hair could have used a washing, and his eyes betrayed a life of resentment. He was probably no older than Paavo, but he carried himself like a beaten down old man.

"Who are these people, Lionel?" the woman, still standing, asked in a voice that said no answer would be satisfactory.

Angie stepped toward her. "We're guests. I'm Angelina Amalfi and with me is my fiancé, Paavo Smith."

"Oh, yes, the guests Ned Paulson imposed on us." She sniffed.

"He said this was a nice place to stay," Paavo countered. "Was he wrong?"

Instead of answering, the woman gave Lionel an icy stare.

"This here's Clarissa Edwards," Lionel said by way of introduction as Clarissa condescended to shake Angie's and then Paavo's hands. "And that's Joey, Hal's son."

"His name is Joseph," Clarissa reminded Lionel.

Hell-on-Wheels herself, Angie thought, suddenly sympathizing with Lionel's characterization. She reached over to shake Joey's soft, moist hand.

"The family came here to wait for the will to be read," Lionel continued unfazed. His smirk only broadened when Clarissa cast him a withering glare.

"That's hardly of interest to outsiders, Lionel," she said through gritted teeth, then turned toward Angie and Paavo with a stiff smile. "This is the week for the ranch's annual cookout, an event that the entire town looks forward to. We're here to assure that, despite Joseph's father's unfortunate demise, this year's event will be bigger and better than ever. Isn't that right, Joseph?"

Angie's ears had perked up at the word *cookout* and she was eager to hear more. "Joseph," however, was too busy looking at the liquor bottles to pay any attention. "Uh-huh," he murmured after too much time had passed.

Clarissa's lips tightened. "Pour some wine, Lionel. The Domaines Schlumberger Gewürztraminer."

Lionel muttered as he put a glass on the bar. Clarissa immediately lifted and inspected it as if expecting dirt, lipstick stains, or at least water spots.

His jaw gyrated as he found the white wine, opened the bottle and poured a little. Clarissa tasted, nodded, and he filled her glass. "You may serve Joseph and our guests also," she said.

Joey was handed a glass of wine. He drained it in a single gulp.

As Angie sipped hers, she thought that while Clarissa seemed to be a terror, she knew wine.

Clarissa glared at Joey when he asked that a bottle of pinot noir be opened.

"This is very good," Angie said.

Clarissa eyed her. "It should be. It's more expensive than Gallo, to put it mildly."

It was one thing for Hell-on-Wheels to look down her nose at her son and Lionel, but Angie wasn't about to put up with it. "It isn't often one finds a dry, crisp Gewürztraminer," she began, then swirled and sniffed the glass. "It's got a wonderfully spicy bouquet as well. Too often, they're sweet and flabby. This is even better than a late-harvest Riesling, which are often overly praised, in my opinion. Do you agree?" She quickly glanced at Paavo, who seemed much amused by her little speech.

Clarissa arched her thin eyebrows. "How amazing to find someone in this area who knows wines."

"I've learned from some of the world's best sommeliers," Angie replied.

"Hmm, interesting. I've learned from my own palate."

Angie's jaw tightened. "You were talking about the annual cookout. When will it be held?"

"On Saturday. Will you be staying?"

Paavo answered. "Yes, we plan to spend the week and leave Sunday night."

"What's the cookout like?" Angie asked, trying to hold in the excitement she was feeling. Paavo

wanted to learn about Hal Edwards's death—
what better way than for her to somehow insinu-
ate herself in with the kitchen staff? "Have you
always been involved in it?"

"In fact, I've done my best to avoid it." Clarissa
lightly patted her hair. "Hal ran it after the snow
birds all went back to wherever they came from as
a thank-you to the town and its people for another
profitable winter. When he left the ranch for a few
years, Lionel somehow managed to keep it going,
to everyone's amazement. This year, Joseph will
preside as host."

Joey, looking pained, gulped the pinot noir.

"It sounds like a wonderful tradition," Angie
said.

"If you like beer, beans, and barbecue." Clarissa
shuddered. "I've asked several people from town
to come over and help, including the women from
the Mexican restaurant, but I'm not counting on
much."

"I see." She couldn't have asked for more. Now
was the time. Angie glanced at Paavo, a question
in her eyes. He caught her meaning and nodded.
She cleared her throat. "Well, if you're interested
in some other food, I wouldn't mind helping out."

Clarissa looked appalled. "Whatever are you
talking about?"

"I studied at the Cordon Bleu in Paris," Angie
said. "I've been a restaurant critic in San Francisco, and I've worked on television and radio. I
know good food."

Clarissa's eyes narrowed. "You're serious?"

"Of course. I'd enjoy it."

For the first time, Angie saw a hint of a genuine

smile on Clarissa's face. "Ah! *Très bien!* My prayers have been answered! To have a competent food person involved would be such a novel change. Personally, I can't abide barbecue. That's such a fine offer, Ms. Amalfi!"

"Call me Angie."

Clarissa didn't call her anything; instead, she seemed to be digesting the news. "You will have the entire kitchen staff to help you. And Lionel, of course. Just tell him what you need. I might even be able to invite a few of my friends from Bel Air. They have very refined taste. I'll have to give it some thought."

Angie couldn't help but smile at this heaven-sent opportunity. She knew that the kitchen was often where the truth about a place was learned, be it a restaurant, a home, or even a guest ranch. In a day or two, she was sure she'd find out whatever Paavo needed to know, he'd be assured that nothing untoward had caused Hal Edwards's death, and they could get on with enjoying Jackpot and their vacation.

"It should be great fun," she enthused.

"Well, why don't we refresh our glasses?" Clarissa said. "And sit down out on the veranda to discuss it further."

Even with Angie and Clarissa and their cookout discussion out of the way, conversation between the men refused to develop. Weather, politics, baseball spring training, and the latest blockbuster movies failed to spark any prolonged discussion. Lionel was drinking himself into a probable paralysis and Joey was sullenly downing too much wine, away from Clarissa's watchful eye. Paavo waited for his chance to move the conversation to Hal Edwards, sure that, given enough time and alcohol, something of interest would be said.

He had to agree with Angie's observation that the way everyone seemed to know one another in this small town, finding out if there was anything suspicious about Hal's death might not be as difficult as he'd first imagined.

Joey's glass was empty and when Lionel didn't notice, he grabbed the wine bottle and poured it himself. Great globs of pinot noir splashed over the rim of the glass onto the floor.

Paavo saw that the toe of one of Joey's boots had gotten a few drops. "The wine will stain," he said. "Better wipe your boots."

Joey didn't make a move. "Who cares? These are already ruined."

"Damn it!" Lionel grabbed a washrag and hurried around the bar to wipe up the floor. "Can't you take care of your own messes? You don't own this place yet, Joey," Lionel said. He got down on one knee to wipe up the floor. "Maybe never will," he mumbled.

Joey stuck out his foot. "Since you're down there . . ."

"Like hell!" Lionel walked back to his side of the bar.

Joey stared unhappily at his boots. They were cognac brown, with hand-tooled shafts and lizard skin toes. They looked dressy and expensive. He turned back to his glass.

"This terrain is rough on boots," Paavo said.

"You a shoe salesman or just have a fetish?" Joey asked.

Lionel chuckled.

It was all Paavo could do to civilly change the subject. "You visit here often?" he asked.

Joey stared hard at Lionel until the bartender, this time, refilled his glass. "From time to time," Joey answered.

"He comes down pretty often," Lionel interrupted. "Joey likes it here, don't you?"

"That makes sense to me." Paavo's tone was indifferent. "Must be great to have a family resort in Arizona, especially in the winter."

"He's turned into a regular little snow bird." Lionel agreed, but his words had a cutting tone. "Especially since he hopes a certain miss will start acting a bit more friendly."

Paavo sensed troubling undercurrents.

"Lionel," Joey said glaring. "I doubt if this stranger is interested in my itinerary."

"Just making conversation, cousin," Lionel said.

Joey looked slightly sick as he turned his shoulder to the bartender, then directed his attention to Paavo. "What do you do for a living?"

"I work for the city of San Francisco."

"How interesting," he remarked, as if the answer was anything but. "Doing what?"

"My agency deals with social and behavioral problems."

"Oh, a social worker." Joey was dismissive. "No offense, but do-good work sounds really boring."

"I suppose." Paavo tried to act friendly. "Say, do I understand that your father took off for five years and no one knew where he was?"

"Yes, you do." Joey looked bored.

"I'm surprised no one worried about him, or thought he might be dead or kidnapped."

"Hell," Lionel interrupted. "First thing Clarissa did was try to get her lawyers to declare him dead so she and Joey could take over the ranch."

"Obviously, it didn't work out," Paavo said.

"Everybody knew Hal was crazy—and he said he was going, so there was no reason to think he was dead. After a couple of years, he started withdrawing money from his account, so we knew he was alive somewhere." Lionel poured himself more Southern Comfort.

"Curious old coot," Joey said, looking into his wine. "He had a severe stroke when he was in his fifties. Took him years of rehab before he could walk and talk again. My mother took over the business—then, got a divorce and took it away from him. All this left my dad a little strange. Or, maybe it was the divorce that did it. Who knows?" When Joey lifted his gaze to Paavo's his expression was surprisingly sad, almost sympathetic. "Hal had to turn our home into a guest ranch just to pay taxes, then, one day, he split. Guess he couldn't handle all that had gone wrong in his life." He downed the wine. "Maybe it runs in the family."

"How old was he when he left?" Paavo asked.

"The first time, about seventy."

Paavo faced Lionel. "When Hal Edwards returned, did he explain why he'd run off?"

"Not to me," Lionel said.

Paavo gazed at Joey.

"I never saw him," Joey said, then stood up and

belched loudly. "I have a headache," he announced, glass in hand, the other extended in wait until Lionel put an unopened bottle of pinot noir in it. "I'm going to my bungalow, Lionel. Tell my mother not to worry. And when the food arrives here tonight, have a girl make up a plate and bring it to me."

He turned and left, ignoring Lionel and Paavo's expressions of concern and farewell.

"Gets lotsa headaches," Lionel murmured into his whiskey glass. "He's kinda delicate like. Same as his old man."

Chapter 4

Angie and Paavo ate dinner alone. Clarissa had decided, like Joey, to eat in her room, and Lionel looked more interested in drink than food. Some silent albeit excellent cook had placed a delicious meal of enchiladas, refried beans with cheese, Spanish rice, and green salad on bowls and hot plates in the dining room. They served themselves.

While Angie got ready for bed, Paavo tried to reach Ned again. He had expected to spend this evening with Ned and then with the people at the guest ranch finding out all he could about Hal Edwards's death, but that hadn't worked out. He was surprised Ned hadn't shown up that evening, since he'd initially sounded so eager to talk to Paavo before Doc did. Paavo's plan was to see Doc first thing in the morning.

He decided to walk around the guest ranch a bit, to see it alone, with no one watching.

Angie put on a sexy black teddy and climbed into bed to wait for him to join her.

And now, here she sat. Alone. She yawned.

No TV. No radio. She didn't want to fall asleep on the first night of her vacation with her lover. How unromantic would that be?

She opened the drawer in the nightstand. Sure enough, there was a Bible, but she also found a map of the state and an old, yellowed booklet entitled, "Jackpot, Arizona—The Town Hal Edwards Made Famous."

The back of the booklet showed that the Arizona Historical Society, Yuma branch, had published it.

Angie fluffed her pillows, and settled back to read. She'd always had a secret love of history. Or, considering that her mother had used a historical theme for her engagement party, maybe her interest wasn't such a big secret.

Clearly written to promote tourism, the sepia-colored booklet was filled with maps and old photographs of the town and the people. Jackpot had been a hard-living, hard-drinking, rough-and-tumble Western town in the early years of its history.

Jackpot's buildings, land, and history were described in rather dull fashion. The only thing of note was a mysterious happening in 1893. Angie quickly realized it was the same story Lionel had mentioned.

A stagecoach had set off from Phoenix to cross the desert, heading for a little town on the Pacific called Los Angeles. Somewhere around Jackpot, it had vanished.

She sat up as she looked at the names of the passengers lost on the coach: Hoot Dalton, cousin of the infamous "Dalton Gang" of train and bank robbers; Daisy Lane, singer and actress; and Willem van Beerstraeden, chef at New York City's Waldorf Hotel.

How interesting, she thought. She'd been to the present-day Waldorf-Astoria many times, and didn't realize it had begun as only "The Waldorf."

She continued reading, and soon came to a write-up about Hal Edwards.

In Jackpot, a young Edwards opened a general store founded on cheap Korean War surplus. It soon expanded to include hardware, farm and ranch equipment, foodstuffs, pharmacy, and optometry services, and before anyone knew it, "Halmart Stores" were all over the state.

She turned a page to find a sepia-toned portrait of Edwards as a young man. Wearing a cowboy hat and bolo tie, he was startlingly handsome, with deep-set dark eyes in an intelligent face. He looked like a movie-star cowboy from the 1940s and '50s, not John Wayne but more of a Gary Cooper type.

The chapter went on to say that Hal Edwards had built a hacienda a few miles from town, and contributed generously to the town and its people until Jackpot grew into a spot tourists went to to get away from harsh, northern winters. Hal and the town prospered until tragedy struck when, as a relatively young man, he suffered a debilitating stroke.

She read, "In keeping with the strong, can-do Edwards's spirit, Hal recovered. Travelers to Jackpot can now visit and stay on his property. Called the Ghost Hollow Guest Ranch"—Angie's eyes began to glaze over at this—"it is renowned for its beautiful grounds and lovely cottages . . ."

Her eyes shut; she could take no more.

The booklet slipped from her lap onto the floor as her head nodded. Images stirred by her readings swirled through her mind.

Visions flickered in slow motion of her first visit to the Waldorf-Astoria with her parents when she was only fourteen years old, of eating at Oscar's Restaurant, named for the famous Oscar Tschirky, the first maître d'hotel who was said to have invented such specialties as the Waldorf salad and veal Oscar even though he wasn't a chef. That was the first time Angie realized she could build a career and a name for herself around her love of food and her skill at cooking.

Like the turning of a page, her dream switched to black-and-white. Suddenly, Oscar Tschirky himself appeared before her in a dapper 1890s tails and top hat. But instead of being at the Waldorf, he was walking down Jackpot's dusty Main Street with a holster and six-gun strapped to his hip. The sun was high, as if it were noon.

Coming from the other side of the block, also armed and walking toward him with arms out at his sides like a gunslinger, walked a young, strong and healthy Hal Edwards.

On a street corner, strumming a guitar, a wine bottle at his side, Joey Edwards sang *Do not forsake me, oh my darling,* from *High Noon.* As he slurred the words "on this our wedding day," even though Angie was asleep, she began to feel agitated and nervous.

She rolled to her side.

The sky was white with heat. Beyond the buildings and wooden sidewalks, a few bushes of sage and tamarisk rose from the hard-packed gravel.

"Where's my chef?" Oscar asked in a clipped Swiss accent. Then louder, *"Where's my chef?!"*

"Your chef?" Hal looked over at Angie and flashed her a brilliant smile. "She'll tell you," he whispered.

"I will, Mr. Edwards?" she mumbled.

"Yes. You'll find him won't you, Angie . . ." His image rippled. "Angie . . ." he repeated, then louder, "Angie, are you asleep?"

She opened her eyes. Paavo sat beside her, silhouetted against the soft lamplight. "No," she replied, shaking the bizarre dream from her mind. As she turned, the covers slipped from her shoulders, revealing the sheer black lace of her teddy. She held out her arms to him. "I'm not asleep at all."

Chapter 5

Angie thought the two-lane road they'd traveled from Jackpot to the Ghost Hollow Guest Ranch was rough going, but it was nothing compared to the narrow, bumpy road they followed early the next morning in the direction of the Colorado River reservation.

The car jostled so badly she had to hold the strap over the door with one hand, the dash with the other. Her stomach flip-flopped. Now she understood why Paavo had insisted that they rent a four-wheel drive vehicle.

After a while, he turned onto a gravel driveway. In the distance was a sprawling white ranch house.

"That's a large home for one man," Angie said. "Doc lives alone, right?"

"He does, and he has every inch crammed. He likes to collect things that interest him."

"I think someone's standing on the porch."

Paavo smiled. "That's him."

As they pulled up in front of the house, Doc rushed forward to greet them.

Angie's nerves bunched. While Paavo, time and again, had met relatives of hers who'd inspected him as if he were a bug under a microscope, she'd never had to experience that anxiety. She'd met his guardian, Aulis, before she and Paavo had become a couple, so it had been easy—along with the fact that she'd immediately liked the kindly gentleman.

Now, though, meeting Doc was different. She cared what he thought of her, and wanted to make a good impression for Paavo's sake. She glanced down at her Moschino jeans, tank top, and red brocade Iisli jacket with Western-looking pearl snaps instead of buttons, and plucked a minuscule speck of lint from her top. She was also wearing a pair of new gray hand-tooled Justin ladies' boots—all bought in San Francisco after a great search. She'd been sure she'd look quite outdoorsy.

Seeing Doc, she was no longer so certain.

From the name "Doc," she'd been expecting someone who looked and acted like a toothless Gabby Hayes. The doctor, however, was a handsome man, a Westerner who could easily give Clint Eastwood or Sam Elliott competition. He was tall and solid with a thick mane of gunmetal gray hair. His long face was deeply tanned, lined and weathered, with blue eyes that probed, and a thin, firm mouth. He wore black slacks and boots, a white shirt and a black string tie, and moved with strength, energy, and purpose unexpected in a man of seventy.

"So what the hell you doing still sitting in the car?" His deep voice boomed impatiently, and carried a hint of a drawl. "Come on out where I can see you."

Paavo and Angie did as told. Paavo's face lit up with warmth and delight as Doc snared him in a crushing bear hug. The two were the same height, and Angie couldn't help but think that if Paavo's father were alive, he'd be much like the man before her.

"Goddamn! It's good to see you!" Doc stepped back and grabbed Paavo's shoulders, looking over the boy he'd known and clearly proud to see the man he'd become. "Grown a bit from the skinny brat I last saw. Guess I can't threaten anymore to take you over my knee if you give me any grief."

"I never dared cause you trouble back then," Paavo said with a grin. "And I still wouldn't."

The two men laughed. Angie smiled, moved by their obvious affection, and glad someone who had been close to Paavo was going to be part of her life.

"Smart kid. I always told Aulis that." Doc patted him on the back as he glanced at Angie and winked. "Looks like you're doing all right for yourself, too. Good job. Beautiful fiancée. I'm glad for you."

"Thanks," Paavo said. "Let me introduce Angie."

"Shame on us for carrying on and ignoring your lovely lady." Doc held out his hand toward her. "I am Dr. Loomis Griggs, but I only answer to 'Doc.' Welcome to my home."

Angie shook his hand as she said, "I'm Angelina Amalfi and only answer to Angie. Thank you for inviting me."

When their hands met, she could feel Doc's scrutiny of her careful makeup, highlighted hair, soft skin, long nails, and clothes. For the first time, she had a clear understanding of how Paavo felt when her parents studied him to decide if he was "worthy."

"Let's go inside," Doc said. The way he eyed her, she hadn't yet been accepted. It must be the clothes. Damn, why hadn't she worn her sophisticated DKNY mauve pantsuit?

Pausing at the front door, Doc's face hardened a moment as steel blue eyes made a quick but thorough sweep of the morning landscape. And in that instant, as Angie studied him, she realized the brash, talkative, almost jolly fellow was a phony. This man was tough as nails, serious to a fault, and with a shell that would be hard to penetrate. Yet, judging from Paavo and Aulis's reaction to him, well worth it if one could succeed.

Doc asked after Aulis Kokkonen as he led them to the living room.

A floor-to-ceiling stone fireplace dominated the room. Wide, deep, high-backed leather chairs draped with Navajo blankets and a monstrous leather couch smothered with colorful pillows competed for floor space with rustic tables and a huge rolltop desk. On walls and shelves were Indian sand paintings, assorted Southwestern antiques, and a great many books. Angie peeked at one of the shelves. Some of the books were in Greek and Latin.

The scent of many a burnt log and countless firings up of Doc's numerous hand-carved pipes permeated the warm, masculine room. No woman's touch was seen anywhere, and Angie's curiosity was immediately aroused as to why such a handsome, eligible man didn't have a woman to share his home.

There were layers and layers to Doc Griggs, she thought, and it was going to be interesting to delve through them.

"Go on and sit down you two, any place that suits you," Doc said cheerfully as he brought out a tray with coffee, cream, and sugar. His joviality seemed forced, and his face bore signs of strain. She knew that Paavo was anxious to learn what was troubling Doc, but Aulis had warned him that Doc opened up only in his own time, and pushing did no good. Paavo needed to be patient, and so did she.

She took a sip of coffee, and nearly spit it right back out. It was so strong and muddy her teaspoon could have stood straight up in it. She reached for the sugar bowl.

"Like it?" Doc asked.

"It's great," she murmured. *Great, if you liked liquid tar.*

Doc grunted in agreement. "Nothing like real coffee to get the juices flowing in the morning. Well, I'm starving. I've usually eaten breakfast by this time. Who'd like bacon and eggs? I've also got toast or English muffins to go with it. We need to eat before we set out."

Set out? Angie's reaction to the phrase was fleeting, almost like a slight tremor of the earth, and vanished with the suggestion of food and a sudden desire for eggs Benedict.

Why would that be?

Then the booklet she'd been reading and her strange dream came back to her, along with memories from some of the culinary classes she'd taken. One of the dishes that Oscar Tschirky, a.k.a. "Mr. Oscar" and "Oscar-of-the-Waldorf," immortalized was eggs Benedict, created—if she remembered right—as a hangover cure for one of the Waldorf-Astoria's guests, a Mr. Benedict, who ordered "toast, bacon, two poached eggs, and a hooker of hollandaise sauce." Oscar had used English muffins and Canadian bacon, and was so impressed with the results he put it on the restaurant's menu.

How odd that in her dream, Oscar was saying, "Where's my chef?" and that the booklet had described one lost passenger as the Waldorf chef. What did it all mean?

Maybe, since she'd agreed to help Clarissa with the cookout—and it was obvious from their little talk that Clarissa had no idea what she wanted Angie to serve—she should consider cooking Waldorf dishes, the ones made famous by Oscar, since there was a connection between the Waldorf and Jackpot. Who would have ever imagined such a thing?

All that aside, at the moment she could all but taste eggs Benedict. And perhaps if she wasn't in the way, Doc would tell Paavo what was troubling him. "Do you mind if I cook breakfast while you two talk?" she asked.

"But you're my guest," Doc replied.

"She's also a gourmet cook," Paavo said, smiling at her in understanding. He might not know about the craving for eggs Benedict, but he'd read her mind about giving Doc and him a chance to talk. "She can make the best Italian and French food you've ever tasted, and just about everything else as well."

"Is that so?" Doc asked.

"I try," Angie stated.

Doc nodded. "In that case, I won't complain."

"Have you heard from Ned?" Paavo asked.

"I'm sorry he stood you two up." Doc sucked in his breath. "I sure as hell don't know what's gotten into him lately. He's been distracted and troubled. It's driving me nuts trying to get to the bottom of it."

"What's it about?" Paavo asked.

"He won't say." Doc thought a moment. "He clams up even worse than you do. All I know is, it seemed to start about the time Hal Edwards came back."

"I'd like to hear about that," Paavo urged.

"The story starts a while ago," Doc said with a grin. "But isn't that the way with most old men's tales? You know how for years Hal Edwards had it all—wealth and honor. But then after his stroke and divorce, he was left with nothing much but his lands in Jackpot. To everyone's surprise, though, with a little help from me as his doctor as well as from physical therapy and the people who worked for him on the ranch, he recovered. He turned the ranch into a moneymaking resort, and seemed content, though he never got over his fury at Clarissa and her lawyers for taking his business in the divorce settlement. But then, for some reason, he became increasingly paranoid. He'd worried for years that Clarissa would come back into his life and take everything else he owned the way she had his business. I guess those worries got the better of him because suddenly, he took off. Vanished."

"He told people he was leaving, didn't he?" Paavo asked.

"He ranted, made threats, but nothing specific. No one heard a word until he contacted his bank for more money. He was in Mexico. He stayed there five years. We thought he'd never return. But then, this past winter—late January—he came back. He stayed about three days, had those female ostriches delivered to the hacienda, and then took off again."

Even though he'd heard all this before, Paavo was still incredulous. "He was gone five years, then out of the blue returned with a hundred ostriches?"

"And left again almost immediately," Doc said. "Or, so we thought. It turns out he didn't leave. He died. And his body wasn't found until a couple weeks ago."

Paavo didn't like it. Not only was Hal Edwards's death suspicious, Paavo thought, this whole story was. "Hal Edwards was a rich man, and you're saying no one looked for him? No one wondered why he'd disappeared again?"

"His family didn't seem to care. Keep in mind, he'd just returned after five years' absence. Everyone assumed he'd gone off again and would be back when he was ready."

The story didn't hold up. Being gone five years gave him *less* reason to disappear a second time, not more. And why would he have brought the ostriches and then left them? Someone, clearly, hadn't wanted anyone to look for Hal—or to find him.

"How does Ned tie in with any of this?" Paavo asked as Angie walked in with the eggs Benedict. It was clear from her expression of interest that although she'd been cooking, she hadn't missed a word.

"From the time Hal Edwards came back," Doc said, eyeing the plate of food Angie placed in front of him, "Ned was a changed person. I don't know why."

"Did they get along?" Angie asked as she refilled the coffee cups—this time with her own brew.

"I didn't think they knew each other well enough to care one way or the other." Doc splashed Tabasco on his eggs and hollandaise sauce. Paavo noticed Angie visibly blanch. She started to stand, but then caught herself, sat back down, and gulped some coffee, trying not to look at the desecration of her delicate sauce. Doc, fortunately, was too engrossed in eating to notice. "Come to think of it, whenever Hal's name came up, Ned looked decidedly unhappy. Angie, these eggs are delicious."

"Thanks," she murmured. Doc reached for a bottle of green chili sauce. She felt the urge to tear it from his hands. "So tell me," she forced herself to ask, "what's Ned like?"

Doc's face lit up, and it was clear he enjoyed talking about the younger man. "He's grown into a fine person. He was just a little guy when his dad passed away and his mother moved here to raise Ned in the country. Ned loved it, but it was too quiet for her. Eventually, she met a man in Phoenix, and they got married when Ned was sixteen." Doc broke off his narrative to say to Paavo, "She passed on a couple of years ago."

"I'm sorry to hear it," Paavo said.

"She was a nice person," Doc added, then turned back to Angie. "Anyway, Ned didn't care all that much for his new stepfather. He asked to stay in Jackpot, and lived with me until he finished high school."

"So it was just him and his mother when Paavo knew him," Angie said.

"Yes." Doc looked fondly at Paavo. "Two little boys who'd already had it pretty rough. They'd both learned what loss was all about at a young age. To me, it helped forge a bond between them. Both paid no attention to the trivial things that so many kids got caught up in, and they valued friendship and honesty. Still do, from what I gather." He gave Paavo a pointed stare.

"He absolutely does," Angie said, touching Paavo's hand with love.

Doc nodded, happy to hear it, and then continued. "Ned worked hard, started his own business. It was rough going at first, but recently, it's been doing well. He's got a good heart, and that's an important thing in a man," Doc added. "Maybe, when all's said and done, it's what's most important."

"We met Teresa Flores yesterday," Paavo said, giving a brief description of the encounter. "It sounds like there's something going on between her and Ned."

Doc put down his fork. "I wish that were the

case. Ned's loved her since high school. Teresa, though . . . she's always wanted more than Jackpot can offer. She cares about Ned, and that's part of the problem. For a while, I thought she'd changed her mind about him, then it ended. He'd be better off, I think, if he could forget about her and find someone else."

"When did it end?" Paavo asked. From the way Teresa looked the day before, their relationship might not be over.

"It was also around winter. Lupe, that's Teresa's mother, invited us over for Christmas dinner, and all was fine. But then, a few weeks later, I remember Ned making some bitter remark that he wouldn't be getting—or giving—any valentines this year."

Doc glanced over at the too-silent phone, as all wondered, yet again, why Ned didn't call. Doc silently finished the last few bites of his breakfast.

Angie tried to lighten the mood by asking Doc about Ghost Hollow's lost stagecoach and passengers, but he dismissed the story as wildly exaggerated.

Doc suspected that no one cared much about the story at all until Hal Edwards realized it might be a way to attract a few more tourists to his resort. Nothing like a mystery to get the curious to visit.

Angie had to agree with him on that. In fact, first chance she got, she was going to find out all she could about the missing stagecoach and its passengers—especially the missing Waldorf chef.

Jackpot probably wasn't large enough for its own museum, but it should at least have a library.

* * *

After breakfast, Doc made several phone calls trying to locate Ned, but no one had seen him. His house was empty, his business door closed, and his motorcycle gone. He hadn't been arrested or hospitalized.

Doc wondered if Ned's latest argument with Teresa wasn't the problem. He wished he knew what was causing their difficulty, and that they'd either break it off completely or resolve their differences. Ned needed to get married and settle down, and frankly, Doc added, so did Teresa.

Doc's fretfulness eased a bit when an older man arrived at the house. Paavo recognized him. Joaquin Oldwater was about five-eight, with broad shoulders and a square build. His hair was nearly white, pulled back and tied with a black thong, and his face was shiny and dark with strong, high cheekbones that gave evidence of his Indian heritage. His jeans, red plaid shirt, leather vest, and battered brown boots looked as old as he did.

Paavo stood. "Remember me, Joaquin?"

As the two men shook hands, Joaquin's creased visage crinkled into a semblance of a smile. "Sure do. Taught you to ride. Taught you to shoot. You were a good kid. How come you don't come down anymore?"

"I got involved in my work—too involved, perhaps," Paavo admitted, then introduced the curious Angie.

She rose and they shook hands.

Oldwater studied Angie a long moment, then Paavo, then nodded at them both before turning again to Doc. Paavo noticed Angie's expression brighten, as if she realized she'd gained Joaquin's approval.

"Hear from Ned yet?" Joaquin asked Doc.

"No. If he's not back this afternoon, I'm calling the sheriff."

"Fat lot of good that'll do," Joaquin muttered with a shake of the head. "Are we still going?"

"Yes," Doc said, then to Paavo. "I've asked Joaquin to lead us to the cave where he found Hal Edwards's body. In fact, it's in the area I was telling Angie about before breakfast—near where the stagecoach disappeared. I'd forgotten about that old story."

"The scene of the crime, in other words," Paavo said.

Doc nodded. "You've got it. Something's going on, Paavo, and I can't figure out what. Joaquin's here—he'll vouch for what I'm saying. I'm executor of Hal's estate. Last week, there were two break-ins—one here, one in my files in Jackpot's medical clinic."

"You're thinking someone wants to know what's in his will?" Paavo asked.

"But there is no will," Doc said. "And that's not what's worrying me—it's Teresa."

"Teresa's in danger?" Angie asked. Her face expressed her concern. She and Paavo had talked about how peculiar the meeting with her had been. Something had seemed "off," but they had no idea what it was or why.

Doc said, "Last winter, after Hal's sudden visit then departure, I heard that strange things had happened around her, like her car losing its brakes, a fire in her bedroom, and attempted break-ins to the Flores home. Then, as quickly as they started, they ended. Were they accidents, or on purpose?"

"Ned knew all this, of course?" Paavo asked.

"He did. He wanted to think they were accidents—we all did—but, then, after Hal's body was found two weeks ago, the strange happenings started up again—all around Teresa. Lupe, her mother, is worried sick about her. Teresa tries to say all is fine, but I can see that she's worried. Ned is, too."

"That's what you meant when you said to Aulis that strange things were going on?" Paavo asked.

"Yes. And there's one more thing—though it might not be connected at all. There was a break-in at the church."

"The church? Was anything stolen?" Paavo asked.

"Not that Father Armand could tell. He found the doors to the sacristy and records area open. None of the chalices or anything of value was taken, but there's no index or even a very good system to tell if anything else is gone, and since Father Armand is fairly new here, he just doesn't know. For all he knows, the break-in might have been simply vagrants, illegals, even some old prospector looking for food or warm shelter for the night."

"But you don't think so," Paavo said, realizing the break-in sounded somewhat similar to what Doc had experienced with his records.

"No." Doc shook his head. "I don't."

Paavo nodded, then said, "You've told me no

one knows the cause of Hal's death—that the body was too decomposed to find decent forensic evidence—but what's the official explanation?"

"Hal had a history of strokes, so the sheriff took the easy way out and said the death was from 'natural causes.'"

Paavo asked the question uppermost in his mind. "Do you think Hal was murdered?"

Doc and Joaquin traded glances. "Yes," Doc said, "I do. Don't ask who or why. I've given it a lot of thought, but I just don't know."

"Enough talk," Joaquin's low voice growled. "Ready to ride?"

"Guess so," Doc said as he took a gun and holster from his desk and slid them onto his belt. Something told Paavo it wasn't four-legged danger that worried Doc.

Doc's gaze fell on Angie. "Can you ride, Angie?" he asked.

A long pause followed. "I've ridden," she replied, lifting her chin.

Uh-oh. Paavo knew that look. "Probably pony rides when she was a girl. I don't know about this."

"That's not true, Paavo," she protested. "I'll be just fine."

"You never told me you knew how to ride," he said. And she'd told him almost everything ... except about old boyfriends, which she kept a deep, dark secret. He always wondered why.

She shrugged. "The subject never came up."

He was ready to argue that that had never stopped her before, when Doc said, "I've got a mare up in years—like me. She's gentle and forgiving. We could take my pickup, but it's tougher to drive over that terrain than it is to ride."

"Believe me," Angie said, smoothing her colorful designer's idea-of-Western-garb outfit. "I know all about riding horses."

Doc and Joaquin glanced at each other.

Paavo knew what they were thinking: clothes like Angie's shouldn't be allowed within five hundred feet of a horse. He hated to think of how her fashionable boots were going to look after a simple jaunt to the stables. "The lady says she can ride." He looked at the men and nodded. "Let's go."

"Oh—wait!" Angie cried. "I'd better get my cowboy hat. It's still in the car."

Chapter 6

Soon, three tall, beautiful horses stood saddled and ready to go. The fourth, an old roan mare with a gray muzzle and bald patches, was much smaller than the others. The mare's hooves splayed outward—the opposite of pigeon-toed—and one ear stood upright while the other was bent forward.

"This is Ophelia," Doc told Angie, patting the mare's neck. "You two should get along swell."

Angie wasn't sure how to take that statement. Wasn't Ophelia Hamlet's crazy girlfriend who drowned herself? As she approached, the horse gazed at her as if assessing her skills.

She'd reassured the men she could ride. She didn't tell them that her only experience consisted of two lessons, English saddle. Eyeing the mare nervously, she plunked a Ralph Lauren Western-style straw hat, dyed a rich red color, onto her head. Just the thought of how difficult it had been to find that hat in San Francisco made her appreciate it all the more.

The mare now wore an expression of complete amusement.

Taking a deep breath, she squared her shoulders. She wasn't about to miss this ride out into the desert. Not if she could help it.

On the other hand, the idea of pleading the need to return to Ghost Hollow in order to help Clarissa with the cookout had a definite appeal. Angie would much rather be cooking than riding.

At least Ophelia had no way of knowing that once, as a kid, Angie had stupidly tasted some canned dog food—not until years later did she learn it was horsemeat.

With one foot in the stirrup, her hands around the saddle horn, she tried to pull herself into the saddle when Ophelia decided to stroll. Hanging on, Angie found herself suddenly taking impromptu hops around the yard. Seeing her dilemma and trying to keep his face straight, Paavo held the mare still and boosted her up.

Once seated high off the ground on the massive beast, all the reasons she'd quit after only two lessons hit her like a sledgehammer. But she'd been about nine years old at the time. She was an adult now; she could handle this.

She gripped the saddle horn rather than the reins and tried to remember how to steer. She and Paavo both gaped in amazement as Ophelia made backward figure eights. What was she, the figure skater of horses?

This time, Joaquin came to the rescue and gave her a quick lesson, assuring her that Ophelia would follow Doc's horse, Achilles, and Angie would be fine.

She doubted it, but nodded.

The others mounted up, and they were off. Angie lagged at the rear until she got the hang of it. Eventually, she began to relax enough to realize how hard the saddle was, and how much she ached.

The four riders headed across the open desert in the direction of the foothills. Since it was spring, there were a few delicate but bright orange and yellow flowers nestled among the scrub, creosote, and jojoba. Higher on the hills were tall saguaro cactus, unique to the Sonoran desert, with L-shaped arms extending upward from the main trunk. Not a tree was seen. In the sand, Angie saw long wavy lines. Joaquin explained that snakes had left them and she should be on the lookout for rattlers.

Rattlesnakes? Angie's head instantly took on the action of a Ping-Pong ball.

Occasionally, lizards, large and small, scurried past. In the far distance, a roadrunner raced on long spindly legs. The sky was high and bright blue, the land quiet with the watery flicker of elusive mirages always just ahead.

Doc and Joaquin looked determined and purposeful, while Paavo, handsome in a black Stetson Doc had lent him, appeared relaxed and calm. Angie was surprised at how comfortable he was on horseback—that was something newly learned about him.

For her, however, the ride was slow torture.

Caught up in the lore of the Old West while preparing for this trip to Jackpot, she'd briefly considered a truly Western wedding theme— maybe even a rodeo. No more! A coach would be as rustic as she'd get, perhaps pulled by beautiful Clydesdales like on TV beer commercials.

As she daydreamed about her wedding, she paid no attention to where the little group was heading until the shifting play of light and shadow across nearby rock formations attracted her notice, and brought her back to the present.

The land was eerily beautiful, but it could be deadly. She couldn't help but contemplate the stagecoach lost in this barrenness, and the terror a Dutch chef must have felt to be stranded out here with his few fellow passengers. A cold chill, almost a premonition, rippled through her as she thought of another who was also missing— Paavo's boyhood friend Ned.

As Joaquin, Paavo, and Doc reached the shadows of a rock wall, they stopped, and Joaquin pointed toward some rises. Angie caught up to them in time to hear Paavo say, ". . . watching us now?"

She didn't like the sound of that, and looked along the direction of Joaquin's finger. She saw nothing.

"We've been watched all day," Joaquin answered calmly. "I spotted the shine of maybe binoculars, maybe a rifle, while we were still on the desert floor."

Paavo and Doc looked around; Doc anxious, Paavo with cool calculation. She felt exposed and suddenly vulnerable. The watcher could be anywhere in the rugged hills around them.

"You won't spot him," Joaquin said after a while. "But he's there. I feel him."

"I've had this feeling before," Doc said, brows locked.

"Are we in danger?" Angie asked softly.

"I don't think so," Paavo replied. "We've been well exposed for a long time."

"I hope you're right." She tried to move closer to Paavo, but Ophelia was more interested in nibbling at a prickly bush. As the silence and emptiness around her went from beautiful to ominous, the thought struck: *What's a city girl like me doing in a place like this?*

"The watcher is a watcher, nothing more," Joaquin said. "He's no shooter—at least, not today."

Everyone dismounted at the bottom of the rocky incline, all too conscious of the secret observer. "There are several caves in this area, but only one big one." Joaquin pointed about six feet up where, behind a scrub brush, the rocks seemed to form a narrow crevice.

That was the cave? Angie thought. No way was she going inside that tiny slit in the rocks.

Joaquin retrieved two flashlights from his saddlebags, handed one to Paavo, and led them up the rough ground. Up close, the crevice opening was larger than it had appeared from below. Joaquin flicked on his light, then bent slightly to enter. Paavo and Doc followed.

Curiosity overcame Angie, and she did the same, her eyes round and straining as she searched for spiders or snakes in her path. Thankfully, there were none.

The walls of the cave were wide and oddly smooth; the cave larger than she'd expected. Even Paavo could stand upright, though the ceiling lowered near the rear.

It was a blessing that Angie wasn't claustrophobic, but the knowledge that this cave had been a tomb or possibly a murder site had her hoping their stay would be a brief one. The smell of death and decay still seemed to linger there, just past the edge of perception.

"Why would Hal have come here?" Paavo asked.

"That's the question," Doc replied.

"Maybe to hide something," Joaquin suggested. "But I don't know what."

After a moment Paavo asked, "How did you find him?"

"These caves are on Hal Edwards's property—it goes on for miles. I was passing through and saw Lionel nearby. I was curious about why. A few days later, I came back and noticed tracks leading to the caves. I found the body."

"Did anyone ask Lionel what he was doing out here?" Paavo asked.

"The sheriff did," Doc said. "Lionel claimed he was being a good manager—checking the property. He said he never went inside the caves. The sheriff believed him."

Joaquin's light illuminated a spot near the far wall. "That's where Hal was. I recognized his ring and belt buckle."

At the realization as to *why* the ring and belt buckle were all that Joaquin could use to identify an old friend, Angie shuddered and backpedaled toward the entrance.

As the three men bent forward like fortune-tellers reading tea leaves to scrutinize the ground where a dead body had lain rotting, the walls closed in on Angie. Lionel's use of the word *skeleton* made visions of bones dance in her head like something from a macabre Halloween celebration.

The cave was dark, chilly, and had far too many nooks and crannies to suit her. She hurried outside, needing air and sunshine.

The sun was warm, almost hot. Above the cave, the hill rose steeply to a ledge. The ledge seemed to be wide and flat; and some distance beyond it, the hill rose up again.

Buzzards circled high overhead. She wondered what they'd found. *You don't want to know,* she told herself.

She studied the landscape, searching for any sign of the watcher. She didn't like it here, not one bit, and could see why people thought the area was haunted. The warmth of the sun left her untouched.

A little ways up from where she stood, a large boulder was shaped like a chair. It seemed almost warm and inviting compared to the cave. She climbed up to the rocky bench and sat. The only good thing about this area was that it had no ostriches to bother her.

She again watched the buzzards, and wished Paavo and the others would finish up.

"What are you doing up there?" Paavo called a

short while later, one hand shading his eyes from the sun's glare.

"I'm guarding you!" she shouted, standing. "Like a sentry. If that watcher showed up, I'd have spotted him."

"Did you see anything?" he asked.

"Luckily, not a thing." She started down to them.

"Did you fall?" Joaquin asked, his gaze jumping from her to the ground near her ledge.

"Me?" Angie stopped, surprised at his question. "No."

"Something happened there." Still studying the soil, Joaquin hurried up to where she stood, then his gaze lifted and he went a little higher.

Something in his expression made the hair on the back of Angie's neck stand up.

Joaquin half walked, half climbed up the steep, dusty slope, following a trail only he could discern. Paavo and Doc glanced meaningfully at each other and climbed up the hill to Angie's side.

She was beginning to get a real bad feeling about this. "Be careful!" she yelled.

Joaquin kept going.

"He's part mountain goat, Angie," Doc said, but looked decidedly worried himself.

Paavo's mouth set in a grim line as he continued to follow Joaquin's progress. Joaquin climbed on steadily and without hesitation. Their relief when he stopped on more level ground was short-lived. Joaquin walked back and forth, halting and kneeling, and then disappeared.

"Joaquin?" Doc called. No answer.

"I'm going up," Paavo said.

Angie looked at the steep slope, the buzzards, then back at the cave. Something was terribly wrong. "I'm going with you."

"Me too," Doc said. "Lead the way."

The climb was much rougher than Joaquin had made it appear. The sun beat down relentlessly. Sand and gravel were stirred by their scrambling, and Angie gulped in mouthfuls of dust kicked up by Paavo just ahead of her. Earth and sweat formed a film on her exposed skin and over her new clothes. Behind her, she could hear Doc coughing, cursing, and sliding.

Finally Paavo, then Angie, reached the level ground of the ledge. They turned to Doc as he struggled the final yards to them. He was red-faced and wheezing as he lurched and fell on his way up. Paavo took his hand and pulled him the last few feet.

They all moved forward, deeper into the mountain. She saw Joaquin at the same time as the others. He was kneeling by some rocks, his head bowed with grief.

Suddenly, all her instincts told her what had happened. Why he hadn't spoken, hadn't called out. Still, she prayed that it wasn't what she feared.

Paavo told her to wait there. *He knows as well.* Even as her heart begged that she was wrong.

Doc froze. Dread shadowed his suddenly pale and haggard face.

Paavo stepped closer to Joaquin, then stopped. His body stiffened. When he turned, the pain and sorrow in his blue eyes confirmed their worst fears. Angie's hope died.

Doc's head bowed as he moved slowly and mechanically forward, like a man in a trance.

Down below, the horses continued to calmly eat sprigs of tender brush near the cave. The hot sun still beat relentlessly on the hillside. But here, Angie felt nothing except the coldness of death.

Chapter 7

A trail of billowing sand kicked up from the desert floor as vehicles raced toward the foothills and the ridge where the four waited. Remarkably, Paavo's cell phone had worked, and he'd called for assistance.

Nearly an hour had passed since Ned's body was found, an hour of silent shock, anger, and grief.

Doc had tried to hide his tears, but finally gave up and let them fall. Paavo sat with him, his arm around Doc's shoulders, his head bowed.

Angie had stayed with Paavo until she noticed Joaquin standing alone, shoulders slumped, sniffling and occasionally rubbing his eyes. Her heart ached and she went to him.

Without looking at her, he spoke in a quiet voice. "I watched Ned grow up, Angie. I loved him, too."

"I know you did." She reached out and lightly held his arm.

Angie mourned for them all: for Paavo, who had looked forward to reuniting with a boyhood friend; for Joaquin, who'd been there, side by side with Doc, helping the boy turn into the fine man Doc had described; for Doc, who had clearly become a father to Ned in everything but name; and especially for Ned, as all the hope she'd heard in Doc's voice about him and his future would never be fulfilled.

Watching their sorrow, her own eyes filled with tears.

In the distance, the vehicles drew ever nearer.

"They're almost here," Paavo said, standing at the edge of the ledge. "Two of them."

"Two?" Doc struggled to his feet. "That means the sheriff is dragging Buster along."

"Buster?"

"Also known as Wallace Willis, the deputy."

Below them, the vehicles came to a halt—a Hummer followed by an old Jeep, both with flashing red beacons and long aerials whipping the desert air. From the Hummer emerged Sheriff Hermann, wearing an oversized beige cowboy hat that shielded his face, a bulky jacket, and khaki slacks over surprisingly short legs and very wide hips. A phone, gun, and nightstick hung from a thick belt.

Slightly behind the Hummer, Buster leaped from the open Jeep and began swatting dust from his clothing. He was nearly a head taller than the sheriff, and more muscular. His uniform matched the sheriff's, though he wore no jacket.

"You all got a body up there?" the sheriff bellowed. His voice, Angie thought, was peculiarly high-pitched.

The four yelled back variations on *"Yes."*

"We're coming up!" the sheriff shouted back.

With fascination, the four watched the progress of Sheriff Hermann and Buster up the steep ridge. The sheriff gasped, swore, and kept slipping, kicking dust and sand in the deputy's face. As the climb grew more difficult, Buster sometimes boosted the sheriff along with a two-armed shove of the buttocks. Near the top, Joaquin and Paavo edged themselves down to offer arms to help yank the sheriff to the flat clearing. Buster clambered behind.

When Sheriff Hermann reached the landing, panting and weary, he took off his hat and then his jacket. Angie gaped. "He" was a woman.

She was in her forties or fifties—Angie couldn't tell—heavyset and solid, with gray-flecked straight brown hair pulled back into a rubber band at the nape of her neck. She wore no makeup, and her face was round, red, and sweaty from the ascent. Her eyes were pale blue, and her lashes and brows so thin they all but disappeared. An upturned, almost pert nose and a tiny mouth were completely at odds with the rest of her build.

Along with the khaki uniform, she wore combat boots and as deep a scowl as Angie had ever seen.

Buster would have been a decent-enough-looking man, mid-thirties with a muscular physique and large blue eyes, if not for his dull expression and protruding lower lip. To Angie's surprise, the collar and front placket of his shirt were edged with maroon piping, and his hat had a small yellow feather stuck in the band. She couldn't help but stare.

As soon as he spotted her, he gazed back with equal fascination.

Eyes bulging, chest heaving as she tried to catch her breath, the sheriff said, "All right, now, where's the body?"

The four pointed, and she marched off.

Buster didn't follow until the sheriff ordered him to. Soon, the sound of vomiting came from behind the bushes. Paavo cringed. Angie knew he was thinking of what the two were doing to the crime scene.

Doc glowered after them. "Our delightful sheriff," he explained, "is the orneriest cuss west of the Mississippi. She got the job because nobody could match her in being mean and hard-nosed. It's a toss-up as to which is worse, her temper or Buster's incompetence."

Doc's little speech made Angie stiffen as the sheriff returned. "Damnation, he's dead," she said, still huffing, jowls quivering, hands on hips and glowering at them as if one of them had been responsible. "What the hell's going on around here? I didn't take this job expecting people to drop like flies!"

"That's Ned! Show some respect!" Doc snapped, and Paavo put a restraining hand on his arm.

"Don't you think I know who it is," she sneered.

"Listen here, Merry Belle—" Doc took a step forward, but Paavo had hold of him. He bit back a curse, and looked away, eyes brimming with tears.

Merry Belle? Surely Angie hadn't heard right.

"Don't you yell none at the sheriff," a green-looking Buster said, patting his mouth with a monogrammed handkerchief—WW in royal purple script lettering. "You okay, Aunt Merry Belle?"

Yes, she'd heard right . . .

"Of course I'm okay!" Merry Belle swatted the deputy in the chest with the back of her hand. "Better than you! Now, make yourself useful and go back down there and radio the county for the coroner and see if we can't get a helicopter from Yuma to fetch the body. Probably can't land, but it could hover and drop a line."

She then cast a sheepishly guilty look at Doc. "Cool off, Doc. I'm sorry about Ned, I really am. But I don't know what the hell's going on around here! Must have been an accident . . . but up here . . ."

Doc shook his head and walked away.

Slowly, as the sheriff looked around trying to determine how the accident might have happened, she revolved in the direction of her deputy, who had remained rooted to the spot. Her face darkened.

"I still see you," Merry Belle barked.

Buster was staring at Angie.

"Have your legs failed you, boy?" the sheriff bellowed. "Or do I have to shoot?"

"I'm going," Buster mumbled. "But who's that woman?"

"I'll do my investigation once you're on your way," Merry Belle yelled, ever more exasperated.

"I do like her red hat, though," Buster mumbled, then went off to begin his downhill slide.

Chapter 8

Much later that day, Angie found her-self back at the guest ranch, alone. She'd taken the SUV and returned, while Paavo did some investigating on his own.

He clearly had no confidence that the sheriff would investigate properly or soon—it was all he could do to stop her and Buster from completely destroying the crime scene. He told Merry Belle he was a homicide inspector in San Francisco and offered to help. She bristled at the suggestion. Neither did she buy that he was vacationing in Jackpot "just by chance."

When Paavo found out Doc had an extra set of Ned's house and business keys, he decided to take matters into his own hands.

Angie expected she'd only be in the way. She decided to leave, let those who knew Ned mourn his loss together in their own way.

She stood in the shade of the little porch in front of the door to her cabin, hunting in her purse for the key.

"Junior!" Clarissa called suddenly. "Junior Whitney, come here right now!"

Angie turned to see what was going on.

Clarissa was on the veranda outside the common room. "Junior" as the man had been called, had been walking toward the stables. Angie wondered if he could be another relative.

As Junior slinked near, Angie saw that his hair was long and unkempt, and his clothes had never known an iron. He seemed to be in his fifties, tall, skinny and blond, with painfully bloodshot eyes and puffy skin.

His jeans and boots were covered with dust, his hands and face grimy.

"Where have you been?" Clarissa demanded, marching to the middle of the plaza. "I haven't seen you in two days! Lionel has some work for you to do."

"Now?" he whined. "I been workin' up at Hal's cattle ranch, an' I'm tired."

"Now!"

Junior spun on his heel and Angie was sure she heard murmurs of "too damned cheap to hire enough help" as he headed toward Lionel's trailer. For some reason, he looked vaguely familiar.

Clarissa looked up to see Angie watching her. "I'm afraid you see, now, what I have to deal with." Clarissa's lips tightened. "Help is so egregious these days! And, by the way, I haven't heard what you plan to prepare for the cookout."

Clarissa sounded as if Angie were nothing more than untrustworthy help herself. She curbed the impulse to stick her tongue out at the woman and felt a sudden sympathy for Junior Whitney.

Suddenly, a memory came back to her. She'd seen Junior in LaVerne's diner the day she and Paavo arrived in Jackpot. And he'd seemed to sneak out as soon as Teresa entered.

Gazing back unflinchingly at Clarissa, Angie stated, "I've been busy."

"Well, pardon me!" Clarissa harrumphed and marched back into the common room.

With a disgusted shake of the head, Angie went into the cabin. The sadness of the morning had cast a pall over her mood, and even the cabin seemed overly quiet and dreary.

Angie began pulling off her dusty clothes. They no longer looked new and designer stiff, but instead seemed nearly as worn and earthy as Joaquin Oldwater's. She used a bootjack to remove her Justins, and even seeing how scuffed-up they'd gotten, had to admit she was glad to have been wearing them to ride horseback and climb rocky hillsides. *What a day!*

What a sad day.

As she headed to the bathroom for a quick shower, she thought she saw something move by the bedroom door—something small, almost like a mote in the eye. A shiver ran down her back as she slowly walked into the living room.

Nothing was there. The room looked untouched. Just her imagination, she told herself.

After a very quick shower, she put on loose and casual Juicy Couture drawstring Capris and a hoodie. Barefoot, she curled up on the sofa with a notepad and pen.

Last evening, speaking with Clarissa, Angie had pointed out that since a lot of meat would be available at the barbecue, her main dish should be something different. She suggested serving a seared cracked black pepper salmon roulade with white leeks and covered with a cucumber sauce.

Clarissa approved, and Angie said she would come up with interesting accompaniments to it.

Now was the time to do just that so Clarissa wouldn't have reason to annoy her anymore—although something told her Clarissa was the type who'd find a reason, no matter what.

Slowly, she began to relax. Her breathing calmed, she yawned, and realized she was tired after getting up so early, the horseback ride, climb, and even the fresh air and sunshine. Between that and the day's emotion, she felt drained. Still, although she tried to think of food, her mind kept replaying the scene on the mountain ledge. Doc's sadness, the conspicuous sheriff, the deputy who gawked at her . . .

She shut her eyes to drive those thoughts away. Food, she told herself, think of food! Something sumptuous. Something she'd find at an elegant seafood restaurant in San Francisco . . .

Something tickled her foot. No. Impossible.

Suddenly, the sensation of feathers brushing against her ankle struck. She opened her eyes. Whatever it was crept higher, onto her calf.

She sat up with a jolt. Alarmed, she looked down at her leg, and saw a slight ripple under the loose material.

Petrified, she gripped the slacks tight around her thigh with one hand to stop the creature's upward journey, while with the other she slowly gathered the pants leg, lifting it higher and higher.

When she saw the three-inch wide, black hairy spider on her knee, she stared at it and it stared at her, both frozen with fright. Everything inside her went still. She opened her mouth to scream, but nothing came out. The spider found its bearings first and ran down her leg, across the sofa, and onto the floor.

That broke the dam, and the sound Angie held came out loud and long at the same time as she sprang up so that she stood on the sofa. Immediately, she doubled over to inspect her skin for a bite, and then rubbed her hand hard over her leg to brush away the "feel" of the spider.

The spider, meanwhile, scurried across the living room to run behind a rolling TV stand.

Without even thinking about what she was doing, Angie grabbed the thick, heavy Phoenix telephone book, shoved the TV stand out of the way, and dropped the book on top of the cowering spider. Then she ran out the door, smack into Lionel.

"There's a spider in my room!" she cried. "A huge, black hairy one."

"I thought I heard some screeching. Hairy, you said? Sounds like a tarantula." He held her shoulders, trying to stop her shaking as he looked her in the eye. "They're real dangerous, and once they get inside a home, it's often hard to find them. If you want to leave now, I unnerstand it. Won't even charge you none extra."

"Leave?" As she looked at him, a suspicion

crept over her. "No, I don't want to leave. I think I killed it."

He went inside to check. And, in fact, she had.

Paavo stood on the dock peering out at Ned's rental fleet. The dam-created lake was of good size, though not nearly as large as he remembered it. As a boy, he'd imagined it to be the size of San Francisco Bay. It didn't come close.

Foolishly, he found himself scanning the water for Ned. Many times as a child he had run to the lake to see a tanned, towhead boy out there waving skinny arms and telling him to "Come on in, the water's warm!" And it was. They'd splash around in it for hours of fun and laughter.

Paavo turned away.

It was easy to see why this business had occupied so much of Ned's free time. His house, a double-wide trailer, was right behind the shop where the boat rentals were made.

The doors to both were locked, and the shop had a sign in the window that simply said CLOSED. A truck was in the driveway and a couple of dogs ran around and barked, but other than that, all was quiet.

Joaquin confirmed that Ned's motorcycle was gone.

As Paavo unlocked the door to the shop and entered, regret flooded him—regret for all the times he'd thought about picking up the phone and calling Ned, but didn't. Regret for not continuing to join Aulis on visits as Paavo grew older; regret for not finding time to visit after he left the army, or even while he was a cop.

Ned had been an important, joy-filled part of his childhood. But he knew nothing of the man his friend had become, and that was the worst regret of all.

The shop was orderly and surprisingly neat for a place that dealt with boat rentals, repairs, and parts. That was typical of Ned. Even as a boy, he'd preferred taking apart appliances and rebuilding them over playing with toys. A memory of Ned taking apart one of Doc's radios swirled in slow-motion in Paavo's mind: Ned sitting on the floor with pieces spread all around him; Doc standing over him exasperated. In the end, Ned had put the radio back perfectly.

But no more.

Everything at the shop appeared strictly business-related, and Paavo moved to the house.

It was sterile. Furniture by Levitz and goods by Target were inexpensive and practical, nothing more. "Every penny Ned made went into his business," Joaquin said, as if reading Paavo's thoughts. "He wanted it to become big and important—to make some money for . . ." Joaquin suddenly stopped speaking.

"For Teresa?" Paavo asked.

Joaquin said nothing, but gave a quick nod.

The trailer consisted of one large living, dining, and kitchen combination in front, and two bedrooms and a bathroom in the back. One of the bedrooms had been made into a den. Paavo tried the telephones first. Stored incoming numbers and last-number redial were boons to homicide inspectors. Unfortunately, neither of the phones in Ned's house had those features.

The answering machine was full of messages from Doc, Paavo, Teresa, and even LaVerne from the coffee shop. Teresa was apologetic and tearful.

There was also a call from Sanderman Stables hoping everything was okay, and surprised Ned hadn't return Lightning last evening.

Lightning, Joaquin explained, was Ned's horse. Paavo expected they would find the missing motorcycle at Sanderman's. That answered another question—how Ned had gotten to the caves.

Paavo searched for Ned's cell phone. At the crime scene, he'd convinced the sheriff to check Ned's pockets for anything that might give some clue as to why he was there. His cell phone wasn't on him.

"You knew Ned well," Paavo said to Joaquin. "What do you think happened to him?"

Joaquin stared out the window at the lake a moment before saying, "He was troubled about Teresa, but he wouldn't say why. When asked, he'd just clam up, and say he'd take care of it. It wasn't like him. Ned was usually open, friendly. He liked to help people. Maybe too much."

Joaquin had nothing more to add, and Paavo continued going through Ned's belongings. In a lamp table drawer he found a small obsidian rock carved in a dog or wolf form.

Paavo held it closer to the light. "Do you know what this is?"

Joaquin stared at the carving then shook his head and looked away. "Just a charm. Tourists like them. You see that sort of thing a lot around here. It's worthless."

Paavo gave the older man a sharp glance. Why was Joaquin suddenly lying? The carving was crude. He placed it back into the drawer.

The den had a number of photos—Teresa alone, Teresa and Ned together in happy times, several of Doc and Ned, and even an old one of Ned, Paavo, Doc, and Aulis, all young and smiling at some long-forgotten photographer.

Paavo felt a pang at the last one. He'd tried as much as possible to treat this like any other murder case; he handled them at work all the time. The photograph, though, was a reminder that this case was different. Ned had been a friend.

Paavo was going through Ned's computer and e-mails when Joaquin gave a shout.

In the bedroom Joaquin sat on the floor by the open closet door. Before him was a box filled with newspaper clippings about the discovery of Hal Edwards's body.

"I heard things last winter, in those few days that Hal was in town," Joaquin said as Paavo looked through the papers. "There was a rumor that Ned hated him; wished he was dead. I couldn't understand it. Why would Ned feel one way or the other about Hal? Their paths hardly crossed. Then, Hal was gone, and the rumors ended. I never told Doc what I'd heard. I doubt anyone else would have either."

"Yet, for some reason," Paavo said, "Ned went out to the place where Hal's body was found, and that's where he was murdered." Paavo flipped through the stack of articles from newspapers around the state. "We need to find out why he saved these, and what he was looking for, because whatever it was"—Paavo lifted his eyes to Joaquin—"I think it killed him."

Chapter 9

Angie rushed over to Doc's house. She'd rather stay there than in the bungalow in case the tarantula was a family man. Not that she had a lot to be afraid of. From the common room, she'd phoned her doctor in San Francisco to ask about tarantula bites and learned they were highly painful, but not otherwise serious. Since she felt nothing, she hadn't been bitten. Tarantulas would rather run than bite, and attacked only if provoked. By the time the doctor finished, she felt guilty that she'd killed it.

Since tarantulas were burrowing animals who lived in soil, to find one in a cabin was highly unusual. She had to talk to Paavo right away.

She expected to sit outside until Doc, Paavo, and Joaquin returned. She tried the doorbell, just in case. To her surprise, Doc answered. Haggard and drained, he looked as if he'd aged ten years since morning.

"Hi," Angie said. "Is Paavo back? I thought I'd come and see how you fellows were doing. See if you needed any help."

83

"He's not back yet," Doc said, wearily. "I'm going into town. You can wait here until Paavo returns."

"To town?" The man looked ready to drop. Doctors, she'd heard, always made the worst patients. "Don't you think you should rest?"

He shook his head. "Rest? Hell. The only rest I'll ever take again is the eternal variety. No, I've got to be the one to tell Teresa. Ned would have wanted me to, though I don't know how I'm going to do it." He briefly covered his eyes then turned toward the door.

"Wait." Angie's heart wrenched at his misery. As much as she didn't want to do it, she knew Doc was in no condition to go off alone. "I'll go with you," she said. "I'll drive."

"No need. As a doctor, I've had to do this type of thing many times, I'm sorry to say. Anyway, you never even met Ned." Even as he firmly set his jaw, she could see a tremor in his lip and knew he wasn't half so tough as he pretended.

"I know—but I've met you and Teresa, and I care about you both. This isn't a time for you to be alone."

Doc looked at her a long moment, then nodded, as if too tired and disheartened to argue.

And just maybe he truly didn't want to be alone.

They decided to leave the SUV for Paavo when he returned, and to take Doc's car, a 1980 black Cadillac Coupe de Ville parked in the garage. Angie had been expecting to drive the old Dodge Ram pickup parked near the stables. Doc, she decided, should meet her father, who owned, loved, and still drove a red 1969 Lincoln Towncar.

As she headed toward Jackpot, Angie quickly realized that Doc was a person much like her. When troubled, he sought out others, needing their warmth, their support, and conversation. She encouraged him, and the two soon formed a warm bond.

How ironic, she thought, that she understood this aspect of a relative stranger so much more than she did her own fiancé. Paavo, when upset, wanted nothing more than to be alone.

Doc told her all about Teresa's family's restaurant, which was named for her grandmother, Maritza Flores. He expected to find Teresa there working.

"So we have Teresa, Lupe, and Maritza Flores— daughter, mother, grandmother, right?" Angie asked, wanting to be sure she had the names and relationships correct.

"That's it," Doc confirmed.

Angie couldn't help but note the fact that since Flores must have been Lupe's maiden name, and Lupe and Teresa still used it, Lupe either was unmarried or had divorced and taken back her own name. Angie also thought she heard a little something extra—a lilt almost—whenever Doc said Lupe's name.

Doc had explained how, as a young widow, Maritza Flores had opened her restaurant in a retired dining car on an empty lot. As it grew in popularity, Hal Edwards loaned her money to build a place in the heart of town. She did, and made the original railroad car part of the front façade.

Yet again, Angie noted, Hal Edwards's name

came up. It seemed he touched everyone's life in this town.

Soon, they reached the restaurant. Angie found that the old train made a distinctive décor. Inside, to the left and right of the entryway were remnants—counters and stools and appliances—of Maritza's original restaurant. Pictures documenting its history covered open wall space, along with colorful Mexican blankets and pottery. Tucked into a corner above a carved wooden chest and high-backed chair were a painting of Our Lady of Guadalupe and a crucifix.

"This is odd," Doc said.

"What is?" Angie asked.

"Maritza isn't in her chair. She usually sits in that corner"—Doc indicated the spot where Angie had just been looking—"dressed all in black, with a black scarf over her white hair. She's slowed down quite a bit lately, and I'm sorry to say her mind isn't as sharp as it used to be, but she enjoys welcoming customers. Everyone knows Maritza."

The hostess headed their way, smiling at Angie, but she froze as soon as she noticed Doc. Eyes wide, she hurried away.

Seconds later, an attractive, elegant woman in a tailored blue dress approached. Her long black hair was parted in the center, then braided and pinned to the nape of her neck. With wide dark eyes and olive skin, she bore a striking resemblance to Teresa.

Her anguished face met Doc's, stemming the words from his lips. Angie knew he wouldn't have to deliver the bad news. This woman had already heard of Ned's death.

"Doc, I can't believe it!" The woman's voice broke. "I'm so sorry!"

"Lupe," he whispered hoarsely as his tears brimmed. Angie had expected the two to give each other comforting hugs, but they held themselves ramrod straight. All comfort was given with their eyes, which—as Angie read them—spoke volumes.

"I . . ." Doc cleared his throat. "I came here to tell you and Teresa, but it seems you already know."

"Yes." She wiped her eyes with a tissue. "LaVerne learned about it from someone in the sheriff's station. She rushed right over—she said it sounded as if someone killed him! Tell me it's not true."

"It may be," was all Doc could reply.

Lupe looked stricken. "My God," she whispered.

Doc quickly introduced Angie.

A couple of diners entered. "Welcome." Lupe greeted them with a forced smile. "Your hostess will be right with you." To Doc and Angie she said, "Follow me."

As Lupe whisked them through the restaurant to the kitchen and the back rooms, she took Angie's arm. She wasn't tall and thin like her daughter, but closer to Angie's height, and her figure slightly rounded. "Teresa told me about meeting you and Paavo yesterday. Thank you for being here with Doc. This hurts him more than he'll let on because"—she glanced at him with such a mixture of warm affection and yet sadness it pierced Angie's heart to see it—"he's a tough, stubborn old bird."

"I've already learned that," Angie murmured.

Lupe glanced at her with somber eyes, then nodded. She led them to a small office space with a desk and four chairs.

"Where's Teresa?" Doc asked.

"After she heard, she went home with her grandmother. I'm worried about her. So many strange things happened around her, and then to have Ned . . ." Lupe bit her lip to stop her words, her face fierce with unspoken anger and distress. "I thought about closing the restaurant, but realized you might come here—and you probably haven't eaten all day."

"He hasn't eaten since breakfast," Angie said, taking a seat near Doc.

"Food's the last thing on my mind." Doc shook his head. "Ned was so filled with hope, Lupe. I keep thinking about that. This past winter had been good for his business. He suddenly had money and hope that his problems with Teresa would work out. And now, it's all gone."

Lupe's mouth tightened, but she said nothing.

"Do you think I should see her?" Doc asked, referring once more to Teresa.

"Yes, but only after you eat." Lupe went to the office door. "I'll bring you both plates. After that, we'll go to my house together. I'll call her and tell her you're coming. Maybe you can give her something to help her sleep tonight. I think, otherwise, it will be very difficult."

"I'll do what I can," Doc said.

Lupe had Carta Blanca beer and crisps sent to them as appetizers. The crisps were large flour tortillas baked with a topping of shredded cheese, mild chili strips, salt, and minced garlic.

Angie had eaten crisps before, but these were lighter, crisper, and spicier than any she'd had. She loved them.

Soon after, they received what Doc said was Maritza's famous stew.

Much as she didn't think she could eat, the stew practically melted in Angie's mouth. No wonder this restaurant was so successful.

With each bite, she analyzed the ingredients. Chunks of pork had been slowly cooked with black beans, roughly chopped poblano and Anaheim peppers, onions, garlic, lime juice, tomato sauce, oregano, and zested with minced jalapeño peppers. The stew was served over rice and topped with shredded cheese, sour cream, black olives, and a piquant *salsa verde*.

Delizioso! And she didn't care that the word was Italian—it applied.

As she ate, Paavo walked in. His gaze took in Angie, and then Doc to see how he was doing. Apparently, when Paavo and Joaquin found Doc's house empty, it had taken Joaquin one phone call to locate him. While Joaquin returned home, Paavo went to Maritza's.

Lupe greeted him warmly, and to his surprise, said she remembered him as a boy. A waitress soon brought him some stew. The way Paavo gulped it down, Angie knew she had to learn to make what would certainly become a Smith-Amalfi family favorite.

Lupe hovered near Doc as he ate, encouraging

him to take another bite. It was strange, Angie noted, how the two were drawn together as if by some magnetic force neither could do anything about and, at the same time, restrained.

Lupe wore no wedding ring, and Angie's earlier speculation about her unmarried state appeared accurate. Which meant that Angie couldn't imagine, since the two so obviously cared for each other, what was keeping them apart.

Chapter 10

Maritza Flores opened the door of the ranch-style house. She had short white hair, onyx eyes, and a strongly sculpted, serene face despite a network of lines and creases. She leaned against a cane.

"*Buenas tardes*, Maritza," said Doc.

"*Mi amigo.* Come in, everyone, please." Maritza stretched out a gnarled hand to clasp Doc's and led her guests into the living room. "My heart is filled with tears. I pray for Ned."

"I know you do," Doc said in a thick, sad voice.

"So much evil in this world." She shook her head with a profound weariness.

Doc quickly introduced Paavo and Angie to her.

"I am happy to see friends of Doc," Maritza said in greeting, then gazed intently at Paavo. "Paavo—I remember you when you were a boy. It was just a little while ago, I think. You would come here with the Finland man"—her eyes glistened—"and would play with Ned."

"I'll tell Aulis you remember him," Paavo said

91

softly. Angie could see that he was touched by the woman's words.

"Aulis, he love my stew! I still cook it . . . I think." She rubbed her forehead as if distressed, then turned her soft gaze on Angie. "And your fiancée. Angie, welcome to my home. I'm sorry this is such a sad time."

"As am I," Angie said quietly, instantly responding to the warmth of the woman.

A voice called out, "Doc."

Teresa stood in the doorway of the living room. She stared at Doc, oblivious of everyone else as tears rolled down her cheeks.

Doc crossed the room and took her in his arms. They held each other tight.

Lupe whispered that she would see her mother to bed and quietly walked Maritza from the room.

Only after Doc and Teresa separated and stood looking at each other, did Teresa seem to remember that Doc was not alone.

Angie and Paavo offered their condolences.

Teresa's gaze deepened as she faced Paavo. "Is it true? Ned was murdered?"

"That was how it appeared." His expression was grave. It wasn't a statement he made lightly.

Her hands clenched. "You're a homicide detective. Find who did this."

"I will," he promised.

"I'm just an old man," Doc proclaimed. "But my new life's work is justice for Ned. And Hal."

"Yes, Hal." Teresa shook her head as though to force away a memory, then sat beside Doc on the sofa.

Paavo and Angie sat on the love seat catty-corner to them. "You and Doc knew Ned better than anyone from what I understand," Paavo said. "I have some questions if you're up to them."

"I am," Teresa said, although the stiffness of her shoulders belied the words.

"First," Paavo began, "do you have any idea who might have done this? Anyone Ned was having trouble with, or who'd threatened him?"

A beat passed before she answered. "No. No one. Ned was a good man, everyone liked him."

Paavo simply nodded. He'd often complained to Angie how both murder victims and killers suddenly became saints when cops interviewed friends or relatives about them. "You heard that Ned died near the cave where Hal's body was found. Do you have any idea why he would have gone there?"

"No."

The answer came too fast. "He seemed to have a lot of interest in Hal Edwards's death and the discovery of his body. Do you know why?"

She visibly flinched. "I have no idea."

Paavo paused as Lupe reentered the room and took a seat in a corner.

Watching, Angie felt herself becoming more and more uneasy. Something was amiss about Teresa, but she couldn't pinpoint it. There was grief, deep-welled, but also something else. Doc had told stories about possible attempts on her life. Now, a man—her lover—had been murdered. Was her nervousness caused by fear? Or was she hiding something?

Paavo continued. "Did Ned mention that he was going to meet anyone yesterday?"

"Only you and your fiancée," she said.

Paavo's questions continued about Ned being concerned or troubled about anything or anyone, about his business, his neighbors, his customers, who his friends were, who he spent time with. Financial problems. Addictions. Everything Paavo could think of. To all questions, Teresa gave monosyllabic answers. Doc cast her looks of concern, but said nothing beyond confirming her replies.

"Let's go back to Hal Edwards," Paavo said finally. "It could be a coincidence that Ned was killed near the spot where Hal's body was found, but I doubt it. We need to look for a link. Do you agree?"

Instead of answering, Teresa turned quiet, as if she'd withdrawn to a faraway place.

"I think she's had enough questions," Lupe said.

"I'm very tired." Teresa put a hand to her forehead. "Could we continue this tomorrow?"

Paavo pressed on. "What was your relationship with Hal Edwards?"

A haunted expression appeared fleetingly in Teresa's eyes. "I used to work at the hacienda. Hal's nephew, Lionel, was supposed to help him manage the guest ranch, but he's . . . he didn't do a good job."

"When was that?" Paavo asked.

Teresa glanced quickly at her mother, then said, "I started working out there one or two days a week when I was only eighteen. It was fun, and it got me away from the restaurant." She folded her hands on her lap, lowering her eyes. "At the Guest Ranch I'd meet people from all over the country and have time to really talk with them, not just take their dinner orders."

Lupe stood.

"You liked working there, then?" Paavo asked Teresa.

"Yes." Teresa showed the first signs of enthusiasm since the start of the interview. "In time, I became the manager and oversaw modernizing the cabins and common room, even the kitchen. Hal was a generous employer, a generous man."

"Teresa," Lupe said, her tone firm.

Teresa stood, then Doc rose and put an arm around her back. "I think she's had enough, Paavo."

Paavo also got to his feet, but he had one last question. "Did you see Hal when he returned to Jackpot last winter?" he asked.

"No, she didn't," Lupe answered. "Doc, could you give Teresa something to help her sleep?"

As Lupe and Doc escorted Teresa from the living room, Angie and Paavo eyed each other, wondering about the bizarre way the interview had ended.

On the way back to their cabin, Angie told Paavo about her strange experience with the tarantula. Paavo's understanding of the spiders was the same as her doctor's. Lionel's frightening words, on the other hand, made no sense, and Paavo soon fell into a brooding silence.

The silence continued in the cabin while he

showered and got ready for bed. Angie put on Paavo's pajama top and climbed under the covers while he, wearing the bottoms, stood by the window, looking out at the night sky.

Finally, he spoke. "I think you should go back to San Francisco."

She sat up and rolled back the pajama sleeves, her eyes flashing. She might usually wear satin and lace, but deep down—she'd never admit it aloud—she really did prefer flannel. "I'm not going anywhere."

He sighed. "Listen, Angie. It could be dangerous here. I thought that at worst I'd find people bickering over an inheritance, nothing more. Instead, there have been two murders, break-ins, the local law is hostile, probably incompetent, and God only knows what else is boiling beneath the surface."

"You need me here," Angie insisted.

"So I have you to worry about?"

"I can take care of myself."

"Really? Like the time a serial killer tracked you to Wings of an Angel restaurant? Or when I found you on a cliffside ready to fall into the ocean, trying to get away from a murderer? Or when that crazy so-called demon trapped you in the old church basement?"

She hadn't joined him on this trip to argue. "If you're going to bring that up, smarty, then what about the time I stopped a newspaper publisher from killing you, saved you from getting blown to kingdom come at the Legion of Honor, and even rescued you from a watery grave on the day of our engagement party?" Then, she smiled. "But, things always worked out, didn't they?"

He frowned. "Barely."

"That was then; this is now. And Doc needs me."

"He does?" Paavo sounded dubious.

"You know he wanted us here to watch these vultures—Clarissa, Joey, and Lionel. Ned's death has only made it even more important. That's why I'm going to help at the cookout."

"Undercover Angie."

She ran her hands over the blanket as she gave him a come-hither look. "Well . . . I am under the covers . . ."

He grinned and walked toward the bed.

"Besides," she continued, "you know I'm good at finding out things. I'm staying."

He sat beside her. "It could be dangerous."

She put her arms around his neck. "Pooh."

"How am I supposed to argue with 'pooh'?" he asked.

"You aren't. Not with this, either." She kissed him.

It was a long kiss, and when they ended their embrace, Paavo chuckled. "No fair."

She grinned. "Ah, but all's fair . . ."

"The last words many a man has heard as he's gone like a lamb to the slaughter."

"You may be many things, Paavo, but you're no lamb. Now, tell me I'm staying."

He tossed back the covers, stretched out beside her, and took her into his arms. "Baa."

Chapter 11

Paavo was glad to walk in the brisk morning air to the sheriff's station after dropping off Doc and Angie at the mortuary to arrange for Ned's funeral. He was thankful Angie had offered to accompany Doc through the process.

Last night and again this morning, they'd searched the cabin for more tarantulas. There were none. Still, he probably shouldn't have given in to her wanting to remain here. The thought of dealing with this without Angie, though, was difficult. Selfishly, he wanted her with him—her smiles, her cheerfulness, and her optimism about an otherwise dismal world.

Now, walking the quiet streets of this old town, it was hard to imagine that any danger lurked here. It amazed him how little it had changed since his boyhood. The town had a few more cars, and definitely more pavement. Some of the motels and trailer parks out at the lake were new, but for the most part, it was a place where time had stood still.

All of which made it that much more unsettling

to be here without Ned. Even seeing how Doc's once thick brown hair had turned completely gray had given him a jolt.

Last evening, before returning to the guest ranch, they'd used their cell phones to call home. Angie talked to her mother, her friend Connie Rogers, plus a sister or two, while he'd phoned Aulis. They'd spoken at length, and Aulis reminded him that he'd met Teresa years ago. She was a shy little girl who hardly left her mother's skirts, but at the same time was quite intrigued by the visitors from the big city. Aulis's words brought back more of Paavo's memories of summers in Jackpot, memories he was glad were awakened.

Up ahead, the sheriff's station looked like something straight out of *Mayberry RFD*. It was a pale yellow wooden building, smaller than he expected.

In San Francisco, the sheriff's department served mainly as bailiffs for the city jail. In this area, with no police force, the sheriff was the law. He needed to know what Merry Belle Hermann—could she have had a more unsuitable name?—had learned in the investigation of Hal Edwards's death as well as how she planned to investigate Ned's.

Inside, the in-need-of-fresh-paint sea green walls gave the room a utilitarian look, as did the gray metal desk where Wallace "Buster" Willis sat. A bottom drawer was pulled out, and his feet were resting on it as if it were an ottoman. Except for a phone and a 3-by-5 notepad, his desk was spotless. One corner of the room, where three plastic chairs formed a waiting area, had a TV angled so that Buster could watch. Paavo did a double take at the screen—a rerun of the soap opera *Eagle*

Crest was playing. He remembered those actors from a past case he'd handled.

Behind the waiting room was an office with the door open. Glancing down the hallway, he could see a jail cell. It was empty.

"Is the sheriff in?" Paavo asked.

"Yup." Buster tore his eyes from the TV and slowly stood, but made no motion to contact the sheriff. "What happened to your fiancée? She go back home already?"

"She's in town. I'd like to speak to—"

"Sit back down, Deputy!" Sheriff Hermann bellowed from the doorway to her office. As pinprick-sized blue eyes glared at Paavo, a deep flush colored her heavy, round cheeks. Her voice turned cold. "Come in to my office, Inspector. I want a word with you."

The office was furnished with two wooden stiff-back guest chairs facing a massive oak desk and a large padded leather swivel chair. She shut the door, pointed to a wooden chair for Paavo, and then walked behind her desk. She looked as if she'd slept in her uniform. Her thin, unwashed hair was pulled back tight, twisted in a circle, and held with a barrette; and the skin around her eyes was puffy. Neither of them sat. She was so angry, her voice quivered. "You interfered with my investigation. I'm considering putting in a complaint to your superiors."

"I don't know what you mean," he said calmly.

She leaned forward, palms on the desktop. She had surprisingly tiny hands and wrists compared to the thickness of her arms. "You sure as hell do!

You went out to Ned's house and his business. You looked at his things, touched them, talked to his neighbors, even the stables where he kept his horse. That's my job!"

"I know what I'm doing around a crime scene, Sheriff," Paavo said.

"That's not the point!"

"I went through no crime scene tape; no deputy was posted to keep us out. Doc had a key to Ned's place and he gave me permission to use it. You and I can pool our findings and work together, or we can debate legalities and jurisdiction."

Her jaw worked as she grabbed the arms of her swivel chair and lowered her heavy body into it. A long moment passed before she said, "I haven't gotten out there yet."

Paavo was stunned. "You haven't?"

Her thin lips nearly disappeared as she pursed them hard while straightening papers on her desk. "I've had other things to deal with first. Ned's house and office aren't going anywhere."

Paavo found her thoughtlessness intolerable. "No, but they could easily have had clues that led to a killer who just *might* go somewhere!"

"But they didn't, did they?" She glowered at him. "I know what I'm doing, Inspector."

Do you? he wondered, even as he warned himself it served no purpose to argue with her. She was clearly in over her head, whether she'd admit it or not. He suspected it was why she was so defensive. Ned's murder couldn't be dismissed as an accident the way Hal Edwards's had been.

This was a sleepy town except when tourists

showed up in winter, and most of them were re-
tirees, not the kind of people who went on ram-
pages or killed each other. "I'm only trying to
help," he said. "This is the kind of work I do
every day."

"All right, San Francisco"—the name was a
sneer—"tell me what you saw."

He gritted his teeth before beginning. "Ned's
fascination with Hal Edwards's death was one
thing, as was"—he hesitated, remembering
Joaquin Oldwater's odd reaction—"a strange black
charm, a wolf carving, that I was told was some
sort of tourist charm. I've never seen one before."

Merry Belle interrupted. "Everyone in Jackpot
is fascinated by Hal Edwards's life and death
both. We all knew that. As for the charm . . ." She
shrugged. "We don't care about tourist junk in this
office, Inspector."

He used all his control to remain impassive,
even as the cop in him mulled over Merry Belle's
words. She knew more than she was telling.
"When is the autopsy scheduled?"

"It's already been done." She folded her arms.
"It's not like our coroner has a waiting list."

"Cause of death?"

"Trauma to the brain. Ned's head was bashed
in, in case you hadn't noticed."

"Time of death?"

"Two days ago." Her eyes narrowed. "The day
you arrived in town asking about him, as a matter
of fact."

Paavo ignored both the sarcasm and ridiculous
implication. "Do you have any suspects?" he
asked. "Know of anyone who fought with Ned?

Threatened him? Doc and Teresa both say there was no one."

"I ask the questions around here, Inspector!" Her response gave him his answer.

"I've heard rumors of some kind of trouble between Hal and Ned," he said. "Have you heard the same, or looked into it?"

"Why?" She sneered. "Do you think Hal's ghost rose up and killed Ned from the grave? Is that the way you investigate crimes in San Francisco?"

"Let's talk, then, about Hal Edwards," Paavo said, holding his ground.

"Forget it." She marched to the door and opened it. "I've wasted enough time with you. Stay out of my investigation!"

He casually hooked his thumbs to the front pockets of his jeans and strolled toward the door. "Since you're a public officer, Sheriff, much of the work you do is open to the public. I'd like to see Hal Edwards's case file."

"That is not public information!"

"I'm afraid you're wrong, Sheriff. I can get an attorney to quote you chapter and verse, if you'd like. Or we can cut out the middleman, and you show me now. And, while you're at it, I'd also like to see Ned Paulson's autopsy report."

Black rage filled her eyes. "Deputy!" she shrieked. Buster nearly fell off his chair. "Give this man the Edwards and Paulson folders. They're in the file cabinet. Don't let him make any copies or take anything out of here." She spun toward Paavo. "You"—her finger was inches from his face—"stay the hell out of my office."

She slammed the door behind him.

Buster handed over two surprisingly thin folders, then sat near the TV, his eyes practically glued to Rhonda Mulholland's sexy body. Paavo used the now empty desk.

Ned Paulson's report held no surprises, and was just as Merry Belle had said.

The autopsy report on Hal Edwards stated the death had occurred some eighty to ninety days before the body was discovered. Cause of death was uncertain due to the body's decomposed and desiccated condition when found. A nick on the rib cavity was consistent with what a knife might have done as opposed to the animal teeth marks found elsewhere. If so, Edwards might have been stabbed through the heart by someone who was facing him.

It took a lot of strength to stab someone to death that way. The killer had to be strong or very, very angry.

Apparently, the sheriff had done nothing with that finding.

Little information was gleaned from interviews with the staff of the Ghost Hollow Guest Ranch—Dolores Huerta, the cook-housekeeper; Sherman Whitney, Jr., ranch worker; Ralph Dittersley, foreman of Hal's cattle ranch some thirty miles east of town; plus maintenance men, gardeners, and several women who assisted Dolores with housekeeping and cooking, all of whom were on call when needed.

The sheriff had interviewed a number of others from town as well as those at the guest ranch. Only Lionel and Doc admitted to having had brief discussions with Hal during the short period between his return from five years absence and his subsequent disappearance and death.

Paavo was surprised Doc hadn't mentioned seeing Hal last winter, but judging from what he'd told the sheriff, there was nothing about the meeting worth recounting.

The file contained no interviews with Clarissa or Joseph Edwards. Nor was there any indication that either of them were in Arizona at the time of Hal's death.

No forensic evidence was gathered. No investigation of the home was made.

Paavo imagined the sheriff and Buster walking around bellowing at people. When no one confessed to foul play, they left, thinking they'd done a proper investigation.

Clearly, since Hal Edwards had been murdered, they were wrong.

Chapter 12

Angie was used to mortuaries. As a little girl, when walking through North Beach with her mother, Serefina would often drop into one or two to see if any of the Italians she knew had gone to their great reward and somehow she'd missed it. When Serefina would find someone she knew vaguely (she'd already know about the death of anyone she knew well, as well as their relatives and friends), she'd cry out, *"Poverino"* or *"Poverina"* as appropriate, and sign the guest book.

Probably, Angie thought, you had to be Italian to understand.

Because of those visits, mortuaries didn't creep her out the way they did some. Still, she was glad to leave it, and thrilled to see Paavo waiting when she and Doc stepped into the bright sunlight.

Since Doc remained convinced that everything that had happened somehow revolved around Hal Edwards, he wanted to meet with Hal's attorney next.

Angie bowed out. She could handle dead bodies, but not lawyers. She asked Doc to point her in the direction of Jackpot's library. She was curious about the missing stagecoach and the Waldorf Hotel's chef, and this gave her an opportunity to look into them.

While following the route Doc had given her, Angie heard a voice call her name. She turned to see Teresa Flores.

"Hi! I saw you as I left the restaurant," Teresa said. "I was wondering if you have time for a cup of coffee?"

Angie wouldn't have turned that offer down for the world.

LaVerne Merritt's face lit up like someone who'd won the lottery when the two women entered her café. As they settled in a corner booth, she grabbed a coffeepot and headed their way so quickly, Angie thought she would leap over tables like a hurdler in an Olympic's race. "I heard your man is a cop from San Francisco," she said as she poured Angie a cup.

"News travels fast," Angie said.

"It's a small town; nothing gets by anyone here." LaVerne sucked in her cheeks, her gaze darting toward Teresa before she added, "Except murder."

"LaVerne—" Teresa began.

"Don't try to stop me," she ordered. "I've been quiet too long about this."

Teresa's eyes rolled upward, as if LaVerne had been anything but quiet.

LaVerne bent forward and stabbed the table with a bony finger to emphasize her words as she said to Angie, "Your man needs to find out why there was no inquiry into Hal Edwards's disappearances. The man was famous! Rich! I'm supposed to believe he just took off and left that worthless Lionel to run things? I don't think so! And then, he came back ready to operate an ostrich farm and next thing you know, he's gone again! Hah! If the sheriff was doing her job, somebody would have been looking for him. Instead, he's dead. There's a reason for that!"

"LaVerne," Teresa interrupted, impatient. "Hal died of natural causes."

Angie's attention bounced from one woman to the other.

"Sure." LaVerne straightened, her shoulders square. "And I've got beachfront property to sell you." With a grimace in Teresa's direction, she turned back to Angie, her lazy eyelid bowing low. "If that's all there was to it, then why is the FBI lurking around? Or maybe the DEA, or INS, or Homeland Security? Hell, I'm not sure who's who anymore these days. We're not far from the border." She leaned close again and dropped her voice. "Terrorists can sneak across all hours of the day and night, you know. A lot of men were showing up here last winter. They looked like illegals, but after Hal disappeared, so did they. I think they were terrorists disguised as illegals. I think they captured Hal, and then killed him when he wouldn't pay up!"

Angie pushed back from the table. "My goodness." The woman's wild imagination astounded her. "Terrorists? I thought I only had to worry about tarantulas."

"You can joke," LaVerne sneered, "but somebody had better find them fast. First Hal, next

Ned. For all we know, we'll all be killed in our beds! And Merry Belle Hermann will say it was due to 'natural causes.' Natural causes, my eye!" With that, LaVerne marched toward the kitchen, leaving Angie gaping.

Teresa waited until LaVerne was out of earshot, then whispered, "She's crazy. Don't listen to her."

"She certainly has a different outlook."

Teresa gazed out the window as if needing to calm herself after LaVerne's comments, but at the same time, she was carefully studying the people walking by as well as passing cars, her expression wary. Angie wondered—and worried—about her.

"How are you doing today?" Angie asked gently.

"I'm all right." Sad eyes met hers. "I don't know why people give me so much attention. It's not as if Ned and I were . . . were engaged or anything. He was just a friend."

"A friend?" Angie hesitated. "I thought he was much more."

Teresa's eyes welled up, but immediately she caught herself, and soon was again composed. "I tried to discourage him, Angie. Since he was close to Doc, my mother would invite him to our home regularly—along with Doc, of course. That's all."

"That doesn't sound like the way he saw it," Angie said.

Teresa rubbed her forehead. "It's . . . complicated. I never told him I loved him. Never."

"But did you?"

"What does it matter?" she asked in return. "Love isn't enough. All I have to do is look at my own family, and I see that love isn't enough."

Angie thought Teresa must have been referring to her father, whoever and wherever he was. She wanted to ask about him, as well as to say that love did happen, and that it was more than enough. But the set of Teresa's face told her any such advice would be unwelcome.

Angie opened her mouth to speak when she noticed LaVerne approaching. LaVerne placed a plate with a wedge of something resembling fruitcake in front of each woman.

"I heard you're a gourmet cook," she said to Angie with a broad smile, as if their recent conversation never happened.

"Yes," Angie murmured. For once, she didn't want to go into a litany of her cooking experience; she wanted to go back to talking with Teresa, whose attitude about love and life was troublesome.

"I'm a bit of a gourmet myself," LaVerne announced proudly. "Not in the diner, of course. People don't come here for fancy food, but when the occasion calls for it, I always make something extra special. This comes from an old family recipe." She pointed at the cake. "I had it in the freezer and zapped it in the microwave to defrost. Don't worry, it's not hurt none. Eat up."

Teresa sat without moving.

Angie simply wanted to get rid of LaVerne, so she cut into the cake with her fork and placed a large bite into her mouth and chewed.

In an instant the food seemed to turn into a giant sucking machine that drained all the liquid from her mouth. Her cheeks were pulled inward, while her tongue stuck against her palate. Her mouth wouldn't open.

"*Mmmurf,*" she cried.

"Ah, she loves it!" LaVerne cooed. "Listen to her *mmm*s of joy."

"*Mmurf, mmmurff!*" Angie said again.

Teresa gawked at her.

"Her eyes are even starting to tear up with joy." LaVerne's hands were clasped near her heart. "I never dreamed a big city gourmet cook would find something I made so delicious."

Angie reached for her water, and somehow managed to pry her lips open wide enough to gulp it down. Chewing and drinking, she swallowed the cake, then gasped in much needed air.

She looked at LaVerne with something akin to horror. "What in the world was in that?"

LaVerne stood tall, head high and proud. "You don't eat something like that every day, do you? Kind of makes your mouth tingle, doesn't it?"

Angie finished her water. Her lips and tongue felt numb, and she hoped the "cake" wasn't doing to her stomach what it had done to her mouth. "It's unique, all right."

"It's cactus," LaVerne whispered, as if giving away a state secret.

Angie glared at the offending slice. "You mean like prickly pear fruit?"

"No, no. I mean boring a hole in a saguaro and pulling out the inside pulp, then mashing it up good and mixing it with pinyon nuts and figs—all good desert food. I call it my Desert Surprise Cake."

"It certainly is," Angie said, her throat and mouth now feeling like they'd been stuffed with cotton. "I think I'll just take the rest with me. Better to enjoy it when I'm not so full."

Smacking her still deadened lips, she was reaching for a napkin when Lupe Flores burst into the coffee shop. "Teresa! What are you doing? You said you were going home!"

"It's just a cup of coffee," Teresa said, standing.

"Go!" her mother ordered. "We'll use my car." She glanced at LaVerne and Angie and, as she rushed Teresa out the door, murmured, "Excuse us."

"What was that about?" Angie asked before gulping down Teresa's untouched water.

"Who knows?" LaVerne cried. "It's always been a weird family. All I care about"—her hips began to sway as she pumped both fists in the air causing Angie to consider a fast dive under the table to get away from the madwoman—"is that I have a winner with that recipe! I'm gonna enter it in the Pillsbury Bake-off."

Chapter 13

Paavo glanced up at the painting over the mirror that ran the length of the bar. Then he looked again.

The bartender noticed and couldn't help but chuckle as she walked over to his table. In her sixties, she was a big woman with big hair, one side clipped with a silver medallion holding a spray of turkey feathers. She wore jeans, a fringed cowgirl shirt, bolo tie with a turquoise slide, and boots. Her holster held a cap gun that had *Hopalong Cassidy* inscribed on the handle. "What's the matter, cowboy?" she said to Paavo. "Never seen a picture like that before?"

"Never," he admitted.

She had a husky chuckle. "That's what happens when you let a gal like me own the town's only saloon. The name's Jewel, by the way."

"Paavo Smith. Glad to meet you."

Her warm greeting to Attorney Jack O'Connell and her sympathy and affection toward Doc confirmed to Paavo that these representatives of the legal and medical professions were frequent, valued, and preferred customers. He alone was asked what he was drinking.

The Stagecoach Saloon fulfilled every city slicker's idea of a Western bar, with sawdust on the floor, wagon wheels on the walls, and a gallery of John Ford classic movie posters. The bar itself was old and made of dark, rich wood. Along the bottom of it stretched a long brass rail. Behind it was a wall mirror with shelves for liquor bottles.

And over it was the aforementioned painting.

Forget the buxom beauties that usually graced bars, this was a portrait of a man lying on hay, buck naked except for a cowboy hat, boots, spurs, and a thickly coiled rope covering his privates. The only other thing he wore was a large and knowing grin.

With a shake of the head, Paavo shifted in his chair to face Doc and the attorney. "Let's begin with money," he said. "Who stands to profit from Hal's death?"

"Good question, Inspector," Jack O'Connell said, "and I'm damned if I know. His property is valuable, and he had a substantial amount of cash and stock market investments, but he was so bitter about Clarissa taking away the Halmart stores, he didn't want her or Joey to get any of it. Still, he couldn't decide who to give it to. His only other surviving family, Lionel, is pretty worthless. Hal would write himself a will, then tear it up before I filed it."

Just then, the two fishermen Paavo had seen at Merritt's the day he arrived in Jackpot entered the saloon. They glanced in his direction, and took seats at the bar.

Jewel's greeting was friendly, but strictly businesslike.

Paavo's thoughts turned to LaVerne's comments about them, and he wondered if she might not have been right. They dressed like a couple of vacationers interested in fishing, but lurked around watching and listening.

He kept a surreptitious eye on them, and couldn't help but suspect that it'd soon be time for a talk. His attention returned to the attorney. "With no will, does that mean Joey inherits everything?"

"Not so fast," O'Connell replied. "I said I never filed a will, but that doesn't mean Hal didn't have one. With him having been gone so long and the paranoid state he was in, for all I know, he could have created a dozen wills—each one designating a different heir."

"Is that why there's been no settling of the estate yet?" Paavo asked.

"You got it." Doc answered instead of the lawyer. "As executor, I want to give anyone who might know about a will a chance to get back to me. Like Hal, I'd hate to see that disloyal son of his get a damn thing. I told Clarissa and Joey that they were just going to have to wait until after the cookout to find out what, if anything, they'll inherit. I swear, if Hal doesn't have a will, before I give all his property to Joey, I'll be tempted to write one up myself!"

"Hello, Miss Angie."

Angie nearly jumped out of her skin and spun around.

Once again on her way to the library, she'd been

so preoccupied thinking about Teresa that she hadn't heard the deputy, Buster, come up behind her. His uniform was starched and pressed so well the creases on his trousers looked sharp as knives, and today the feather on his cowboy-style hat was red rather than yellow.

"You surely do look pretty this morning," Buster said with a smile. Smiling, he didn't look quite as witless as usual. "Prettiest thing to come to Jackpot since like forever. Is that what you call a designer outfit?"

Angie wasn't sure which surprised her more, his compliment or his question. She glanced down at the multicolored pastel zigzag striped sundress she was wearing. "It's a Missoni."

"I've heard of that." He pointed at her four-inch lime green wedgies with ankle straps. "What about your shoes?"

Angie's eyebrows rose. "Manolo Blahnik. Why?"

"Why? Why she asks!" he said with a chuckle. "Do you realize how awful people would look if it weren't for clothes?"

She blinked a couple of times.

"I mean, what if all these people were running around in just their underwear, or god forbid, with nothing on at all? How ridiculous would that be?" Angie glanced at the few rather scruffy people wandering around Jackpot. She wouldn't argue. He continued, "So, since we need clothes, why not make them as beautiful as possible?"

Her sentiments exactly, she had to admit.

"Do you know how rare it is to find good fashion in Jackpot, Arizona?" he asked. "Or anywhere in Arizona for that matter, though I did see some nice things in Scottsdale once." His brow scrunched as if he were thinking hard. "You know, Clarissa Edwards wears some really good clothes now and then. No matter, though. I still do all I can to keep away from her. Can I walk you someplace?"

Her head was spinning. "I'm just going to the library."

He smiled, falling into step beside her. "My pleasure."

As they walked, Angie said, "That's a very nice maroon trim on your uniform."

"Thanks." Preening, he patted his collar. "I did it myself. I even have a checkered maroon handkerchief that matches. I used to wear it tucked in my chest pocket, just like they do in *Gentlemen's Quarterly*, but Aunt Merry Belle didn't like it. Too fancy for a uniform, she said."

"You sew?" Angie couldn't hide her amazement.

"Sure. I got a Singer Quantum XL-6000 for only two grand on eBay. It does everything. That's why I like looking at good clothes. Gives me ideas. Unfortunately, Aunt Merry Belle doesn't like me fussing with her outfits—not that she has many. And the few times I've had girlfriends, they never liked it that my clothes were so much more stylish than theirs were."

It took Angie a few seconds to wrap her mind around that tidbit of information. She opted to change the subject. "Speaking of friends, did you know Ned very well?"

"Not really. We were in school together. Not the

same class. I was held back a couple times, and Ned kept going."

"What do you think happened to him?" she asked.

"Damned if I know. The only person I ever saw him fighting with was Teresa Flores," Buster said, then stopped walking. "Here's the library. Guess I'll have to say good-bye. Going inside with all those books gives me the willies."

"I'd like to find out about the stagecoach that disappeared in the 1890s," Angie said after introducing herself to the librarian, Doris Flynn.

The public library was very small, but charming, and situated in a back bedroom of a private home that had been converted into Jackpot's City Hall. The library walls had floor-to-ceiling bookshelves, and several freestanding ones crowded the middle of the floor. Books that couldn't fit on shelves were stacked against them.

"I've got a wonderful collection about it." Mrs. Flynn led her to a bookshelf in the far corner. "This is the best collection in the state. There were a lot of newspaper articles at the time because one of the passengers was very famous."

Angie thought back to the booklet she'd read. "That's right, there was an actress on the coach."

"Actress?" The librarian chuckled and shook her head. Her voice dropped as she said, "I believe that was simply a euphemism for what she really was."

Angie got the picture. "Then, it must have been the chef from the Waldorf Hotel in New York City."

"The Waldorf? Nobody out here had any idea about a place like that. No, it was Hoot Dalton. And with good reason. The Dalton Gang had robbed a bank in Coffeyville, Kansas, in October 1892 and all were killed except Emmett, who was captured and imprisoned. He was later released, by the way, and went to California. People say their cousin, Hoot, gathered up all the money after the gang ended and tried to run off with it."

As Doris spoke, she pulled out two oversized volumes filled with newspaper and magazine articles from the time of the disappearance, and put them on the one free table in the room. "The most likely explanation for the coach's disappearance is that the drivers realized who Dalton was, believed that he had the gang's cash, and turned on their own passengers, robbing them and running off with the money."

"Why is there any doubt?" Angie asked. She sat and began to leaf through the scrapbooks.

"Because the drivers never contacted any of their family, or anyone else, and they both had large families. Maybe the drivers also died, or killed each other, over the money. Nobody knows for sure. All that's known is no one who was on the stagecoach was ever heard from again."

"Could the stage have been lost by natural causes? I've heard flash floods, when they hit, can be deadly in the desert. And what about Indians?"

"No. We had treaties with the Indians by then, and if there was a flood, something would have been found when the water receded."

Angie inhaled sharply. "And nothing at all was found?"

"Just a few pieces of clothing and odds and ends out by Ghost Hollow. A few things were found near the creek, others up in some caves in that area."

"The caves? Where Hal Edwards' body was found?"

"Yes, as a matter of fact. Those caves are said to be haunted."

"So I've heard," Angie murmured.

"Let's see." The librarian flipped to the back of one volume where letters to the sheriff and mayor of Jackpot had been filed between clear plastic sheets. "These are all inquiries that came here from friends and relatives seeking information." She turned the pages. "Most are from relatives of the drivers, as you can see. None are for Hoot Dalton or the so-called actress. Ah, look here"—she pointed at a page—"these were for the chef you mentioned."

Angie stared, awestruck, as all her student-of-culinary-history juices stirred. The letters were from the famous Oscar Tschirky, himself. Handwritten, no less. And signed. Her heart pounded at the sight.

The first, dated September 1893, was a short inquiry as to the state of the investigation. On the second line, it was written that if Mr. Willem van Beerstraeden's journal or recipe notebook were located, they should be sent to Tschirky immediately, in care of the Waldorf Hotel.

"Look at that!" Angie cried. "My God! Oscar Tschirky!"

"Who?"

"The recipe notebook mentioned in this letter," Angie said, "was it ever found?"

"I don't believe so," Doris replied. "You'll see more inquiries, but then I suppose the letter writer gave up."

Angie paled. "Thank you."

Doris knew when she was no longer needed and wandered away.

Angie read through the three remaining letters from the famous Oscar Tschirky. Each became increasingly desperate to find the recipe book, saying things like "the family name and honor" were at stake, and that "it should not get into the wrong hands."

What must those recipes be like to cause such a reaction? The family name and honor . . .

Her mind raced. What could he possibly have meant about "wrong hands"?

How she'd love to see that notebook! This part of Arizona was a desert. Things could be preserved forever in this type of climate. Look at the Dead Sea scrolls, for example. Original recipes from one of the first chefs of the Waldorf Hotel . . . recipes that Oscar-of-the-Waldorf himself wanted . . . might still be buried there somewhere!

She read the letters again, word by word. Then she read them a third time.

With painstaking care, she closed the album and sat back in the chair. A thought struck her. A completely jarring, earth-shattering, mouth-dropping-in-amazement thought.

Her heartbeat quickened. Her stomach fluttered. And suddenly, it all came to her like a bolt of lightning.

Eyes shining, face flushed, she smiled until she couldn't stretch her face any farther.

Chapter 14

After the meeting at the Stagecoach, Paavo and a feeling-no-pain Doc Griggs went to the library and found Angie pouring over the Internet where she was apparently reading about some New York City chef. It made no sense to Paavo, which was nothing new where Angie was concerned.

As they headed for the rented Mercedes, Angie was just about to explain some discovery she'd made, when Sheriff Merry Belle Hermann came marching toward them.

"Hold on, you all!" the sheriff thundered. Her cell phone, nightstick, holster with gun, mace canister, and whatever else she managed to attach onto her belt flounced like a tutu as her short legs and wide hips gave her a waddling gait. Buster trailed behind.

"What's the problem?" Paavo asked.

"I got some info for Doc," she said with a scowl.

Buster moved next to Angie. "Say, did you bring any other designer clothes, or just that Missoni?"

Paavo stared at Buster. Had he just said what Paavo thought he said?

"Shut up, Buster!" Merry Belle ordered. "I got business."

"What's your news?" Doc asked.

"Ned's horse turned up out at Hal's cattle ranch. The foreman out there gave me a call."

Buster walked around Angie, taking in her dress and shoes from all sides while Merry Belle talked. Paavo put an arm around Angie and glared in Buster's direction.

The deputy never even noticed.

Doc said to Paavo, "This is mighty odd."

"What do you mean?" Paavo asked.

"It doesn't figure the horse would show up way out there. It's all wrong."

"Mind talking to me?" the sheriff growled. "I'm the law around here."

"Don't trouble your blood pressure, M.B.," Doc said. "I was just thinking out loud."

"If you've got questions, ask me," Merry Belle insisted.

"Try this, then. The cattle ranch is some twenty miles away from where Ned was murdered. Most of those miles are high, rough ground. It would have made more sense for the horse to cross the flatland."

"You think like a horse now?" she jeered.

Doc glared at her. "That's more than you can do!"

Paavo decided to interrupt before this got out of hand. "Sounds to me like Doc has a point, Sheriff."

At the sheriff's derisive stare, Angie chirped up with a loud, "That's right!"

Merry Belle's small eyes seemed even smaller as she folded heavy arms across her bosom. "So, you two city folks are experts on horses, too? What an outbreak of experts I got on my hands!"

"But isn't that what you said earlier, Aunt Merry Belle?" Buster asked.

"Shut up!" Then, to the others she added, "Let's say I don't know. The killing spooked the horse, damn it, and it ran off without consulting you all."

"Or was taken away," Doc offered.

"Who's to know?"

"It may be worth looking into," Paavo suggested.

She squinted at Paavo. "I'll give the horse the third degree."

"I wish you could," he said coolly.

Her jowls quivered. "The investigation is progressing thoroughly and professionally, Inspector. Pleasure to talk to you all." She turned away, then halted and shouted, "Buster!"

He reluctantly left Angie's side and followed.

Angie took the SUV and returned to the guest ranch while Paavo went with Doc out to the cattle ranch to retrieve Ned's horse. As she hunted for the key to unlock the door to the bungalow she thought of how ecstatic Paavo was going to be when she told him her wonderful discovery about Oscar Tschirky. What luck! What—

"Well, speak of the devil!" Clarissa said, coming out of the common room and spying Angie. "You didn't give me a single detail about finding

Ned Paulson's body! I had to hear about it from LaVerne Merritt."

"There wasn't much to tell," she said.

"That's not what I was told." Clarissa made an about-face to stand in the shade of the veranda. "The whole town is buzzing."

This town was even smaller than Angie thought. "Yes, I—"

"Such a pity. He was a young man, too, I understand. Oh, well, such is life. Now, we've got a cookout to plan. Have you done anything at all?"

"I've given the meal quite a bit of thought, actually," Angie stated. "And, I just learned that at the turn of the century a famous chef from New York's Waldorf Hotel was lost near here and—"

"Turn of the century? I take it you're talking about the prior century, not the twentieth. That doesn't sound very modern or exciting. Oh, well, if you can't come up with anything better than that, LaVerne Merritt will help you."

Angie blinked a moment. "The woman from the coffee shop?"

"That's right. She told me that she's a gourmet cook herself, even though, for the restaurant, her cooking is rather dull. Not that I've ever eaten in a cheap diner, of course. Anyway, she's quite chatty and friendly, you know, so I told her about your background, and she'd be thrilled to work with you. She's also agreed to prepare some special dishes for me."

"You want Laverne Merritt to help me? The woman who makes poisonous cactus cakes?" Angie was sure steam was coming from her ears.

"That's not necessary. As I was saying about the Waldorf's chef and Oscar Tschirky—"

"I'm afraid I don't know the man," Clarissa insisted. "Perhaps he doesn't frequent my friends."

"He's dead!"

"That explains it, then." Clearly exasperated, Clarissa stood. "Let me show you the kitchen. Maybe it will help inspire you."

Angie gave up and followed. They walked around the main house and across a small herb and vegetable garden to a wooden building that Clarissa called the cookhouse. The outside looked plain and uninteresting, but inside was a kitchen with professional appliances and a storeroom stocked with food. It appeared to be a pleasant place to work.

"Teresa Flores did a wonderful job here." Angie ran her hand over a granite countertop as she remembered that Teresa told her she'd worked on updating it.

"Teresa Flores?" Clarissa asked.

"Hal's manager," Angie said.

"I vaguely remember her—her grandmother runs the little Mexican restaurant." Clarissa patted her hair as if to make sure every lacquered, golden strand was still in place. "I don't believe she was ever a manager. A housekeeper is more like it."

A middle-aged woman appeared at the entrance carrying a bag of groceries. As soon as she noticed Clarissa, she froze, bowed, and bobbed a couple of times and looked ready to back right outside again.

Angie quickly introduced herself.

The woman appeared surprised, then greeted her warmly and put down the grocery sack. Clarissa didn't say a word.

Dolores Huerta was of medium height, with a broad build, muscular arms, and square, competent hands. Her black hair, with a few gray strands, was short and curly, giving her face a pleasant, but serious demeanor.

Clarissa explained to Angie that Dolores, with some kitchen helpers, would be preparing the traditional fare for the cookout. Angie found Dolores to be a pleasant woman, and she was sure they could share the kitchen with no problem.

With a baleful look at Clarissa, Dolores hurried from the room, leaving Clarissa to show Angie where the supplies were kept, and to demonstrate her woeful ignorance about everything that went on in the kitchen.

Chapter 15

Hal Edwards's cattle ranch was northeast of town, where the land rose high and could be used as pasture. Miles from the caves, Paavo understood Doc's surprise that Ned's horse had ended up way out there.

Apparently, the horse hadn't traveled that far on his own. The foreman found him on the desert flats just east of the cattle ranch, hungry and thirsty. The saddle and bridle were gone. The horse was tame, so he loaded him onto a horse trailer and brought him to the stables. After hearing about Ned, he called the sheriff.

Paavo wondered about the missing saddle and bridle. Ned's cell phone was also missing, and the odds were good that it was in the saddlebag. The horse had no cuts or gashes that would indicate the harnesses had been torn from its body, so someone must have removed them.

Paavo wanted to find that saddlebag. The question was how?

* * *

"Want to see what you'll ride on at the cookout?" Lionel called out. Angie had left Clarissa and was now sitting on a rocking chair in front of her bungalow, thinking about what to serve with salmon roulade and waiting for Paavo to return.

"What do you mean by 'ride on'?" she asked skeptically.

"Didn't nobody tell you? The cooks come riding out onto the plaza with the chuck wagon filled with food just like in the old West. It's a, *uh*, a tradition." He smiled as if glad to have found the word.

He led her to a huge garage. Inside were a truck, tractor, some farm equipment, and an old chuck wagon that looked like something out of a movie set. She stared at the rickety wagon with its high bench seat. "It looks ancient."

"That's 'cause it is. A genuine antique from cattle drives that used to go through this area. Chuck box and all. 'Course, it could be dangerous."

He steered her to the rear of the wagon. The back consisted of a hinged lid that dropped down to serve as a work surface. When opened, it revealed the chuck box. Large, square, and wooden, it contained a number of shelves and drawers to hold whatever the cook might need. Dutch ovens were in the boot of the wagon, and a water barrel was attached to the side, along with an assortment of tools and boxes, hooks, brackets, and a coffee grinder. Numerous side drawers stored even more supplies.

Angie was impressed with the compact and utilitarian setup.

"I'm sure it's fine," she said running her hand

over the weathered wood. The wagon was living history, as was much of Jackpot. She felt as if she'd stepped back in time. It reminded her of the missing stagecoach and the caves—and Willem van Beerstraeden's journal. "This chuck wagon is like history come to life—like the missing stagecoach you talk about. As a matter of fact, I'd love to learn more about the stagecoach. I've heard some belongings from it were found around here."

"Yes, ma'am. It's true." He scratched his belly. "Some at the creek, but mostly up at the caves where Uncle Hal died. You can go up there anytime, you know. Might find something interesting yourself."

"Do you really think so?"

"Why not?" Lionel gazed at her with a definite twinkle in his eye. "Just be careful you don't get to liking treasure hunting too much. If gold fever gets hold of you, Miss Angie, you'll soon be wandering around these hills like some old withered prospector with nothing but a donkey, pickax, and shovel."

"I know why I'm here!" Angie cried the minute Paavo walked into their cabin. She threw her arms around his neck, got up on tiptoe, and kissed him.

"What's all this?" he asked.

"I couldn't wait to tell you!" She spun away and was all but dancing around the living room. "It all came to me at the library. Paavo, I can *feel* it. This time, finally, I've discovered the thing that's going to make my name in the culinary world!"

"Angie—"

"Don't Angie me in that tone! I know what

you're thinking, but I'm telling you, it's going to happen."

He sat down on the sofa. "Okay."

She sat on the arm beside him. "It all has to do with Oscar Tschirky!"

"Who?" He looked completely befuddled.

She gave him a quick history, explaining that Oscar was one of William Waldorf Astor's first employees when the Waldorf Hotel opened in March 1893.

Later, in 1897, cousin John Jacob Astor IV erected the Astoria next door, and the hotels combined to become the Waldorf-Astoria. In 1929, the original hotels were demolished to make way for the Empire State Building, but reopened at the current site in 1931. Throughout all that time, Oscar Tschirky was the maître d'hotel, renowned for his fabulous gourmet concoctions.

All this bit of history did was to make Paavo look at her with something akin to deep concern.

She then told him about Chef van Beerstraeden and the missing journal of recipes, pointing out that van Beerstraeden disappeared in the summer of 1893—the same year that the Waldorf opened. "I started thinking about this coincidence," she concluded. "Oscar Tschirky, you see, wasn't a chef, he was a maître d'hotel. So why would he be so interested in someone else's recipes?"

Paavo had no answer.

Angie's voice turned conspiratorial. "Everyone had marveled that Oscar was so good at creating tasty delights when he wasn't a cook. Yet, his most famous creations were developed in the early years of his reign at the Waldorf, shortly after he'd been working with Willem van Beerstraeden . . . shortly after a real chef disappeared!"

"Oh?"

"Don't you get it?"

"No," he admitted.

She leaned closer, practically nose to nose, her hands gripping his shoulders. "What if, for example, veal Oscar wasn't created by Oscar of the Waldorf, but by another man—a man who disappeared on a stagecoach in the middle of the Sonoran desert in the 1890s? Do you realize what a tremendous stir that would cause?"

"You're kidding me, right?"

She looked at him as if he was crazy. "Of course not! And if I'm the one to discover that the culinary world has been wrong about Oscar Tschirky all this time, it'll make me famous."

He had no comment.

"On top of that," she continued, "if I find his recipes, I can publish them myself! I can see it now—a bestseller. Oprah might start talking about cookbooks on her show. Or Letterman. I'd love to do Letterman. What are the top ten reasons for buying Angie Amalfi's cookbook?"

Paavo gaped. "I don't know."

"Neither do I. But I'll come up with them. First, though, I've got to find that recipe book. Lionel told me people still find things from the missing stagecoach out near the creek or in the caves." She glanced at Paavo's expression. "What, you think I'm joking?"

"No, not at all." He shifted her onto his lap.

"Matter of fact, I think it's a great idea. You should pursue it," he said, wrapping his arms around her.

She frowned. "Really?"

"Absolutely. Just make sure you're careful out there in the desert. Take Lionel or someone with you."

She frowned at this sudden turnaround. "What am I missing?"

"Missing?" He tried to look innocent, but failed. "Nothing. Nothing at all."

They headed for the dining room with Angie practically dancing with excitement and shooing ostriches out of the way. She went from one plan to another on how to retrieve the lost cookbook. Paavo had to smile at her enthusiasm, secretly thankful that it just might keep her occupied while he tried to find out who killed Ned and Hal.

As soon as they reached the common room, she dropped the subject. Not that it mattered—no one was there to overhear it.

Dolores served T-bone steaks, baked potatoes, squash, and a green salad for dinner with pinot noir to wash it down. As Paavo ate the thick, tender steak, he had no doubt this was cattle country.

Clarissa and Joey had again asked for dinner in their rooms, and Lionel was eating, as he usually did, in the kitchen with Dolores and Junior Whitney.

Right before dessert, however, Lionel and Junior ventured into the dining room. Junior looked even more like he'd been rolling in cow manure than when Angie first met him.

The two men regarded Angie and Paavo almost

shyly. Their eyes lit up, though, when Dolores brought in a cheesecake covered with huckleberry preserves.

"Are we all going to have dessert together?" Angie asked.

"Sure," Lionel said, a mischievous glint in his eyes. "But our guests always go first. This is a treat. It was sent over by LaVerne from Merritt's Café. She's quite the gourmet cook, you know."

Angie frowned. "So I've been told."

Paavo wasn't sure what was going on.

Dolores cut the cake, put two pieces on dishes for Angie and Paavo, and then she joined the men watching them. He noticed Junior, who'd clearly been drinking, give Dolores an appreciative glance and move over next to her. She, however, shifted away.

Paavo bent near the cheesecake, then pushed his plate away. The strong odor of goat cheese was unmistakable. What in the world was LaVerne thinking?

Angie, to his surprise, took a bite.

"How interesting. Cheesecake *au chèvre*." She smiled at the three who were now gawking at her with amazement. "This cheese is wonderful in *bûchette charcuterie*, you know, an appetizer made by wrapping pancetta around a small piece of cheese and chives, then sautéing it. It's also delicious in tarts."

Lionel and Junior stared, open-mouthed, their eyebrows high, as if they didn't know whether to believe her or not. She took another bite, and murmured, "*Ummm.*"

Lionel licked his bottom lip.

Junior began to drool.

"Marvelous!" Angie cooed. "Too bad I'm too full after that T-bone to enjoy it."

"Cheesecake-oh-shever?" Lionel asked.

"It's all the rage in San Francisco," Angie replied, putting down her fork.

"Hey, I'll try some," Junior said.

"Me too," Lionel added, as Dolores cut three big slices, obviously deciding to join in herself.

As Angie whisked Paavo from the room, he noticed the others taking big forkfuls of LaVerne's specialty. Immediately, their mouths wrinkled in disgust. Dolores gagged the food down while Lionel and Junior spit it into their hands.

And then Paavo heard Angie's soft cackle.

The last customers had gone home, and Teresa Flores stepped onto the dark, empty parking lot that surrounded Maritza's restaurant. She had visited the restaurant that evening just to get out of the house, to see people who were untroubled enough to want to relax over a good meal.

She'd been that way once herself, an eternity ago.

The next day was Ned's funeral.

Just the thought of it made tears form once again. She fought them back, tucking her long black hair behind her ear, squaring her shoulders as she hurried to her car. But Ned's face shimmered before her, especially his intense blue eyes, and the way they'd followed her with a sad mixture of desire and hopelessness. If only she had been able to love him the way he did her, if only the way she'd wanted to live her life was different . . . if, if, if . . . would he still be alive?

Would she no longer feel this oppressive guilt whenever she thought of Ned . . . or of Hal?

Would everything, still, be her fault?

She took long-legged strides, forcing herself to hurry. The lot seemed somehow darker and quieter than normal. The lights from the restaurant burned bright as the kitchen helpers cleaned up for the next day's business and her mother took care of the day's receipts. She wondered if she should have waited for them so that they all could have left together.

No, that was silly. She knew the restaurant and this parking lot as well as she did her own home. She continued toward the back of the lot where she always parked in order to leave the prime spaces for customers.

She was halfway across when something told her to go no farther—to hurry back to the restaurant.

She fought it. She didn't believe in "intuition," in "second sight," in any of that ESP-type nonsense her mother and grandmother placed such store in. It was all superstition.

Her heartbeat quickened, and suddenly she was running. She didn't know why, couldn't think, all she knew was that she needed to hurry back to the restaurant.

At that moment, behind her, a truck engine roared. Its headlights were off, but even in the darkness she could see the truck, like an enormous black monster, bearing down on her.

She ran faster, reaching the restaurant's back

steps, grabbing the metal handrail, and pulling herself up off the parking lot and high onto the staircase just as the truck sped by.

Hand to her chest, hoping to still her pounding heart, she stared into the darkness. Had it come as close, and was it going as fast, as she'd thought? Or was it, once again, only her imagination?

Chapter 16

Angie and Paavo were alone in the dining room, drinking coffee and eating waffles from the breakfast buffet when Lionel entered. He took one look at them and started to back out.

"Join us," Paavo called, his tone making it more an order than a request.

Lionel hesitated, but then poured himself coffee and sat at their table.

"Sounds like your fishing plans fell apart." His eyes shifted warily. "Guess you folks are gonna be leaving us soon."

"No, we'll stay." Paavo's voice was low, the words firm.

"It's nice here," Angie said to Lionel, trying to lighten the mood. "Despite all the ostriches, and even hairy spiders. I found out tarantulas aren't nearly as dangerous as you said."

"Really? I been bit once. Hurt to high heaven." He glanced at Paavo. "I just didn't think you'd stick around after finding a dead body. Sort of a busman's holiday, seems to me."

Paavo grimaced. "What I'd like to know is why Ned was out at those caves," he said. "Do you have any ideas?"

Lionel looked surprised. "Me? Hell, no."

"Funny," Paavo said, "that Ned was found near the place your Uncle Hal died. Did Ned ever talk to you about Hal?"

"Ned and me didn't talk about nothing." Lionel loudly sipped his hot coffee. "He was kinda uppity, having his own business and all. Guess I wasn't his sort."

"Weren't Ned and Hal friends?" Paavo pressed.

"Ned and Hal?" Lionel chuckled. "Hell, Hal couldn't stand the guy!"

"Really?" Paavo wanted to hear Lionel's take on the relationship. "Why not?"

Lionel shrugged. "Beats me."

"Did they see each other when Hal returned?" Paavo asked.

Lionel lifted an eyebrow, then dropped his voice. "I'm surprised no one's asked me that afore now, but then ol' Mighty Butt didn't ask much at all."

"Mighty Butt?" Angie repeated.

"M.B. The sheriff," Lionel explained with a scowl. "Anyway, I saw Ned and Hal having it out right out there on the veranda." He nodded toward the windows. "Come to think of it, though, that don't mean a hell of a lot. Hal always argued with folk."

"Ned was here?" Paavo asked, then his eyes hardened. "What about Teresa Flores? Did she come out here, too?"

Lionel grimaced and nodded. "I 'spect she was here trying to get her old job back. I think my uncle had had it with her, though. She weren't nothing but a gold digger. It took him a while, but Hal finally figured it out. He run her off."

That was new information, Angie thought.

"When did he run her off?" Paavo asked.

"Round about a day or two afore he took off for Mexico, some five years ago." Lionel scratched his chin a moment, shifting nervously in the chair, as if thinking he might have said too much. Suddenly, he told them he had work to do, drained his coffee cup, and left.

"If Lionel was telling the truth," Paavo said, once he and Angie were alone, "it means Teresa lied to us. And Ned must have lied to Doc, or I'm sure Doc would have told us that Ned and Hal had had words."

Angie met his gaze. "The questions are, why was Ned lying then? And why is Teresa now?"

"I think I'll go pay a visit to the sheriff," Paavo said, standing. "Do you want to stay here, or head into town?"

"I should finish up the menu for the cookout," Angie said. "And maybe afterward, I'll take a little walk down to the creek."

"Be careful," Paavo warned.

"Don't worry about me," Angie said with a grin. "Around Mighty Butt, you're the one in danger!"

"There's no evidence of squat," Merry Belle said a bit later as Paavo sat across her desk going through the information she'd gathered. At her side was an enormous cup of caffé mocha with a whipped cream topping. Not that Jackpot had a

Starbucks or that Merritt's had become creative. Merry Belle had bought herself a Saeco espresso machine and made it there in her office.

Saecos were expensive, Paavo thought, as were Hummers. It made him wonder how Jackpot's sheriff could afford them.

He read over the forensic reports on the finger-prints, blood, hair, and fibers from Ned's home and office, the cave, and the rocky ledge. They'd picked up all kinds of samples, and all of them came back with no match. Paavo was puzzled un-til he learned that Buster was the one using the crime scene investigator kits for analysis.

If there ever had been any good evidence, it was gone now.

"You should have sent the samples to Phoenix and had them analyzed in the laboratories," he said, unable to hide his disgust at the mess.

"Is that so, San Francisco? And have them say what? That we can't figure out how to use the kits they spent good money to send us?" The sheriff sipped some coffee, then wiped whipped cream off her upper lip. "We used the kits just fine. It's simply that all the spots had plenty of activity with people coming and going."

"The skill comes in knowing how to separate out the usual activity from the crime. For example"—he pointed at fingerprint samples—"looks like you've got a couple hundred, but they aren't even marked as to where they're from. Do you know?"

Merry Belle stuffed them back into a folder. Out of sight, out of mind. She glowered at Paavo, dar-ing him to say more.

Paavo suppressed a sigh. Accusations after the fact were not going to help anyone. "Have you requested Ned's phone records?"

"Oh . . . his phone records." She went to the door. "Buster, did you get Ned's phone records?"

"No, Aunt Merry Belle."

"Well, why not? Do it!"

"You didn't tell me nothing about getting no phone rec—"

"Be quiet, Buster! Do your job." She slammed the door shut. "Satisfied now, San Francisco?"

Paavo took a large swallow of his plain black coffee. It was going to be another long day.

Angie went to the cookhouse to look over the supplies and spices. She was pleased with the menu she'd come up with.

Along with the salmon, she planned an appetizer of *fois gras* with poached apples, and two salads—one of beet, orange, walnut and arugula, and the other of shaved fennel, mushroom, and parmesan. For vegetables, she'd have butternut squash timbales, and orange dal made by crushing lentils with ginger and garlic. She still had to check with Clarissa to find out if she should prepare a dessert or not.

Now, she needed to see what items to ask Lionel to buy. Some ingredients, like the fois gras, arugula, and fresh fennel might require a trip to a town a bit larger than Jackpot.

A very sheepish Dolores was in there cleaning up the breakfast dishes. "I'm sorry, *senorita*, about last night's cake. Lionel, he said it would be a good joke. But the joke was on us."

"It's all right," Angie said. "I guess LaVerne tries."

"She is very trying," Dolores added, and both women laughed.

As Angie made her list, she chatted with the head cook and housekeeper. Dolores had worked on the ranch for over twenty years. She'd never married, and lived in rooms in the cabin behind the hacienda. Back when Hal Edwards ran the guest ranch, there were many cooks and house-keepers, and all had rooms there. Now, she was the only one left. She would hire kitchen helpers and housemaids as needed when more guests than she could handle arrived, which wasn't very often anymore. Right now, she had a girl come in to clean and change linens in the guest cabins each day, but she alone prepared the food.

"Does Junior Whitney live in one of the rooms the way you do?" Angie asked.

"No. He has an old RV, and mostly lives in it—thank goodness," Dolores said with a shudder.

Angie couldn't help but agree. "You don't mind being alone?"

Dolores shook her head. "After the way I lived so crowded with my family when I was growing up in Mexico, I like it."

Just then, Clarissa walked in and Dolores pressed her lips firmly shut.

"I've just returned from my morning ride," Clarissa said, getting herself a bottle of Perrier, eyeing Angie and ignoring Dolores. "I heard you were in here. Have you been able to come up with any more ideas at all for the cookout?"

"I've been thinking about making an Italian dish, *strozzapreti alla puttanesca*," Angie said. "How does that strike you?"

Dolores looked quizzically at Angie, then quietly asked, "Is that anything like *puta* in Spanish?"

Angie smiled. It was an uncomplimentary term for a woman. "You've got it," she whispered back.

Dolores glanced at Clarissa and nodded.

"Whatever," Clarissa said, drinking some water. "Give Lionel your list. Let's go have some chilled wine. It's very warm today." She left the bottle on the kitchen counter, and headed for the common room.

Angie waved good-bye to Dolores.

The sun was bright, and the day already warm. Angie wondered if she'd ever before seen a sky as high and blue as that in Arizona. Even the rather smelly ostriches looked magnificent against the horizon.

"Do you ride often?" Angie asked, marveling that at Clarissa's age she still rode at all.

"I try to do so every day when I'm here," she replied.

"You seem quite at home," Angie added.

"I should! I lived here for twenty-five years. Even though I can't stand this backwater, to turn it into an ostrich farm is beyond appalling! If somebody hadn't beaten me to it, I might have killed Hal myself."

Angie was astonished to hear anyone finally being honest about what happened to Hal Edwards.

"I'm surprised you didn't get the house," Angie

said. "Most of the time, it seems, that goes to the wife, especially when there's a child involved."

"I wanted to return to California. Instead of the house, I took the business."

"That's even more surprising."

They reached the common room and Clarissa made a beeline for the bar. She began going through bottles in the wine cooler.

"Why? After his stroke, Hal couldn't run it anyway," Clarissa called. A moment later, she stood with a bottle of chardonnay in hand. "He couldn't walk, could hardly speak. What he needed was a home, which I allowed him to have. I thought getting the business was a good deal. Was I ever fooled! The business should have provided Joseph and me with a fabulous income for years. But Joseph is having trouble. The manager he hired couldn't run a shoebox. We fired him, but the damage was done. Other grocery chains began moving into Arizona, and we've lost more stores than I can count."

Like a pro, Clarissa uncorked the wine and poured.

"How terrible," Angie said.

"It is." Clarissa handed her a glass. "It makes me furious! I've taken care of myself with investments, but I worry about Joseph. Unless he turns it around, Halmart stores are looking at bankruptcy."

"What will it take to reverse course?" Angie asked. She wasn't a fan of chardonnay, but this one was exceptional.

"Hmm, very nice." Clarissa topped off her glass before answering. "From what Joseph tells me, the stores need an infusion of money. That's why I wish we'd get this silly reading of the will—if there is one—over with. Hal had lots of money. Look at all those stupid ostriches. They're expensive! And I understand he planned to buy a few males, which are even more expensive, to breed with them! God, the man makes me sick!"

"I take it your divorce was acrimonious," Angie said.

"Acrimonious." Clarissa gave a dry, mirthless laugh, then gulped down her wine and poured more before heading out to the veranda to sit in the shade. "It was so 'acrimonious' we didn't simply divorce, he had the Catholic Church annul the marriage! Can you imagine?"

They took seats at a wicker table. "How could he do that?" Angie asked. "You have a child."

"When we married, I was a divorced woman."

"I see." Herself a Catholic, Angie guessed Hal had argued that he never had a legitimate marriage to Clarissa. Even in such cases, though, when children were involved, church annulments were extraordinarily difficult to get. She didn't understand why Hal would go through all that. "Was Mr. Edwards very religious?"

Clarissa's laugh was loud and harsh. "God, no! What a funny image! No, Hal used his Catholicism the way he used people—when it suited his own selfish purposes. He was quite the character, Hal was."

"I'm sorry," Angie said, fingering her engagement ring. "I'm sorry to hear you were unlucky in your marriages."

"My first marriage was a mistake," Clarissa said. "Nothing more. A college romance." She swirled the wine in her glass. "He was just a poor boy, on scholarship. Of course, my parents objected and convinced me to leave him. They took care of the divorce. I transferred to another college . . . and never saw him again."

"Did you ever wond—"

"No!" Clarissa snapped. "Of course not."

"But then you met Hal," Angie said.

The distant brown mountains were sharply etched against the sky. "A cowboy from Arizona," Clarissa's voice was soft. "My family found out how rich he was and suddenly decided cowboys were quaint and colorful. What better reason to marry, right?"

Angie couldn't find any words. How strange that this harridan, who so carelessly bossed other people, had herself been pushed into making life-altering changes—and had spent her life paying the consequences.

"Don't look at me like that!" Clarissa said. "You're young. You think married life is a bed of roses. I'll tell you—it's a bed of thorns. Someday you'll thank me for the warning. People here feel I took advantage of Hal's illness. They thought Hal was a saint, but in truth, he was a spiteful little man who never passed up an opportunity to make money no matter the cost."

"I'm sorry," Angie murmured.

"It's life. Remember that, and expect that someday you could easily come to hate your handsome fiancé. And him, you."

Angie was so shocked and appalled by the sudden personal attack, her voice shook. "I don't believe that."

"Realism is an asset in marriage. The biggest asset."

"So are love and trust and the will to persevere."

Clarissa smiled disdainfully, then emptied her wineglass. "Perhaps we should speak again in, say, ten years."

"You're wrong, Clarissa."

"You *hope* I am." Clarissa stood. "I've got to go get cleaned up. I can't abide the smell of horses."

As Angie watched her leave, she found herself torn between anger at the lonely, bitter woman and feeling very, very sorry for her.

Chapter 17

Angie was looking for Lionel to get directions to the creek area, where remnants from the stagecoach had been found, when she noticed Junior Whitney scrubbing out the plaza's center fountain. Clarissa had demanded that it sparkle for the cookout.

Several ostriches were around him, fascinated by what he was doing.

The second time Angie saw Junior take the handle of his mop and hit a wayward ostrich with it to get the big bird away from him, she decided to do something.

Ostriches, she'd learned by watching them, weren't quite as free ranging as she'd originally thought. They were herd animals and tended to stay together in flocks. As long as a mound of food was kept in an area behind the workhouses, the birds mostly stayed there. The problem was that they were also curious. If their interest was piqued, simply because they were so large, their legs so long and fast moving, in just a few steps they were in the plaza.

They were surprisingly good-natured, as well. If startled, though, they tended to run blindly in straight lines, which meant smacking into trees, buildings, or even people in their way.

Only when cornered were they dangerous. Then, their enormously powerful legs could kick a man to the next county.

That was why Angie saw no reason for Junior to hit or jab them, when simply taking the time to shoo them away worked just fine. As another ostrich ventured near, Junior raised the mop again.

"Is that bird being stubborn or is it you?" Angie asked, marching toward him. "I'm sure she'll follow corn kernels if you sprinkle them back toward the flock."

He scowled. "You herd ostriches in San Francisco, do you?"

"No, but I've watched Lionel do it."

"He don't know nothing."

As Junior stepped toward the bird, Angie grabbed hold of the mop. "You don't need to do that."

The way he looked at her, she wondered if he wasn't going to whack her with it. Suddenly, though, his expression changed. He stared over her shoulder, and his face went from white to red, and then angry and vicious. He shoved the mop at her. As she stumbled back a few steps, he stomped off.

She turned to see what had caused the change in him, and discovered Lupe walking toward her.

"Are you all right?" Lupe asked. Dislike and something else were in her dark eyes as she glared after Junior.

"Fine," Angie replied. "I'm surprised to see you out here."

"I need to talk to Paavo," Lupe said. "It's important."

"He's off somewhere with Merry Belle, I think."

Her hands clenched, Lupe spat out the words, "Someone tried to kill Teresa late last night. She says I'm overreacting, but I saw the whole thing. If she hadn't turned back, a truck would have hit her."

"Whose truck?" Angie asked, alarmed.

"I don't know. It was too dark to tell—and it didn't have its headlights on. But I know . . ."

"What?" Angie asked.

Lupe shook her head. "I'll go back to town. I'll try to find Paavo."

"Give me a minute to change clothes," Angie said. "I'm coming with you."

Paavo stopped at the foot of the hills where the caves were located. He was searching for the saddle and saddlebags.

He tried to think like Ned's killer. The man—or woman, although it wasn't very likely that a woman had killed by brute strength—had probably premeditated the murder, and lured Ned up onto the ledge knowing the chance of anyone finding his body up there would be almost nil. Out in the open like that, with the kinds of scavengers in the desert, there was a good chance he'd never be found.

But then, the killer had to do something with Ned's horse.

He couldn't leave the horse there at the caves. That would be a sign that the body was near. So the murderer led the horse out to the open desert, took off his saddle and bridle, and spooked him. A strong horse like Ned's could go a long distance before he'd stop running, and even afterward, he'd continue moving, enjoying his freedom before hunger and thirst set in.

So, unless the killer brought the saddle and saddlebags home with him, he most likely hid them somewhere in the rocks before the desert turned flat and sandy.

That was what Paavo hoped.

As he sat thinking, he realized this area was quieter than anywhere he'd ever been, so quiet he could hear his horse breathe. It gave him an idea.

Patting the horse to calm and quiet it, a five-year-old roan gelding named Bucky from the guest ranch, he took out his cell phone. For some strange reason, out in this area, there was cell service. He wasn't sure why, but he could take advantage of it.

Even before dialing, he had to admit the idea was probably silly. Chance of him being within miles of Ned's phone was pretty remote.

Still, what would it hurt to try?

He punched in Ned's number. The phone rang once, twice, and then a voice said, "Hello?"

Angie tried to phone Paavo while Lupe drove, but she had no service on her cell phone.

How did people exist in an area where they couldn't be reached any time of the day or night?

Hmm . . . come to think of it, that sounded rather nice.

When Angie and Lupe returned to the restaurant, Teresa was there. She ignored her mother's concerns to the point of rudeness, and said no one was trying to harm her.

With that, she stormed out of the restaurant.

Seeing how unhappy and stressed Lupe looked, Angie offered to stay, but Lupe declined, saying she wanted to talk to Doc.

Astutely, Angie excused herself.

Paavo thought he was going to die. He choked, wheezed, and gasped. Tears formed in his eyes, and fire roiled down to his guts. "You call this medicine? It's criminal," he managed to croak. He handed back the brown glass flask of Wainwright's All-Genuine Medicinal Elixir.

Lucius Wainwright twisted the cap back on the bottle. "It most certainly is medicinal!" The middle-aged, florid-faced man put the bottle by his side, then turned the wieners on the spit over the butane heater while licking his lips.

They sat on lawn chairs in the shade of a van. A sign painted on each side showed a covered wagon and above it, in flowery writing, the name Lucius Wainwright, Esquire.

"My elixir relieves headaches in men, and for the ladies, whatever ails them," Wainwright said. "Most women I've known have a great many ailments." He took a moment to tsk-tsk. "My great-grandfather sold Lydia Pinkham's Compound to the ladies for their female complaints. He made a fortune from it. It's become the family tradition."

"A family tradition of selling eighty proof?" Paavo asked skeptically.

"Now, sir, you should know that at least twenty percent alcohol is not atypical of an herbal tincture, which is all this is. Indeed, my good man, an herbal extract with less alcohol is pharmacologically unstable! The alcohol is necessary to disperse the medicine, especially to the uterine tissues, where the little ladies seem to suffer their gravest discomfort." He bowed his head.

"Okay," Paavo said. "Forty-proof, then."

"Actually, it is eighty. But it even helps with depression, which is quite common in bleak areas such as this." He spread his arms wide.

"I'm not here from the FDA," Paavo said. "And I don't care what you're selling. But I do need to take the saddle and saddlebags with me."

Earlier, the peddler had relayed how he'd been driving his van when he heard ringing and realized it was coming from the cell phone in the saddlebags he'd found. That was when he'd answered.

"Finders' keepers," Wainwright said with a smile, removing the frankfurters to buns. He offered one, which Paavo declined. "That's the way of the West."

"This is a murder investigation," Paavo pointed out. "You don't want to be withholding evidence."

"Evidence? Damnation! Why is it that whenever I come across something useful, I can't use it?" He pouted. "Of course, even if I were to keep the phone, I have no one who would want to call me. Is it worse, I wonder, to have a cell phone and have it remain silent, or to not have one at all?"

That was a question for which Paavo had no answer. "Have you come across anything else useful recently?" he asked.

Wainwright munched on his hot dog. "Depends

on what you consider useful. Do you mean the coyotes and illegals who used Hal Edwards's property and hid in the caves last winter? Or the fact that the man who was killed—the boat rental owner—was out here a couple of times going through those caves?"

Now that, Paavo thought, was definitely interesting. "You saw him?"

"Yes. Including the day he was killed, poor fellow. As a matter of fact, I saw two horses out there that day. One black, and the other looked just like the one you're riding."

Ned's horse was black, and people at the hacienda all rode Bucky from time to time.

"I didn't know who they were," Wainwright continued, "and I was heading back to town. If I'd have known the dénouement, I most certainly would have stuck around. Maybe even received a reward for my troubles. Unfortunately, I did neither." He opened an ice chest at his side. "My elixir is actually quite good over ice." He made up a glass for himself and another for Paavo. "Want to talk about any of that?"

Paavo took the glass he was offered. "Absolutely."

Wainwright clinked their glasses together. "Cheers."

Angie stuck her head into the sheriff's office to see if Merry Belle or Buster had any idea where she could find Paavo. The sheriff wasn't there, but Buster was.

"Oh, my God!" he cried, jumping up as she walked in. "Is that a Dolce and Gabbana dress?"

"My goodness, you do know your designers!" Angie said, amazed.

"I love their clothes." He took her hand, lifting it high and twirled her around so he could get the full effect of the white summer silk. "Casual, sometimes funky, and so classy."

"Well . . ."

"I'd love to go shopping sometime in San Francisco. Maybe when you're back home . . . ?"

She was speechless.

"Oh, that's all right! You don't want me bothering you. I can understand that." He flopped back down at his desk, his expression pouting. "Sometimes I think it's only me and Teresa Flores who realize just how small and uninteresting this town is. We're two peas in a pod—adventurous people, trapped here like rats in a cellar."

"You and Teresa?" Angie gasped.

"Not as a couple. She never cared for me that way, I'm sorry to say." His pout grew deeper.

"No. I guess her heart was with Ned," Angie said softly.

"Ned?" Buster took a handkerchief from his pocket and used it to buff the buttons on his shirt. "How about Joey?"

"Joey? You're joking."

"Nuh-uh! But Teresa knew Clarissa would have skewered her like a pig on a spit if she ever made a pass at Clarissa's little boy."

"Teresa . . . and Joey?" Angie could scarcely imagine it.

"Think about it. Teresa used to work for Hal. She even lived at the hacienda, and if you ask me, that was the happiest time of her life. Now, Joey comes here every winter, and he has everything Teresa ever wanted. Personally, I always figured Teresa was just using Ned to make Joey jealous, hoping that'd make him get up the gumption to tell Clarissa to go . . . uh, to leave him alone."

Angie was beginning to put some of the pieces together. "Do you know if Joey was here when his father returned this past winter?"

"Likely as not. He was in and out all winter. I'm not sure of the exact days, though. Never asked him, come to think of it." Buster looked down at his shiny buttons and smiled with satisfaction. "Enough about all that nastiness! I want to hear all about Manolo Blahnik. Have you ever met him? Do you think you could introduce me?"

Doc heard the kitchen help and waitresses gasp as he grabbed hold of Lupe's arm and hustled her out of the kitchen to her office. She, too, stared at him as if he'd lost his mind. Maybe he had.

"What's this about Teresa nearly being killed?" he asked when they were alone in the office, the door shut.

Lupe folded her arms and turned her back to him. "I'm afraid! I'm so afraid for her . . . I told myself I was wrong, but when Ned . . ."

He took her shoulders and spun her toward him, then stopped as he realized how close she stood, how dark and deep her eyes were, how the faint scent of both roses and spice that always lingered about her now curled around his senses. Whatever was between them, always there lurking beneath the surface, suddenly burst forth. His fingers tightened. She stiffened, but he knew she felt it, too. "I lost Ned, but I'm not going to let you lose Teresa! What's going on, Lupe?"

"I'm not sure."

"You know you can trust me."

"I know," she said. Her eyes glistened as she lightly placed her hand on his chest, whether to hold him back or to simply touch him, he had no idea—and he didn't care.

Without thinking, he drew her into his arms.

"No!" She pulled away, head bowed as she drew in a deep breath. After a moment, eyes averted, she said, "I've made promises. Promises I must keep."

He slid his hands into his pockets so he wouldn't make the same mistake again. "Then send Teresa to my house," he said. "No one will know she's there. She'll be safe."

She looked up at him, and then nodded. "That's a good idea. I'll ask her, and hope she'll do it." She stepped even closer. "Doc . . ." Her expression was so sad, so troubled, that it was all he could do not to reach for her again. He was certain that if he did, she'd allow it.

But she'd made it clear over the years why nothing could happen between them. He respected her reasons and knew that if he ever managed to break through her will, the end result would only be that he'd lose her.

She was always the strong one in the past. This time, it was his turn.

"I'll be waiting," he said as he walked toward the door. "Whenever you're ready."

Angie wasn't in a good mood. She'd spent the entire afternoon and evening—including dinner at

Merritt's—with Buster. As she told him about shopping at Bergdorf Goodman, Barney's, and Saks, he was like a man dying of thirst who'd just found artesian springs. For her, it was boring.

When Paavo finally did show up, he was in far too happy a state of mind to suit Angie. His evening had been spent with some snake oil salesman who had nothing better to do than ply him with "medicine" and tell stories about Jackpot. Angie wasn't impressed.

But at least he'd found Ned's cell phone and saddlebags. The morning before Ned's death a call had been made, which Caller ID showed was from "Hal Edwards." That was the last phone call Ned ever answered.

When Angie and Paavo finally returned to the guest ranch, they discovered that the phones in the common room and the dining room—and most likely in several other locations throughout the ranch—all had two lines, a public one and a secondary number. The secondary line had been used to call Ned. Anyone could have used it— anyone who worked there, or anyone who visited.

The common room was empty as they checked the phone numbers, but Angie couldn't shake off an eerie feeling of being watched. "It's just the ostriches," Paavo said. "Those birds have you spooked. They have nothing to do all day but eat and watch us. Don't worry about it."

"I think the one with the cowlick has a crush on you," Angie said, forcing a laugh. "It's always nearby."

He wasn't amused.

Since Paavo hadn't had dinner, and admitted the

so-called medicine was doing him more harm than good, Angie had him join her in the cookhouse where she made him a cheese and chorizo omelet, toast, and iced tea. He felt a lot better after eating.

As they walked back to their bungalow, the feeling Angie had of being watched grew stronger with each step. Paavo seemed oblivious, though.

It's not the ostriches, she told herself. Looking around the dark plaza, it was empty. That was the problem, she realized; the plaza was absolutely dark. Usually, until midnight, floodlights brightened the fountain. "Why aren't the lights on?" she whispered.

"Maybe Lionel doesn't want to waste money on electricity when we're the only guests," Paavo said.

"He doesn't want us here," Angie murmured. "He keeps trying to scare me."

"There's nothing to be afraid of. And you don't have to whisper." He unlocked the door to the bungalow and pushed it open.

Angie walked in as Paavo switched on the lights. Afterward, they realized the door must have hit a spring release lever. At the time, though, all Angie knew was that as she entered the room something long, scaly, and ropelike fell from the ceiling onto her head and shoulders.

It was a rattlesnake, so recently killed it was still pliant and flexible. It dangled from a bungee cord attached to the ceiling, bounding up and down, and seeming to wriggle about as if alive.

Angie nearly fainted from fright. If Lionel was the one who was trying to scare her into leaving, he'd just succeeded.

Chapter 18

It was the day of the funeral.

Angie headed for the kitchen, where she was going to bake a traditional favorite, a chocolate bourbon pecan pie, for the reception at the Flores's home after the funeral. With this hard-drinking town, the dash of bourbon in the pie would probably be appreciated.

And after the snake episode, the reason why the town was so hard drinking was becoming ever clearer. In fact, she was sorely tempted to join the boozers herself.

Last night, she was still loudly telling Paavo what she'd like to do to whoever put the snake in their room when Joey and Lionel ran over to find out what all the commotion was about. They denied any knowledge of what had been done, and both swore pranksters from town liked to play tricks like that on visitors. Looked like the work of teenagers, they insisted. Harmless, they swore. The snake was dead, wasn't it?

Lionel then pointed out that if Angie was too upset to stay, he'd refund their money.

The smirk on Lionel's face as he said that was all it took to get Angie to change her mind about leaving. Paavo, in fact, was the one she had to work hardest to convince to let her stay.

Now, she detoured to the common room for a cup of coffee. Joey was inside, his face flushed, his eyes glassy as if he'd already been drinking more than coffee that morning—or was nursing a horrendous hangover. *"Hola!"* he called, lifting his cup as if in salute. "Seen any snakes lately? Or tarantulas?"

"Very funny," Angie said as she served herself, wondering how he'd heard about the spider. "Are you going to the funeral?"

"I don't think I'd be welcome." His demeanor turned glum. "Poor bastard."

Angie decided baking a pie could wait a few minutes, and sat near Joey. "Did you know Ned well?" She didn't bother to ask if he knew Ned at all, as she truly believed everyone knew everyone else in this town.

"Of course. I went to school here until I was fourteen. Then my parents divorced and I moved to California."

Angie remembered Buster making reference to Joey and Teresa. Looking at Joey now, Angie was even more certain that Buster was completely wrong, but some innate curiosity made her ask, "Do you think Ned and Teresa Flores would have gotten married?"

"Does it matter?" His face tightened.

"Just curious," Angie explained, then drank more coffee before saying, "it must be hard for you being here, first losing your father, and then a friend."

"Ned and I weren't exactly friends," he said. "And I hardly knew my father." He downed his cup, and before Angie could say another word, he left the room.

Paavo had insisted on driving Doc to the funeral. This was the kind of day the doctor would get through by doing a fair amount of self-medicating, and Paavo didn't want him behind the wheel of a car.

They stopped at the Flores home. Doc wanted to escort the women to the church, and Angie wanted to drop off her pie. A few people were already there to leave flowers and food dishes.

"It's so wonderful to have another gourmet cook in town!"

Paavo turned as the sound of LaVerne Merritt's voice cut through the room.

"I brought something special," LaVerne was saying to Angie as she held up a Saran-wrapped Pyrex container. "You'll have to be sure to try it."

"What is it?" Angie asked.

"Javelina-noodle casserole." LaVerne beamed.

Others immediately began to walk away. Far away. Several left.

"What's a javelina?" Angie asked.

"It's kind of like a skinny pig," LaVerne said. "We have all kinds of pigs and wild boars in the area, you know."

"They're black and bristly," Paavo added, "with

tusks. They're ugly things. Some people call them musk hogs."

"I think I get the picture." The dismay on Angie's face left him no doubt that she did.

"It's delicious. Just like pork." LaVerne licked her lips. "Wait until you try it! Lupe, can I refrigerate it?"

"Yes, of course," Lupe replied.

"I hope LaVerne's javelina is better than her goat cheesecake," Paavo whispered.

"I'd rather not find out!" Angie added, just as all talking in the room ceased. Even LaVerne stopped in her tracks.

At the door stood Joey Edwards, looking in not much better condition than when Angie last saw him.

No one said a word to him. His gaze searched the room until he found Teresa. With no more than a nod to the others, he approached her.

Lupe immediately left Doc's side and stepped between them. If her eyes were daggers, Joey would be dead.

Teresa put a hand on Lupe's arm, stopping her. Teresa then walked out the patio door to the garden, Joey close behind.

Lupe watched them, her face thunderous.

LaVerne interrupted. "Lupe, there's a problem with your mother. She's in the kitchen."

Lupe and Doc hurried to Maritza, Angie and Paavo following. "What's wrong?" Lupe asked.

"There's something . . . I can't remember," Maritza said, head bowed and resting her hand heavily against the sink. "I try, but . . ."

"Sit down." Doc slid a chair beside her.

"I'm sorry," Maritza said, as tears filled her eyes.

Lupe stooped low, eye level with her mother. "Sorry for what? What's the matter?"

Instead of answering her, Maritza gazed up at Doc. "Hal come. He talk to me. He give me something."

"When was this?" Doc asked.

Maritza's face contorted in thought. "Yesterday. No, not yesterday, but soon."

"She's confused." Lupe stood and patted her mother's shoulder. "All this." Lupe haphazardly waved her arm, clearly referring to the recent deaths. "The last time my mother saw Hal was at least five years ago."

"Poor Hal. Poor Ned," Maritza began to cry harder.

"I think it might be best if she stays home," Doc said softly. Lupe nodded.

"I want you to lie down, Mama," Lupe murmured. "This is too much for you. You stay here and keep an eye on the food. We'll be back soon."

"No. I should come. For Ned."

Doc took Maritza's arm and slowly walked her to her bedroom. "Ned wouldn't want you getting sick. You rest at home. He'd understand, I'm sure."

Maritza nodded and lay down on her bed, her tears had stopped, but her expression was dazed. Lupe kissed her cheek and walked out, quietly shutting the door behind her.

Teresa was alone in the living room, her eyes wide with worry.

Lupe stared hard at her a moment, then turned to Doc. "Let's go to the church now."

* * *

Nuestra Señora de Guadalupe, a small version of the classic adobe and wood missions of the Southwest, held an aura of permanence and serenity. To one side of the church was a building that might be a school or large meeting hall. Set back on the other side was Father Armand's rectory. The mission wasn't directly in town, but slightly above it in the foothills, a rustic setting with a vista of the Colorado River.

The day was overcast and chilly. A film of gray covered the sun and made the surroundings as somber and glum as the people who filed into the church. They came from the town, the lake, and the reservation. Angie was amazed at how many knew who she and Paavo were. People she hadn't met told Paavo that they remembered when he came to Jackpot as a boy and would play with Ned while "the Finnish man" visited Doc.

Paavo seemed surprised and touched by their memories. He spoke movingly with them about Ned. More than one strongly hinted they were glad "a real detective" was in town. Although the sheriff had swept Hal Edwards's death under the rug, everyone knew she couldn't do that with Ned's.

Inside the church, gardenias, hyacinths, and carnations surrounded the altar. Candles had been lit and incense burned. Paavo scrutinized the crowd, his face hard, looking much like a detective searching for a suspect. Merry Belle hovered near the door as if ready at a moment's notice to rush off in her Hummer in case there was an outbreak of crime in Jackpot.

Buster was near his aunt, and when Angie noticed him, he was watching her. He raised his
hand, waggling his fingers in a slight wave in her
direction. She nodded back. He pointed to her
navy blue Oscar de la Renta suit and gave two
thumbs up. Despite herself, she smiled.

She and Paavo remained in the back, not wanting to intrude on those who had been close to Ned
all these years.

Doc was seated in the front row of the church
with Lupe on his left and Teresa on his right. Behind him was Doc's good friend, Joaquin Oldwater. Father Armand, a young priest who Doc had
introduced earlier to Angie, was speaking quietly
to the little group, offering consolation.

The two fishermen Angie had seen the first day
she was in town, the ones LaVerne had called FBI,
stood in the back of the church, perusing the
crowd much as Paavo was doing. LaVerne was
probably right. Just who did they think they were
kidding?

Angie then searched for people from the guest
ranch, but didn't see anyone until Junior pushed
his way through the crowd. As unkempt as ever,
he stared hard at the mourners in the front row,
then took a seat.

It seemed the whole town had turned out except
those from the guest ranch. It was odd that
Clarissa didn't have the sense to get herself and
Joey there, or at least Lionel. If, as she'd said, she
wanted the town to accept Joseph as Hal's heir
and new neighbor, someone should have had the
decency to show up.

The service began. But halfway through, the

peace of the church was broken by the town's fire siren, its loud wail an ominous call for the volunteer fire department to gather.

Suddenly, Merry Belle's voice boomed out, "Fire! Main Street is burning!"

Chapter 19

Merry Belle probably didn't mean to cause a commotion, but she had. As one, people rose from their seats, frantic.

"Go," Father Armand told them. "I will finish here."

Immediately, everyone streamed from the church. Some were volunteers who helped the town's two professional firemen; others were townspeople with businesses in the area. Whatever the reason, a problem for one was a problem for all. An unchecked fire in the dry desert could spread quickly

"It's near our restaurant, or at it!" Teresa cried, a catch in her throat, as she scanned the horizon.

"*Dios!* We've got to go!" Lupe hurried to her car. Doc got in beside her while Teresa climbed into the back.

"We'll follow," Paavo said. He took Angie's arm and they hurried across the parking lot. Fishing in his trouser pocket for his car keys to no avail, he realized he must have put them in his sports jacket pocket. He reached in, and found more than car keys. Lifting out a small piece of paper, he read, bad grammar and all . . .

Ned Paulson killed Hal Edwards. So he had to die. Keep your nose out or your next.

Teresa had been right about the fire's location. Smoke streamed from the back of the restaurant.

Lupe and the others arrived in time to see the firefighters carry her mother out on a stretcher. Maritza was unconscious, apparently from smoke inhalation.

Lupe nearly fainted at the sight and tried to follow, but Doc reminded her of her other duties. She quickly steadied herself and asked Doc to take care of her mother. He got into the ambulance with the paramedics.

Fortunately, the damage to the restaurant wasn't as bad as it first appeared. None of the workers were inside; they'd all gone to the funeral service. Lupe's office was burned, and the fire had just reached the kitchen when the fire truck arrived.

Lupe's responsibility to check on her workers' safety done, she left Teresa to deal with all that was happening in the restaurant, and headed for the medical clinic.

Seeing how distraught Lupe was, Angie stopped her and insisted on driving. Paavo would stay at the restaurant with Teresa and try to learn what had caused the fire.

"Do you have any idea what your mother was doing there?" Angie asked Lupe as she drove. "I thought she was staying at the house?"

"It's crazy!" Lupe cried. "She's never wandered off before without telling me. Never!"

"She seemed confused earlier," Angie pointed out.

"She's been troubled by something lately, but can't say what it is. She easily remembers things that happened twenty years ago, but last week is another story. Sometimes, she doesn't remember that Ned is dead, or Hal. I try to watch her, Angie." Lupe fought to control her emotions. "I really do. She's never done anything like this before. I wonder if she caused the fire."

Angie had wondered that as well. "Your office seemed to be where the fire started. If it was in the kitchen, that would make sense, but it wasn't."

"I agree," Lupe whispered. "It makes it look like, whatever happened, it was deliberate."

"Gasoline." Fire Chief Manny Gonzalez walked up to Merry Belle. Paavo and Teresa were with her. "Looks like somebody wanted to destroy the office."

"Where was Maritza found?" Paavo asked after introducing himself to Gonzales.

"In the hallway between the office and the kitchen. She must have been overcome by smoke and collapsed. The gas canister was at her side."

"You're saying she might have done it?" Merry Belle asked.

"That's crazy!" Teresa cried.

"Hard to imagine, but if her prints are on the can . . ." He didn't need to complete the sentence.

"Or, someone set things up to look that way," Paavo offered.

"Anything's possible." The chief looked over the building and shook his head. "I can't believe

Maritza would want to destroy her own restaurant. I've gone to that place my entire life. The whole town has."

There was a problem. Angie could see it on Doc's face as he crossed the waiting room of the medical clinic where Maritza had been brought. Angie and Lupe stood as he approached.

"It's not only smoke inhalation," he said. "Someone hit her. Her skull's been fractured, and she's in a coma."

"Like Ned," Angie whispered.

"Not exactly." Doc's expression was grim. "Whoever did it didn't want her dead—they probably hoped the fire would do that, and make us look no further for a cause of death."

"Why?" Lupe looked ready to pass out. Doc had her sit, and Angie got her some water, but neither could answer her question. "How is she?"

"It's a simple fracture," Doc said. "No surgery will be needed unless she develops an intracranial hematoma. I'm going to go back with the doctors. I want to observe as she undergoes tests."

Lupe looked at him blankly.

"It'll be a long wait."

She nodded, and watched Doc leave.

Angie sat beside Lupe. "None of this makes sense," Angie said softly. "Why would anyone do this to your family?"

"I don't understand it either," Lupe said.

"If there's anything I can do . . ." Angie began.

"No, but thank you for staying with me now, and for being there for Doc," Lupe said as her gaze traveled to the door to the medical offices where

Doc had gone. "I appreciate you and Paavo being with him through all this. He's a good man."

"I think so." Angie hesitated to say more, but then added, "In fact, it's so obvious that you two care deeply about each other, I'm surprised you aren't an item."

"An item? Such an old-fashioned word to be coming from you." Lupe forced a smile before her face turned serious. "I guess no one's ever told you . . . I'm married."

"Married?" Angie was stunned. "I'm sorry . . . I mean, I assumed you were divorced or . . . I mean, your last name . . . and Teresa's."

Lupe folded her hands on her lap. "I understand. Legally, I am divorced. He divorced me, in fact, and I must admit I'm glad he no longer has any legal claim over me or my belongings. I didn't want anything to do with him, not even his name. Teresa felt the same. But that doesn't change the fact that I'm one of those old-fashioned Catholics who believes I married for life. Talk about strange, right?" Her eyes, even as she spoke those words, were calm. "I take my faith seriously, Angie. Some say too seriously—but God has sustained me through many harsh, bitter days. I will not turn my back on him."

Angie's mother was also a very traditional Roman Catholic—strict, one might say—in her beliefs. Angie understood what Lupe was saying.

"Where is your husband?" she asked gently.

"He's here, in Jackpot. He's here when he's not in jail, or alcoholic rehab for the umpteenth time. His life is a mess, Angie, and after years trying to straighten him out, I finally gave up."

"I see."

"His name is Sherman Whitney, but everyone calls him Junior."

Angie couldn't believe it. "Junior . . . who works out at the Ghost Hollow Guest Ranch?"

"Yes. He and Lionel went to school together. Since Lionel took over the guest ranch, he lets Junior work out there when Junior's on the wagon. Then, when he falls off, Lionel fires him, and the cycle starts all over again. At least when he's working he doesn't come bothering me for money."

Angie thought of the raggedy fellow who poked ostriches with mop handles. "You give him money?"

"I can't let him starve, can I?" Lupe asked.

Might not be such a tragedy, Angie thought. She was curious about Lupe and Junior. "I guess Junior wasn't always the way he is now."

"I thought he had promise," Lupe admitted, "though my mother never saw it." At the mention of Maritza, Lupe bowed her head and paused a moment before continuing. "Anyway, Junior worked in his father's cantaloupe business, but when it fell on hard times, Junior was no help. If anything, he was a hindrance. Finally, Sherman Senior sold what remained of the business to Hal Edwards, and left town."

"Hal was involved in cantaloupes?" Angie asked.

"Hal was involved in everything," Lupe said wryly. "Junior liked to say Hal had robbed his father, but it wasn't true—Junior did."

"So Junior disliked Hal?"

"Hated him. He always said he knew Hal's dirty little secrets, and that Hal had better think twice about disrespecting his family."

"What did he mean?"

"Who knows? He's a blowhard. All talk, no substance."

"Does Junior see much of Teresa?"

Lupe shook her head. "He was never a father to her, though, in his way, he cares about her. I've always wondered if Junior isn't the reason she's so resistant about love." Tears filled Lupe's eyes as she said, "I feel so bad about her, as if I failed in the way I raised her. Because, even though it didn't work out for me, Angie, at one time in my life I truly did love him. I'll always have that, and because of it, Teresa. I wish she could understand the way I feel. Unfortunately, she never has. And I doubt she ever will."

Chapter 20

"Boomer can't lift any prints off the gas can." Merry Belle stood to make her pronouncement as soon as Paavo entered the office. "He tried, but said they were all smudged. I think he made things worse by trying, if that's possible."

"Take it away from him and send it to Phoenix." Paavo had had it with the incompetence in the sheriff's department. "If there's any evidence on it, we need to know."

"You're right." Her round face scrunched into a frown. She hesitated, then dropped back into her chair as her entire demeanor took on a weary, almost defeated air. "Smith, can we start over?" Her voice was uncertain.

"What do you mean?"

"Sit down and listen." The words were bossy as ever, but the tone softer. Something in her eyes made him curious enough to do as she requested. "I know I come on strong. I'm not big on outside cops interfering with my work."

"I understand," he said. No cop likes outsiders poaching, not even if they are other cops.

She nodded, and continued in what was for her a muted manner. "I got two people dead, and now an old woman got knocked around. Too much old nasty stuff is coming to the surface."

Paavo waited.

"This isn't easy to say, San Francisco." This time, there was no sarcasm in the nickname. She took a deep breath then added, "I could use help. Another professional. You're a good homicide cop. I checked."

Merry Belle's look of embarrassment almost made Paavo smile. It figured she had vetted him, but for the first time, she did something right. She needed help. The question was, could he trust her?

"I'd like to help, but . . ."

"I know, I know," Merry Belle interrupted. "You think I'm corrupt." The sheriff allowed herself a sly smile. "I may do favors for campaign contributors—as a courtesy, you understand—but that's all." She went on in a firm voice. "I'm not bought and paid for. Don't ever think that."

To his surprise, Paavo believed her. This bellicose woman seemed to have her own goofy set of ethics.

"Look, I took this job because I needed work and nobody else wanted it. Besides, I knew more about being a cop than any ten men in town put together. I watch every police procedure show on TV, including the ones from the BBC, and every episode of CSI no matter where it takes place—New York, Miami, Las Vegas, Nome. Hell, I even wrote and told them they should put a show

right here in Jackpot." Her plain features soft-
ened, her voice lowered. "I can roust drunks and
testosterone-laden teenagers with the best of
them, but I never expected to deal with murders
in Jackpot."

Paavo relented, although a part of him enjoyed
Merry Belle's discomfort. Doc would probably
say she was eating huge slices of humble pie. "I'll
be glad to work with you."

"I appreciate that," Merry Belle said, hastily
adding, "it'll be purely unofficial."

"However you want to play it. And I've got something here for us to start with." He then took out
the note he'd found in his pocket, holding just one
corner, and laid it on her desk. It was block printed
which was considered one of the easiest ways for a
person to disguise his or her handwriting. "Someone slipped this note in my jacket. I don't know
when. In this warm climate, I spend more time
carrying the jacket around than wearing it."

Her eyes widened as she read the note. "Someone is trying to warn you off the investigation,"
she murmured, and he could tell it rankled her
that no one was trying to warn *her* off as well.

"It seems to be saying that Ned's death was revenge for Hal's murder," Paavo suggested.

"That's right!" Her round face lit up brighter
than a full moon. "And who'd want revenge . . .
except his son! It's telling us Joey killed Ned!"

"I'm not so sure," Paavo said. "Look at the
grammatical mistake on the note—it shows *y-o-
u-r* rather than *y-o-u*-apostrophe-*r-e*. Any ideas
who might make that kind of mistake? I'm not
sure Joey Edwards would," he said.

"Mistake?" She studied the note. "Uh . . ."

He didn't pursue it. "Let's bag this, then I'd like you to send it to a crime lab in Phoenix for a fingerprint analysis." To emphasize his point he added, "Don't let Buster touch it."

"Thank the good Lord you got back!" Lionel panted, more red-eyed and scraggly than usual. He met Angie as she pulled into a parking area at the guest ranch. "Clarissa's raising holy hell."

"Why's that?" Angie asked.

"'Cause you ain't here, that's why!" Lionel exclaimed. "And the cookout's in three days. Miss High 'n' Goddamn Mighty wants you to give me your list of supplies."

Lionel and Clarissa's concerns were the last thing Angie cared about at this point. Maritza was still in a coma. Doc had insisted that Angie and Lupe go home while he and Teresa kept the vigil. And Paavo had to leave to work with Merry Belle and Buster.

Before each went their separate ways, however, they had gathered together at the cemetery for a brief but tearful prayer for Ned, and to put flowers on his fresh grave. The emotion at the grave site had been heartbreaking.

"It's late, and I'm tired." Angie stifled a yawn. She was emotionally and physically exhausted. "Doesn't Clarissa know what happened today?"

"You mean about Maritza going nuts and trying to burn down her restaurant?"

"I doubt that's the real story."

"Whatever." Lionel grimaced. "You don't think Superbitch cares about that, do you?" Angie wondered if Clarissa had scared Lionel into being stone-cold sober, because he was that now.

"Does she harass everyone this way?" Angie asked.

"Sure does. Dolores has been here since before Hal had his stroke, and Clarissa treats her like she don't know shit; and Junior, who's been here on and off for over ten years, is treated like he knows even less!"

That got Angie thinking. "Interesting," she murmured. "Well, good night. I'm going to bed."

"What about the supplies?" he demanded.

"I'll give you a list tomorrow."

"What you going to cook for us, anyway? Is it any good?"

She stopped in her tracks and slowly turned. "Is it *good*?"

"Hell, when LaVerne cooks fancy, I wouldn't give her food to the hogs."

Angie's eyes narrowed. "For you, I'm going to make something really special."

"Is that so?"

She put her hands on her hips. "Sliced rhubarb and okra in a nest of alfalfa sprouts."

"Goddamn," he muttered to himself as he walked off. "She really does sound like a gourmet cook."

Chapter 21

It was late, too late for a priest who would be giving a mass at six A.M. to still be up and reading. Father Armand sighed and closed his book, an often-read collection of Chesterton's Father Brown stories. He stood, stretched, and went to the rectory's bedroom.

In bed after his evening prayers, Father Armand found it hard to sleep. The priest had few illusions about the desperate troubles people could get themselves into, but the web of ugly secrets, vengeful passions, and violence that gripped his small community disturbed him greatly. He felt useless— a failure. He should know his people better. He'd been here four years—an eternity in some parts of this country, but in Jackpot, he was still considered an outsider. The former priest, Father Benedict, had been there sixty years. It was with thoughts of Ned Paulson's murder and the attack on Maritza Flores that Father Armand finally drifted into a restless slumber, wondering if a better or more experienced priest might have been able to unravel the mysteries that lay hidden behind this trouble.

The grinding of truck tires digging into gravel woke him. His eyes opened in the darkness and he lay unsure that he hadn't only dreamt the noise. He rolled over, hoping to go back to sleep, but uneasiness filled him. He got out of bed in the moonlit bedroom and put on his robe, slippers, and glasses. Perhaps some troubled soul had come to the church in need of comfort and counsel.

The priest walked to the front room that served as his office and opened the door. The parking lot was empty.

Okay, he told himself, his imagination had become overactive. With all that was happening in his parish, that was no surprise. He turned to go back to bed when the squeal of old door hinges being opened shocked him. He stood on the porch unable to believe that anyone would be breaking into a church a second time in the same number of weeks. What was going on?

He headed toward the mission, baffled and angry.

It could be illegals crossing the desert and looking for food and water. They should have just come to his house; he'd give them aid.

But they wouldn't have had a car . . .

It might be someone here to steal the sacred vessels, especially the silver chalices! That made him pause, but outrage overruled prudence.

All was quiet when he reached the sacristy. The door lay open. The priest stopped and looked all around. He heard no sound, saw no one. Fear for the sacred vessels filled him and he crept inside.

The room was empty, the storage area undisturbed, and the chalices safe. Whoever was here must have heard him and run.

Breathing easier now, he looked around and noticed that the door to the room where the parish records were archived was no longer latched shut. Soundlessly, he headed for it, staying clear of the doorway. The windowless room should have been deep in darkness, but a small penlight flickered.

Curious, he entered, peering hard into the dimness. Only after his eyes adjusted did he reach over and flip the switch to turn on the overhead lights.

The shrill, insistent ringing broke the night's deep quiet. Paavo, shaking the sleep from his head, glanced at the nightstand clock. He was accustomed to being awakened by the police dispatcher back home.

1:12 A.M.

He groped for his blaring cell phone. Next to him, Angie stirred.

"Smith," he mumbled into the mouthpiece.

Angie sat up in bed, flicked on the lamp, and turned toward Paavo, blinking owlishly at the light.

"Yes. Do you need anything? . . . Okay, I'm on my way."

Paavo clicked off his cell phone and got out of bed.

"What's happening?" Angie asked groggily.

"That was Father Armand. Teresa's at the

church. He caught her going through the archive records. He doesn't want to disturb her mother. Doc's still at the clinic and gave the priest my number. He wants me to talk to her."

"She broke in?" Angie was fully awake now. "That doesn't make sense! Did he say why?"

"I'll know soon enough," Paavo said as he began to dress.

"I'll get dressed, too," Angie announced.

"No, you're staying here."

"But . . ."

"I'm going alone." His voice was stern and inflexible. "You stay here with the door locked."

One glance at Paavo's hard, no-nonsense expression made it clear that any arguing was futile. "I'll stay, but you call me as soon as you find out anything."

"Angie, I'm sorry about the way this trip has turned out," he said grimly.

Her heart seemed to stop as she watched him pull his Beretta and shoulder holster from the dresser drawer. "It's not your fault," she said. "But I'm planning our next vacation."

Angie's phone remained silent as she finished a cup of coffee. Of course, Paavo never phoned when he was on a case in San Francisco, so why should it be any different here?

The night was chilly and the coffee warmed her, but she feared the onset of caffeine nerves if she kept this up. Her mind raced, and her imagination conjured increasingly improbable scenarios for Paavo as the waiting wore her down. Her mother

had always told her that she was by far the most
impatient of Serefina's five children.

Angie got up from the sofa and meandered
through the rooms of the bungalow. Each time she
passed the coffee table in the living room she
would glare at her cell phone, willing it to ring. At
the living room window she stopped and stared
across the plaza toward the dark hacienda.

Something flashed. Was it her imagination or
something else? *Calm down,* she told herself.

She saw it again. Was it a flashlight? Somebody
was on the second floor of Hal Edwards's home.
Every muscle stretched tight as she watched the upper rooms' windows. Her eyes strained as if trying
for X-ray vision. Despite her best efforts, though,
she couldn't achieve Superwoman powers.

If she could only get a wee bit closer . . . the instant the idea occurred to her, so did Paavo's
warnings about avoiding danger.

She quickly put on jeans, a shirt, and her boots,
then ran back to the window. The light flashed
once more. Her mind warred. She would phone
Paavo—that was a condition of her staying after
the snake incident. Frankly, though, he was too far
away to help.

No excuses! She should phone him, and she
would.

She picked up the cell phone and dialed. The
message came back to her that the party she was
calling was outside the cell area. At least she knew
why he hadn't phoned. She thought a moment. If
she simply waited and watched from the bungalow
for whomever it was to leave, it'd be too easy to miss

seeing the prowler in the darkness. She wanted to know who was sneaking around in there.

What choice did she have? It wasn't as if she had to go *inside*. Just close enough to see who'd broken in. She'd be cautious and avoid danger, of course. That decided it. She switched her cell phone to go straight to messaging so that, if Paavo did phone, he wouldn't wonder why she wasn't answering.

She slipped out the front door. As much as she tried to tread soundlessly, the crunching of the gravel beneath her boots was like machine-gun fire. Hurrying across the open plaza, she felt safer once within the hacienda's shadows. She could only hope no one had seen her on the moonlit square. Her breathing grew heavy.

Relax, she ordered herself.

She worked her way to the side of the hacienda, and froze.

A dark shadow loomed before her, then slowly moved toward the moonlight.

After a moment she let out a breath of relief. It was just an ostrich.

She darted around the corner of the hacienda to the rear. Inching along, she stayed as close to the wall as possible, her every sense magnified. The feeble breeze in the night air seemed to rush, the tiny scampering of small animals and insects sounded like a stampede, and when the high cry of an owl shrilled, she jumped, convinced Gabriel had sounded the Last Trumpet. Her mouth and throat were dry; she was breathless and sweating in the cool night air.

Steps led to the veranda. The entry door was ajar, inviting and beckoning.

Maybe if she simply went up to the opening she could hear voices from inside. She ascended the steps. Beside the door lay a crowbar. Somebody means business, she thought.

She listened, but didn't hear a sound. What harm would one quick-as-lightning peek do? Who would even know?

With Paavo's admonitions thrumming in her ears, she touched the door. Like magic, it swung open to the kitchen, dusty and distorted by shadows cast by the moonlight streaming in through streaked windows.

The house was quiet. Had she imagined the light?

She moved past the kitchen and into the moonlit dining room. A single place mat lay atop the table. It was spooky—as if Hal had eaten there alone and would return any second. The presence of the angry, bitter, fearful, and lonely master of the hacienda loomed over the room, and she couldn't help but contrast it with the vibrant, charitable, and clever man the historical society had written about. A surge of pity for Hal rose, followed by a deep, gnawing uneasiness. This is where a murdered man would haunt, she thought.

Outside the dining room was a hallway.

She paused.

Upstairs, soft noises could be heard. As her nose twitched from the dusty, stale air, she crept through the shadows until she reached the base of a staircase.

Clutching the banister with painful caution, she started up. Midway, a crashing sound reverberated through the house, and she came to a startled halt.

"Goddamn it!" grumbled a male voice.

"Don't curse, Joseph."

It was Clarissa.

"I bumped my leg on this damn dresser."

"Stop whining!"

"This is a fool's errand," Joey cried, louder.

"Then you're acting well-suited for it! Get busy. I want to get out of this room. Look at this jewelry, these clothes. The place reeks of Hal's cheap women."

Angie eased her way down a couple of steps, but stopped, curious, when they began to speak again.

"Mother, for cryin' out loud," Joey said, his voice climbing with each word, "it's clear Dad didn't hide it here. We've searched this place high and low. I'm not tearing up any more floorboards! It's not here!"

Angie listened hard, not wanting to miss a word.

"If we can't find it, we might just have to burn the house down." Clarissa's voice was cold and deadly serious.

"That's crazy!"

"Don't you dare talk to me that way!" Clarissa snapped. "You seem to forget that you wouldn't have anything if it weren't for me!"

All talking stopped. *Go on*, Angie urged silently.

"Are you just going to stand there and rub your leg all night?" Clarissa demanded.

"It hurts, Mother. When will you get it through

your head that other people have feelings, even if you don't?"

The sound of a slap rang through the dead air of the house. Angie listened, horrified, as a deep silence settled over the hacienda and a weighty sense of oppression pulsed in the gloom. Her breathing became so shallow she was growing light-headed. Her body ached from the strain of silent immobility, her nose continued to itch from the dust, but she wouldn't miss this for the world.

Clarissa's voice turned low and menacing. "You will stop acting like a vulgar weakling! You wonder why your father despised you? Why wouldn't he? You acted scared of him even when he was a bedridden drooling wreck."

"Stop, Mother," Joey pleaded.

"Stop, Mother," she repeated in a mocking tone. "You'd be nothing if it weren't for me, and don't you ever forget that!"

"I should never have come here."

"Listen to me." Clarissa spat the words. "If we can't find the will, I'll use his computer, his letterhead, and printer, and we'll create one for him."

"But, Mother," Joey said, "if we can't find it, no one else can either, and I'll still inherit everything. Why are you bothering?"

"It's insurance," she said. "Who knows what your father did when he was away? Over the years, I learned to never trust him. Never!"

There were footsteps as the two moved about in their search. Angie waited. If the steps grew louder or seemed to head her way, she'd run. Besides being achy and miserable, the tingling pressure in her nose was mounting, demanding an explosive release. She rubbed it until the feeling passed.

"Damn! This odious computer still won't work," Clarissa cried. "Why is nothing simple?"

"How many times do I have to tell you, it's password protected?" Joey snapped.

"And how many times do I have to tell you that you ought to know how to break into it! It's your generation that deals with computers, not mine! I want to use it."

Angie's nose suddenly took on a life of its own. Twitching, wrinkling up, the need to sneeze built inexorably. She squeezed her nostrils, holding them shut, continuing to listen.

"All right, then." Angie could all but hear Joey pout. "But it's a waste of time."

The sound of a chair scraping the floor reached her, along with the *oomph* of a weary man sitting down.

Soon after the tingling began, Angie's nose went back to normal.

Joey and Clarissa seemed to be doing nothing but squabbling, and she needed to get out of there. She started slowly down the stairs.

"I can't do it," Joey cried, his voice loud as his frustration grew at not being able to get into Hal's computer.

"And maybe I can't help you turn the Halmart stores around?" Clarissa jeered.

"For all your talk, you haven't been much of a help to me so far!" Joey's tone was beyond indignant.

"Not much help? You wouldn't even have the stores if it weren't for me! Now, get busy with that computer."

"Stop ordering me around!" Joey cried.

"Don't you dare use that tone with me!"

"I can't take it any more!" Joey yelled.

And right then, Angie sneezed.

Chapter 22

"What are you doing here?" Teresa stood as she saw Paavo enter the rectory's living room. She spun toward Father Armand. "You said I'd be left alone. You lied!"

"You can stay, Teresa," Father Armand said quietly, "but you refused to talk to me. You've got to speak with someone about what you're doing. What you've been saying."

She looked about wildly as if trying to decide if she should run. "I haven't been saying anything."

"Yes, Teresa, you have." The padre's tone was firm.

"What were you looking for?" Paavo asked her.

She turned away, and he looked to the priest for an answer.

Father Armand shook his head. He didn't know. "I allowed her to continue to search the records. In the end, though, she came away with nothing."

Her eyes darted from one to the other, and slowly, her face became hard and stony, devoid of all emotion.

"What's this about, Teresa?" Paavo asked.

"It's about . . . nothing. Everything was a lie. All that's happened—" She stopped speaking and covered her mouth with a shaky hand.

Father Armand took a chair and gestured toward the sofa. "Teresa, sit down, please. You need to tell us what's troubling you. How can we help if we don't know?"

"You can't help!" Even as she said the words, she sat dejected on the edge of the sofa. "I'm beyond help!"

"Never—"

"It's true!" Silent tears fell. "Please, leave me alone."

"Doc thought you should talk to me," Paavo said, pulling up a chair to face her. "Why is that?"

"I have no idea!" she said, trying to stanch her tears.

"Yes, you do. Doc knows something or he wouldn't have told me to come."

"If he knew, he'd hate me . . ."

"Tell us, Teresa," Father Armand urged. "Tell us together, or me alone. Whatever you'd like."

She stared at him a long moment, then whispered, "It's my fault, Father. It's all my fault."

"What is?" he asked.

"Everything." Her voice was grating and desperate. "Hal's death, Ned's, the attack on my grandmother. It's all because of me."

"What do you mean?" he asked. "Why do you think that?"

"I know it! I should be the one who's dead, not Ned! And my grandma, if she dies too . . ."

A sob fell from her as she ran out of the rectory.

It was as if all she'd kept bottled up inside had finally broken her.

Paavo saw her stop at the edge of the desert and look up at the starry night. He knew he would somehow manage to get her home, but first, he had a question for the priest.

"Did she say anything to you that you're able to pass along?" he asked.

The padre shook his head. "She refused to say anything at all, refused even to make a confession. She said she doesn't deserve absolution. That if she died now, she'd be damned. And that she deserved it."

Clarissa froze. The sneeze echoed through the old house. Hal was always sneezing and coughing and complaining of how tired and sick he felt. She couldn't help but look around guiltily, almost expecting him to walk through the door, accusing and angry. "Did you hear that?" Clarissa whispered.

"I think so," Joey said, his voice small.

Clarissa yelled, "Who's in here?"

"It s-sounded like a sneeze," Joey stammered.

Anger—anger at Joey for his weakness, at Hal for all he'd put her through, even at herself for her mistakes—caused her to sneer. "That's so astute, Joseph. Now, why don't you find out who it is?"

"Okay . . . I'm going to look around."

Duh, she mouthed, much like young people on TV. Like her own grandchildren would be doing, if she had any. "Move it, Joseph! You couldn't catch a statue!"

Slowly, she followed him down the stairs. How

she hated being inside this house. It held too many memories, especially with Hal dead . . .

She wished she could think back to at least one time when she'd been happy here. Hal tried, she had to give him that. But he didn't hold her heart. Someone else did. She hadn't thought about him in years, not until she talked to that young woman, that Angie, so happily in love. Her hand slid along the smooth railing as regret filled her. And strangely, the regret was about Hal, of how she'd taken advantage of him, how she'd never even given him a chance to make her happy. How differently would her life had been if she'd opened her heart to him, just a little bit?

How differently would things have turned out for Hal as well as for her?

Clarissa stepped out the back door to find Joseph on the veranda. "Why are you still here?"

"I don't know where he's gone. He was fast."

Clarissa stared into the darkness, then snorted. "He? *She* is more like it. Look." Just then, the ostrich with the cowlick ambled toward them. "You idiot! You were chasing an ostrich!"

"I wasn't! Anyway, ostriches don't sneeze."

"How do you know?" she demanded. "It was probably standing at the door. You left it open, didn't you?"

"Well, yes, but—"

"Stop." Sudden weariness overwhelmed her. "As things stand now, you should inherit everything, but to be absolutely safe, we're going to return tomorrow and type up a will. You have all night to figure out how to do it. Once we've got it, the sheriff will declare it official. We'll be fine as long as that homicide detective doesn't get involved."

"How can you be so sure the sheriff will go along?"

"She has to." Just the thought of Merry Belle—what an outrageous name!—made the words curdle on her tongue. "For years I've been a heavy, unofficial contributor to her campaign and, no doubt, retirement funds."

"You aren't saying, Mother, that you took money from the business to buy yourself a sheriff?"

"Some expenses were necessary—such as giving her that Hummer she's so proud of." Clarissa frowned. "The problem is the homicide inspector. It's no coincidence he chose this spot for his vacation. I'll have to make sure the sheriff doesn't allow him to interfere any more than he already has."

Angie didn't believe she was fast enough to run all the way across the plaza without being seen, so, spotting some bushes to the left of the hacienda, she ran to them and dived inside.

As she crawled for cover, all the scary things she'd heard about desert creatures came back to her. She couldn't help but wonder where live rattlesnakes slept. Dead ones were bad enough!

She stopped, laid low, and listened to Clarissa's continuous berating of her son. No wonder the man was such a basket case.

Eventually, Clarissa must have grown tired of being a harridan because she abruptly said good night and left for her cabin. Joey slinked off to his.

Angie decided to wait a short while to be sure they'd retired for the night. She didn't want them to catch her.

Unfortunately, in the silence following Clarissa and Joey's departure, Angie became aware of strange noises and scurrying in the undergrowth. Hadn't someone mentioned that there were wild boars in the area? Surely they didn't come this close to the hacienda, she told herself. That had to be true.

Except that, somewhere in the brush behind her, she heard the sound of stirring, breaking branches, and distinctly unfriendly snorting. Something was crashing over the terrain, gaining speed. The snorts were urgent and insistent as a horn on a feral train. Angie began to scramble through the brush. *This must be what Miss Piggy's like after a bad review.*

She reached the clearing and stood, listening, scarcely noticing the twigs and stickers that had attached themselves to her hair and clothes. All was quiet for a moment, but then, suddenly, the noise began again.

As if she were setting a record for the hundred-yard dash, she crossed the plaza to her bungalow. The window was open. She didn't bother with the door, but dived in, head first.

Cowering behind the window, she peered out to see the deadly fiend that pursued her.

It was a pig, all right. But not a wild one.

It was a young pig, probably one that had some-how broken out of the pig sty. Her monstrous wild boar turned out to be about the size of a chubby cocker spaniel.

Chapter 23

"What's Teresa up to?" Angie asked. Although half asleep when Paavo returned, she became fully awake and alert after hearing how Teresa blamed herself for Hal and Ned's deaths and Maritza's injuries. "How could she blame herself unless she had a part in the deaths?"

"I don't think that's the case," Paavo said.

"But why else would she be so guilty?"

Apparently, that was Paavo's question as well. He put it aside to listen with interest to Angie's story of eavesdropping on Clarissa and Joey. She left out the part about the piglet, however.

"I guess it's about time I saw where Hal Edwards lived," he said. "It sounds as if everyone else has. Want to join me?"

"Aside from being worried about you," she said with a grin, "why else do you think I stayed up so late?"

"Lead the way."

Quietly, they crept across the plaza.

The back door had been left unlocked.

Once inside, Paavo turned on the small penlight he usually carried, but soon found a larger flashlight nearby—perhaps the one Joey had used—and switched to it. They followed Angie's earlier path to the stairs, and she walked partway up. "This is where I stood."

They hurried up the stairs to Hal's bedroom.

Feminine toiletries had been pushed to one side on the dresser. Angie stared, surprised to see them. She wondered what Clarissa had made of them. In the closet was a jumble of strewn clothing, as if someone had taken everything off the hangers, and then tossed them in there.

"I don't get this at all," Angie said, looking in horror at the clothes.

"Did they do all this?" Paavo asked.

"It didn't sound like it." She went to the closet. "Why would anyone throw around Hal's things this way?"

The first garment she pulled out was a brown cowboy shirt, then a pair of Wranglers. Beneath them was a brightly patterned teal and yellow material. She lifted it high. A dress.

"Size ten." She looked at the label—Merona. "I don't recognize the designer. It's not expensive."

"Not Clarissa's, in other words?" he asked.

"Not a chance. She's a size two at most."

There were two other dresses, same size and colorfully patterned, in the pile. A prickle played along Angie's spine.

"These look like something Teresa would wear," she murmured.

"Teresa? That doesn't make sense," he said.

"Doesn't it? I wonder . . ." Angie began. They exchanged looks.

Paavo checked the other bedrooms. Two were practically empty, but the third was used as Hal's office.

Paperwork was scattered everywhere, files opened and riffled, and the computer left on. Angie moved the mouse. Sure enough, a log-on screen appeared. She had no idea how to get past it.

Paavo began sorting through the paperwork quickly, Angie peering over his shoulder. It looked business related, but old. Probably the last time Hal Edwards used any of it was five years ago.

Why had Hal Edwards walked away from a home and business this size? Angie could only imagine that he'd been truly mentally deranged, or truly scared.

As Paavo continued with the papers, she took his penlight to look at the dining room and kitchen—she was a cook, after all.

There were no surprises in the dining room. Silverware, dishes, table linen.

She moved onto the spacious kitchen and went through cabinets and the pantry. At some point, someone had cleared out foodstuffs that could spoil or attract vermin, for which she was grateful.

The refrigerator was not only empty but off. When she had opened the door, however, she realized there was something odd about the way the kitchen was set up.

A large pedestal table and chairs were in the middle of the room, but not centered. In fact, they were so close to the refrigerator, that it was impossible to open the door all the way. At the same time, the far wall was empty, yet roomy enough for the kitchen table and chairs to fit into nicely. Mind racing, she pulled the chairs out of the way and shoved the table toward that wall.

Directly under the spot on which the pedestal had stood, a large stain discolored the oak floor. It had a whitish cast, but some darker flecks seemed to have seeped through the old, porous boards.

She drew back. "Paavo!"

As soon as he reached the kitchen, Angie flashed her light on the hardwood. "What do you think happened there? It looks like someone tried to clean it, maybe using bleach."

He looked at how she'd pushed the table aside. "If blood was there, it'll show up with Luminol. I'll get the sheriff to run tests."

"It makes me wonder"—Angie swallowed hard—"if this is where Hal died."

A strange voice filled the room. "What the hell's going on in here?"

"Junior!" Angie turned and stared at the gun in the man's hand.

"Put the gun down," Paavo said. "We aren't dangerous. We're just curious."

"Curious enough to break into someone's house? I think I should call the sheriff."

"Fine," Paavo said. "There are things in this house the sheriff needs to see."

Junior snorted. "Yeah, I heard about you. You're some kind of expert, they say."

"Homicide, San Francisco."

"Homicide?" His eyes darkened. "Nobody

wants you snooping around here. This is none of your damn business. Get out!"

"Who are you trying to protect, Junior?" Paavo asked.

"Nobody."

"Yourself? Or is it Teresa?"

"Leave Teresa out of this!" Junior yelled.

"Why? Because she's your daughter?" Angie asked. Now, studying Junior, Angie could see a slight resemblance to Teresa, especially in the eyes. She'd wondered where Teresa had gotten those green eyes, now she knew. Junior's were always so bloodshot, it had been hard to discern their true color.

"She's in danger," Paavo said. "Someone tried to kill her. Two people have already died. We've got to find out what's going on before anyone else is hurt."

"I don't believe you," Junior snarled.

"Believe it."

He raised the gun.

"Put the gun down, now!" Paavo repeated in his most forceful tone. "You don't want the kind of trouble this will bring you."

Just then, Junior was knocked from behind. The gun flew from his hand across the kitchen. He landed face-first on the floor.

Standing in the doorway, where Junior had been, was the ostrich with the cowlick. Her black eyes gazed adoringly at Paavo, and the edges of her beak seemed to curl into a proud smile.

Chapter 24

The next morning, Paavo drove Angie to Jackpot's medical clinic, only to learn that Maritza had been moved to the nearest hospital in Blythe, California. Knowing Paavo was going to pay a visit to Merry Belle, Angie excused herself to walk around town.

She was probably going shopping, he thought, and frankly, he couldn't blame her. This whole trip had been no kind of vacation for her.

He continued on toward the sheriff's station with Hal's computer snugly strapped to the backseat of the SUV. Merry Belle should have access to someone who could crack the password, and something on the computer might give a clue as to why Hal left five years earlier, and maybe even a last will and testament.

The night before, after the gun had been knocked from Junior's hand, Paavo grabbed it. Junior ran off saying Lionel would hear about their break-in, but Lionel never showed up.

Paavo then removed the computer from Hal's office. Back in San Francisco, he would have needed a judicial search warrant and permission. Here, he was quite certain Merry Belle paid no attention to such legal niceties. In fact, he had to admit to rather liking the way she did things. Some things, anyway.

Despite that, he decided against telling her about his visit to Father Armand until he had a better idea of what Teresa was doing there, and what she meant by saying the deaths were her fault. Her confessions might have been only the ramblings of a distraught woman who'd put up with more loss than she could handle, and he didn't want Sheriff Hermann to go off half-cocked because of Teresa's "guilt" sentiment.

Now, as he neared the station, he saw something that made him quickly turn the corner. He locked up the SUV, then, staying close to the buildings, edged along the street.

As he reached the parked pickup truck, he bent low and inched his way to the driver's door. Once there, he yanked it open.

"Hello, gentlemen," he said.

Joey Edwards was leaving the Flores house as Angie approached. She ducked behind a telephone pole. Her conjecture about Joey being the reason a couple of Teresa's dresses were left at Hal's was looking ever more correct.

She needn't have worried about Joey noticing her. He seemed preoccupied and barely glanced at the street as he drove off in the opposite direction.

The whole scenario suddenly became quite clear to her.

Somehow, Ned found out that Joey and Teresa

were having an affair and were using Hal's house for their tryst. He saw movement in the house, broke in, and attacked someone he thought was Joey. Instead, it was Hal.

He killed Hal and brought him out to the caves. Why Ned would want to do that, she didn't know—yet.

After Hal's body was found, for some reason, Ned waited a couple of weeks, then went back to the caves to make sure he hadn't left any evidence. But Joey, who realized what had happened, followed Ned and killed him.

The note that someone had left in Paavo's jacket pocket confirmed her theory.

Everything about it made sense—except that she couldn't see either Ned or Joey as a murderer. But then again, if killers were obvious, Paavo wouldn't have a job.

Now that she had everything figured out, Angie decided it was time to resolve these murders—for Doc, for Paavo, and even for herself and her vacation.

She was going to confront Teresa—woman to woman—and convince Teresa to admit to Paavo all that had been going on between her and Joey.

With firm determination, she marched up to the house and jabbed the doorbell hard.

Drapes at a nearby window fluttered, as if someone was peeking out. A moment later, Teresa pulled the door open. "This is a surprise," she said. She seemed nervous. "Are you here to see my mother? She's at the hospital."

"I'm here to see you," Angie replied. "There's something I want to talk to you about."

Teresa invited her in. They went into the kitchen and Teresa got them both some iced tea.

"I saw Joey leaving," Angie said.

"Yes. He's an old friend." Teresa's voice and expression remained glum. "Angie, please tell Paavo I'm sorry about last night. I never should have gone through the church archives without permission. I thought it could help, could end all this quickly, but it turned out I was wrong. Everything I believed was wrong. And I was ashamed. Too ashamed to face Father Armand."

That wasn't exactly what Angie had expected to hear. "What do you mean?"

"It doesn't matter. It means nothing now."

Angie's irritation skyrocketed. She needed an explanation now! So many of these people wouldn't open up, wouldn't tell everything they knew, that it was absolutely frustrating. She wanted answers. "No, Teresa. It means a lot." She told Teresa about the clothes she'd found in Hal's home. "They look like they're your size, your style."

Teresa sat back in the chair without speaking for a long moment, then gazed at Angie. "Yes," she said, her expression at once resigned yet almost relieved. "They're mine. I suppose you're wondering how they got there."

Not at all, Angie thought. "I know how they got there. Your affair with Joey."

"Joey?" Teresa nearly laughed. "Of course not! It was Hal."

"Hal?" Angie couldn't quite imagine what Teresa was saying.

Teresa sighed. "I wanted to tell, but my mother

said no one would believe me—that they'd say I was just doing it for the inheritance, and I needed proof." She chuckled sadly. "But I can't find any."

"Proof of what?" Angie was beside herself with these riddles.

Instead of answering, Teresa looked lost. "I often think my own family didn't believe me, either. Who knows? It turns out they shouldn't have. I feel like such a fool saying this"—Teresa drew in her breath—"but I truly believed Hal and I were married."

At the sound of Paavo's voice, one of the "fishermen" automatically reached for the gun under his vest.

"No need for guns," Paavo said. "Let's talk. You can start by telling me who you are."

The two men had been parked a half block from the sheriff's station and watched it so intently they didn't notice Paavo sneak up from behind.

"Mackenzie," the older man said.

"Cragin," replied the younger. "FBI, Tucson." They showed their badges.

"Any good at cracking computer passwords?" Paavo asked as he looked over the IDs.

"I've been known to, Inspector Smith," Cragin replied, even before Paavo introduced himself. "Whose computer is it?"

"Hal Edwards's."

"I'll definitely do it."

"Good," Paavo said, adding, "and, since you know me and why I'm here, how about giving me some information? What's your interest in all this?"

"Border security," Mackenzie said. "Nothing more."

"Since when does the FBI back up Border Patrol?" Paavo asked. "And aren't you a little too far north for that?" Even as he chided them, he remembered his conversation with the snake oil salesman who said he'd seen illegals on Edwards's property last winter.

"Not necessarily," Cragin answered.

Paavo really hated dealing with the Feds. They wanted all the answers and gave none. "What brought you here?" he asked, trying again.

Cragin looked at Mackenzie and waited. Mackenzie nodded.

"This." He took a small, carved obsidian stone from his pocket. "Have you seen one before?"

"Yes."

"Where?"

"Why don't you tell me what it means first," Paavo replied.

"It's a coyote. It's the name and symbol of the people illegals pay to help them cross the border and hide in safe spots as they work their way deep into the U.S.," Cragin began. "They turned up in this area last winter and caught our interest, along with Hal Edwards, a once prominent man in this state. He disappeared, the illegals took a different route, and we left."

Mackenzie picked up the story. "Then we learned Edwards's body had been found, and it seemed he'd been murdered. We wanted to see if his death was linked to the human smuggling. Maybe someone else in this town was also involved. The way the sheriff was bungling things, though, we thought we'd have to work the cases ourselves. Good thing you're here, Inspector."

"Glad to be of service," Paavo said sarcastically.

"That computer you were talking about might help both of us," Cragin added. "Let's take a look at it. And anyway, I've been wanting to see if Sheriff Hermann is as bad in person as she seems from afar."

Angie nearly fell off her chair at Teresa's pronouncement. "You thought you were *married* to Hal Edwards? But he was old!" Good grief, she'd been a bit off in her theory, hadn't she?

Teresa smiled, misunderstanding Angie's mortification. "Yes, he was. But you need to understand, Hal was very special in this town, not only because he gave people jobs in his stores and donated lots of money, but he'd help people he hardly knew. He saved my grandmother's business, and helped my mother when she was having terrible problems with my father. He was always very kind to me, and I grew up practically worshipping Hal Edwards. When he asked me to marry him in secret, how could I refuse? I felt safe around him. Does that make any sense at all?"

It did, Angie realized, because this was the only world Teresa knew, and Hal Edwards was king here. "It makes sense," she admitted. "But why did he want the marriage to be a secret?"

"I can only tell you what he said—that he was afraid Clarissa would badger him over Joey's inheritance if she knew he'd remarried, that he was private and increasingly paranoid about everything legal and involving his estate, that he wanted to look after me and see that my future was secure. And I believe that part of him was embarrassed to have such a young wife. He didn't want to deal with the behind-the-back snickers and taunts. And also, something had made him afraid. He denied it, but I could tell. I'll admit I'd hoped that after the wedding he'd see that those reasons were thin, and we could let our marriage be known. Instead, his fear grew. He honestly believed he was in danger, blaming everyone, even me. After only a month of being married to me, he left without a word."

Angie shook her head. She couldn't imagine anyone getting married and not being able to tell the world about it. In fact, she was trying to figure a way to get one of those big nuptial write-ups in the Sunday *New York Times*. Hal's attitude didn't make sense. "That's hard to believe, Teresa. In this small town, where everyone knows everything, how is it nobody figured out about the marriage? They must have suspected something."

"Some did. But remember, I'd been working for him since I was eighteen. People knew we were close, but saw it as a father-daughter relationship, nothing more. If anything, they suspected something between Joey and me. Joey isn't all that interested in women, however—not men, either. He's simply a loner. And lonely. Sometimes, I think I'm the closest thing to a friend he's ever had. And that's all we are—friends. Anyway, Hal and I kept separate quarters on the ranch, though, obviously, a few of my things ended up in his room. It wasn't"—her face reddened—"a very physical relationship."

Angie's head still couldn't get around this young woman and Hal Edwards as husband and wife, secret or otherwise. "There are public records and announcements of marriage. Hal Edwards was well known. How could he hide it?"

"There's also something called a 'confidential' marriage," Teresa explained. "Certain criteria need to be met, and Hal told me his friends in Yuma would arrange a marriage that was sealed from the public. They were most often used when people lived together and told everyone they were married, and then decided to make it quietly legitimate. I was young and foolish enough to think the idea was romantic."

A secret marriage. Something like that would certainly help Angie with her wedding plans! Maybe there was some merit to the idea.

Go off to Yuma; don't tell a soul. No special destination locale to find. No reception to plan. No wedding planner hectoring her. No caterers demanding decisions. No music that had to please three generations of listeners.

But also, no beautiful wedding dress . . . no special jewelry . . . no memories of Paavo waiting for her at the altar while she walked down the aisle on her proud father's arm . . .

Teresa's next, bitter words pulled Angie from her daydream. "I never even got a marriage certificate."

"But you can get one now," Angie insisted.

Teresa shook her head. "I tried, but the record, it seems, was lost. And Yuma hasn't gotten around to computerizing 'oddball' records as they called it. Or—and I have to accept this as a possibility—

there never was a real marriage. Hal might have paid someone off. He was capable of doing just about anything."

The thought of a sham marriage had Angie horrified. Beyond horrified. "That's absolutely despicable! Why would he do such a thing?"

"I don't know, except that he knew how strictly I follow my religion, and I'd never marry a divorced man. He told me he'd had his original marriage annulled, but that might have been a lie, too. We went to Father Benedict to have the marriage blessed, and last night, I learned there's no blessing record either." She shut her eyes a moment. "I can't imagine Father Benedict would have been a party to a lie, but I don't know what else to think. It's a nightmare."

"Clarissa told me about the annulment, so she thought it was legitimate as well," Angie said. "And I can't believe an old priest would have lied to you. Also, Doc said there'd been a break-in at the church last week."

Teresa was stunned. "I hadn't heard. What was taken?"

"Father Armand didn't know."

Teresa made no comment; her mind seemed to be whirring.

Angie had to ask, "Did Ned know about the marriage?"

Teresa's mouth tightened. "Three months ago, when Hal returned, he asked me to forgive him, to go back to him." She twisted her hands. "I didn't know what to do, because of Ned. Ned confused me. He loved me. He made me realize the way a marriage should be, but mine never was."

Finally, Angie thought, Teresa was making some sense about marriage. Yet, one thing confused her. "You told me once that you didn't love Ned."

"I don't . . . I don't know." Teresa's green eyes met hers, pleading for understanding. "I was an abandoned wife, stuck here helping my mother make ends meet at the restaurant. Ned and I had an affair, I'll admit that. And then, Hal came back." Her face was stricken. "I had to choose, Angie. I had to choose between two men who meant very much to me. And I chose the man I believed was my husband."

"Oh, Teresa," was all Angie could say. She couldn't imagine being in such a situation.

"I told Ned," Teresa said quietly, "and I was going to return to the hacienda, when Hal . . . suddenly, Hal wasn't there. I couldn't believe he'd run off, not after the things he'd said to me, the promises he'd made. But everyone said he had. I'd hated that once again, I'd been so stupid as to believe him."

Angie took a deep breath. "What did Ned do?"

"What could he do?" Teresa stood and walked to the edge of the pergola, looking out at a succulent garden. Angie didn't allow herself to say a word or make a sound. She only listened.

"Hal only returned long enough to turn my life upside down," Teresa said. "Soon after he left, though, strange things began, as if someone was trying to kill me. God, I feel like Hal saying that! But Ned believed me. Then, as quickly as it began, it stopped—until Hal's body was discovered. Suddenly, it all started once more. My truck breaking down out in the desert. Losing its brakes. Fires.

Once, I even thought I heard a gunshot. Ned was furious. He began searching, asking questions. I begged him to stop. It was too dangerous. Someone is crazy here.

"My mother believes Clarissa and Joey are behind it—that they found out about the marriage and want to stop me from inheriting Hal's money. That was why I went to Yuma to get my marriage certificate, to openly claim what was mine and to end the fear my mother had. But there was nothing.

"I told Ned I was going away. He wouldn't stop investigating; wouldn't listen." Her tears began to fall. Angie realized what was coming next, and despite herself, she felt her own eyes well up.

"We fought," Teresa said, "and then, before I had a chance to right the situation, before I had the chance to make amends, or make it up to him, or do anything at all to save him . . . he, too, was dead."

Chapter 25

Angie could scarcely believe it when she saw Paavo and Merry Belle head to head and side by side in the sheriff's office. That the two fishermen were with them, on the other hand, didn't surprise her at all. Even she knew their spotless L.L. Bean and Patagonia gear was just a cover. All were pouring over Hal's computer and the sheets of papers spitting out of the printer attached to it.

"I don't mean to bother you," she said to Paavo. "But I'd like to return to the guest ranch. Can I take the car?"

"If you need wheels," Merry Belle quickly interjected to Paavo, "you can use Buster's Jeep."

"Thanks," Paavo said, and handed Angie the SUV's keys.

Before leaving, Angie quickly told everyone about Teresa's admission of marriage to Hal. Her face filled with smug satisfaction at being the one to spring this important bit of information on the professional investigators.

She then returned to the ranch. She had made

out the list of supplies for Lionel and thought she'd double-check it before giving it to him. She'd come up with a few substitutes for her more exotic ingredients. Such as if no fennel, then leeks; if no leeks, then white onions. Somehow, she'd make this work.

She was still a few feet from the cookhouse when she heard voices coming from it.

Quietly, she approached. Peering in the door, she saw Clarissa and Dolores in deep disagreement over what Dolores would be cooking on Saturday.

Angie backed away. That was one fight she didn't want to get involved in.

"You're doing the smart thing," Lionel said behind her.

She jumped and turned around.

He smirked. "I wouldn't get in the middle of that, either. There are too many cleavers and butcher knives close at hand."

"You've got a point," Angie said. She took a folded piece of paper from her pocket. "Here's the list of supplies I need. Do the best you can, and let me know soon if you can't find some ingredient."

"Will do." Lionel stuck it in his shirt pocket. "Say, did you ever go treasure hunting?" He looked ready to laugh at her.

"You think I'd wander the desert talking to myself like some old withered prospector?" Angie asked.

"That depends on how interested you are in finding something from the missing stagecoach."

"Oh. Well, I am interested, but I haven't found the time."

"No time like the present. I'll take you."

That surprised her. "Really?" She couldn't imagine Lionel wanting to do anything more than absolutely necessary.

"We should take horses," Lionel said.

Angie's memories of her last riding experience—the horse going backward, sideways, and in figure eights—struck. Without Paavo and Joaquin Oldwater's help, she didn't know if she could manage. "How about a truck?"

He chuckled and agreed.

She changed into boots and jeans, and soon, they were off.

Brimming with excitement over her good luck at finding Lionel in such an agreeable mood, she couldn't wait to see the place where some of the belongings from the missing stagecoach had turned up.

The chance that Chef van Beerstraeden's journal might still be lost out there was remote, but possible. After all, how many treasure hunters would care about a book filled with recipes? They'd probably toss it away.

She remembered how her sisters and her friend Connie had laughed when she told them she was going to vacation with Paavo in a little desert town in Arizona. Words like "tenderfoot" and "greenhorn" were mirthfully thrown at her.

Well, if her idea worked out, she'd get the last laugh, that was for sure.

And even more so if she brought them out here to her destination wedding site. She was like Mustang Sally compared to them. And she wasn't talking about Mustang cars.

Or—considering that she was riding in a black GMC truck rather than a ranch horse—maybe she was.

At a bullet-ridden saguaro, Lionel turned off the road and onto a dirt path that was no more than a couple of ruts in the desert sand. Doc had been right when he'd warned that driving over that land was a lot worse than horseback riding. Angie feared the fillings in her teeth would rattle loose before they ever got there. She had no idea the desert was so bumpy.

In the distance, she spotted three flat rocks. The one on the bottom was the largest, the middle was in-between size, and the top was smallest. Her breath caught. The way they were stacked made them look like layers on a . . .

Could it be?

Small rocks covered the ground. Little whitish ones about the size of candy-coated Jordan almonds so often used as favors at a . . .

Yes!

The creek wasn't far, and near it she saw a willow with small, shimmering leaves covering branches that bowed low, sweeping the ground much like a bride's . . .

Perfect!

A stand of saguaro looked like a reception line; a small distant hill was shaped like a church organ; a barrel cactus looked like a ring bearer's pillow.

Her heart filled. Even Mother Nature wanted her wedding to be held here.

"I haven't quite figured out where you could

find things from the stagecoach," Lionel said, "but everyone thinks those people used the caves for shelter. That'd be a place to start."

His words broke her reverie. "You aren't talking about the cave where Hal was found, are you?" she asked.

"I sure am." He gave her a toothy grin.

Joyful wedding thoughts fizzled completely. "No way! There's nothing there and it's spooky."

Lionel, however, didn't turn back. Going across Hal's property to reach the caves, she discovered they were much closer to the hacienda than she'd thought.

The atmosphere around the caves felt even creepier than the first time she was there. "I'm not so sure about this," she said as she got out of the truck on the flatland and looked up the incline to the narrow cave entrance.

"Prospectors gotta have a sense of adventure," Lionel said, beginning the steep walk. "Let's see what we can find." Before long, he plunged inside.

She took a deep breath before entering the cave, then stopped near the entrance. It took a moment for her eyes to grow accustomed to the dark. Then, without moving, she scanned the area. The ground was rock hard. Nothing could have escaped anyone's observation in here.

"Hey!" Lionel was on his hands and knees, deep in the cave. "I see something." He was brushing aside some dirt on the ground, near a cave wall.

"You do?" She could scarcely believe it. "What is it?" she asked, stepping nearer.

"I don't know. It's shiny. Like money—or gold coins!" he cried.

"Gold coins?" She was agape. How lucky was this? Forget the cookbook—maybe they found the treasure!

He picked up the object and sat back on his heels as she squatted beside him. "I was wrong. Sorry about that." He held out a brass strip curved into a half circle.

"What in the world is that?" she asked.

He stood, and they both walked outside into the sunlight. "It's just a heel rand. I wonder how in the world it got back there? Maybe this place really is haunted!"

"What's a heel rand?" she asked, taking it from Lionel before he tossed it away.

"Cowboys sometimes put them on the back of their boots, where the leather meets the heel. It protects the leather. More common is when we put metal caps over the toes of our boots. It's all the same thing."

"Oh, my God! I think I know who it belongs to." She'd seen one of those—only one, in fact, on Joey Edwards's boots. It was the same brass color, the same curved design.

"You do?" He looked at her skeptically. "I'd keep a lid on it, if that's the case. It just might belong to Hal's murderer."

Her eyes widened. "It looks like something that might belong to Joey Edwards. If so, he probably came here to look at the site where his father was found. I can't imagine that Joey would kill his own father."

"Don't be so sure." Lionel's mouth twisted into an ugly grimace. "For one thing, they hated each other. For another, all Joey's money is tied up in the Halmart stores, and word has it they're going down. When Hal showed up with all those birds, Joey might have seen the ruin of this guest ranch and everything else Hal built suddenly staring him in the face. Maybe he got tired of waiting; tired of watching his inheritance going down the drain. That's just my speculation, mind you," Lionel added.

"Are you saying Hal and Joey met when Hal returned in the winter?"

"They sure did."

Why had Joey lied? Angie wondered. "Despite that, though, Hal was his father."

"Yeah, but that only made matters worse. Hell, Hal was twice the man Joey is, especially in the ladies department."

How much, Angie wondered, did Lionel really know?

"All that aside," she continued, "if this heel thingy was here since the time of the murder, don't you think the sheriff would have found it?"

He looked at the brass object a moment. "Ordinarily, I'd be inclined to agree with you. But you've met Monster Bum and Ball-less Buster. Hell, Buster wouldn't want to dirty his slacks looking under dirt like I did!"

"You may be right," she whispered as elation slowly built. Suddenly, she grabbed him in a bear hug. "We've done it, Lionel! I can hardly believe it, but we solved the case!"

"If you're right," Lionel said, disentangling himself, "then you'd better get that evidence to your man, pronto."

Chapter 26

An hour later Angie entered the sheriff's station. Buster greeted her warmly and directed her to Merry Belle's office.

"All this damn stuff is getting in the way of me doing my regular chores like writing out traffic tickets and such." Merry Belle was complaining to Paavo, her words muffled by a mouthful of chocolate-glazed doughnut.

"Not to worry," Angie announced as she waltzed inside. "Help is on the way." With a big smile, she placed the heel rand on the desk in front of Merry Belle.

"What the hell's that?" the sheriff asked. "Something for cowboy boots?"

Merry Belle's eyes narrowed as Angie explained how Lionel had found the heel protector in the caves and that she believed it matched the one Joey Edwards was missing. She also said that Joey had lied, according to Lionel, and that he had met and spoken with his father.

As the sheriff listened, her face blazed a deep

crimson. Paavo shook his head. The FBI agents looked disgusted.

"What's wrong?" Angie asked.

Paavo explained. "By removing the metal from the crime scene, there's no chain of evidence. We can't use it to connect Joey—or anyone else—to the location with Hal's body."

"Oh," was Angie's chastened reaction.

Merry Belle put down her half-eaten doughnut, stood up, glared at them, then stomped over to the window. Her back was to them and they could see her shoulders start to quiver. "*Arrrrgh!*" A visceral, jungle cry erupted from her.

The window glass in front of her seemed to shake and bow. The room quaked as if from a sonic boom. Angie could swear that somewhere in the far distance, a dog howled. She, Paavo, and the FBI agents sat in utter silence, gaping at the sheriff.

"*I can't stand it!*" Merry Belle sounded angry and on the verge of tears at the same time. "I just want to go back to taking care of my sweet little town, but everyone's against me!"

There was the pounding of footsteps, then a fearful-faced Buster stood in the entry. "Is something wrong, Aunt Merry Belle?"

His words hung suspended in the air as Merry Belle slowly faced him. "GET-THE-HELL-OUT!"

Buster beat a hasty retreat.

Merry Belle's attention turned to her stunned audience. She was breathing in great gulps of air, then she stiffened, closed her eyes, and inhaled slowly. Opening her eyes, she marched back to the desk and seated herself as she stared at the four gawking onlookers.

"What else is wrong?" she whispered with a mixture of hope and despair.

No one said a word.

"You tell me," Merry Belle roared.

"Your name?" Angie said meekly.

It took the three men all they had to keep the sheriff from flying across her desk at Angie.

Teresa hung up her cell phone. She used the excuse that the connection was becoming weaker as she drove. The truth was, she didn't want to hear anything more from Joey.

He was upset that the sheriff had come by to inspect his father's home. There was a stain on the floor that Merry Belle wanted to run tests on. And then she took his boots. She made it clear she wanted to tie him to the caves, to his father's and Ned's murders, and acted as if he should simply confess and get it over with. He swore he had nothing to confess.

He called to insist he hadn't killed anyone. Not Hal, not Ned.

Teresa knew that. Joey was a dear friend. No one took the trouble to understand him; they expected him to be like his father, and when he didn't live up, they dismissed him as weak and inconsequential. She felt he could be more than that, and for that reason, they'd become close. Joey was no killer.

Once, the thought had crossed her mind that a jealous Ned could have done Hal harm. But that

wasn't true either. Ned's only mistake was that he
loved her and tried to find out who wanted to hurt
her. She still couldn't believe he was gone, that
she'd never again see his deep blue eyes, the way
his sandy blond hair rippled in the breeze on the
lake, his strong hands, his arms reaching out for
her . . .

Tears shimmered. She had loved him, but not
enough.

It was the same with Hal. He'd offered her
hope. Hope to be free of life in Jackpot, of the boring sameness of it. Once, he'd accused her of using
him, of marrying him for his money. She'd denied
it, but if she were being honest with herself, she'd
say he was right. She'd been selfish. She'd loved
him in her way, but in her heart she knew she
hadn't ever truly and completely loved anyone.
Not the kind of love she saw in Angie's eyes whenever she talked about, or looked at, her fiancé.

She turned onto Doc's driveway. Her mother
was remaining at the hospital and didn't want
Teresa home alone. Her thoughts turned to Doc
and her mother, and how happy they were simply
being in each other's company.

Teresa wondered if she'd ever find that with
anyone. That's what was wrong—the curse of her
life, the thing she'd have to learn how to change if
she was ever going to be happy. Her problem
wasn't Jackpot, not its people, not even the loneli-
ness of life in the desert. Her problem was her in-
ability . . . no, her *fear* . . . of trusting enough to
open her heart to another human being. Her problem was simple: she was afraid to love.

Chapter 27

Early the next morning, Paavo went to Doc with news of the latest discoveries. Teresa had already left Doc's house to relieve her mother at the hospital.

Doc was stunned. "A part of me suspected something was going on between Hal and Teresa, but I dismissed it due to the age difference. I decided he was a father figure, nothing more. God knows, after Junior, she needed one. I never imagined they were married, though. And I don't think Hal would have lied to the girl about it. He did some shifty things in his life, but never anything that low. If the marriage records are missing, it's because someone took them."

"Did you know Ned had met with Hal?" Paavo asked.

"No," Doc said, and clamped his lips together as if he refused to speak more on that subject.

"Fine." Paavo didn't want to pursue it either. "We know that Lupe is afraid someone wants Teresa dead. If that's the case, and if there once were marriage records, then we know someone besides the Flores women knows about the marriage."

"I see what you're saying," Doc said. "Someone who doesn't want Teresa to inherit."

"Someone—and I'm afraid that someone has to be our sheriff—will have to go to Yuma and find out what happened to those records."

"Do we really want to let her in on all this?" Doc asked. "If you're talking about official documents, this could be an inside job."

"We have no choice." Paavo's words were firm. "For some reason, I trust her."

"For some reason, I do too." Doc's jaw tightened.

"I know that Teresa and her whole family are strong Catholics," Paavo said, his words cautious and wary. "You realize, don't you, that it meant that if Ned couldn't convince Teresa to divorce Hal, there was only one way he could ever marry her."

"Don't go there, Paavo," Doc said, threateningly. "Ned would never kill anyone."

Paavo wanted to agree, but after all he'd seen on his job, nothing surprised him anymore.

Angie headed for the cookhouse. The day before, as she went to the sheriff's office with the heel rand, Lionel had gone off in search of supplies. She had no idea how far he'd gone, but after breakfast that morning, a grumpy Lionel told her he'd gotten everything she wanted except *fois gras*. Of course the fact that he pronounced it "foys grass" might have been the reason for his lack of success. Or not. She'd do without the appetizer.

The next day was the big cookout. This morning, she was going to do as much of the preparation as possible in order to make tomorrow easier.

Dolores was making pie crusts. "If you're looking for Señora Edwards," she said, "she just left to go horseback riding. I'm sure if you hurry, you can join her."

The thought of getting back on a horse gave Angie jitters. Between horses wanting to run off with her, ostriches pecking at her, and wild boars—so to speak—chasing her, not to mention encounters with tarantulas and rattlers, she wasn't having a great time, zoologically speaking. "No rides for me," she said. "I'm going to cook the lentils for the dal today; peel, seed, and boil the butternut squash; and make a sauce for the salmon."

"I don't know exactly what your dal is, but generally, the longer food marries, the better it tastes."

"I'll show you what it is as I make it," Angie said.

"Good. Mr. Edwards used to like my Mexican cooking, but sometimes I'd surprise him with special dishes. He always appreciated them. He said I was the best cook he'd ever known." Dolores smiled fondly at the memory.

Angie was impressed. "That's high praise for a man who had the money to go to many of the top restaurants in the country, I'm sure."

"I thought the same thing," Dolores said emphatically.

As they worked, Angie remembered that Dolores had lived here over twenty years. There had to have been a lot that she'd seen. "You knew Mr.

Edwards well," Angie began. "After he came back last winter, did you think he'd leave so soon?"

"I don't know," Dolores said.

"Were you surprised to learn he hadn't left, but that he'd died?"

"Oh, yes." Dolores nodded. "I was very surprised."

Angie would have really liked to know what Dolores thought. She tried again. "The sheriff said his death was from natural causes, but now people think he was murdered. What do you think?"

"He was a good man, a good boss," Dolores said. "I don't think anyone would kill him."

Well, this was going nowhere fast, Angie thought. She proceeded to work on her dishes, and the two chatted amiably about food and cooking techniques.

The time passed quickly, and Angie was surprised when Clarissa entered the kitchen. "There you are," she said to Angie. "LaVerne brought over something special for you to try."

Again? Angie thought. The woman should have been named Lucretia Borgia. "I'm working on the meal for the cookout."

"Doesn't matter. You've got to taste it while it's warm."

"I'm not falling for that again," Angie said.

"What does that mean?" Clarissa asked, but before waiting for an answer, added, "come on, you don't want to disappoint LaVerne. She especially asked for you. You're a gourmet cook."

"Like she is?" Angie asked.

"Exactly."

"Try it yourself." Angie went back to her dal.

"I plan to." Clarissa marched off.

Angie and Dolores looked at each other in astonishment. This, they couldn't miss. They hurried after Clarissa.

Lionel and Joey were already in the dining room. Near the back door, Junior was watching from safety. He obviously remembered LaVerne's goat cheese.

Junior must have felt Angie's scrutiny, because he seemed to grow uncomfortable and left the room.

LaVerne stood proudly over a bowl. "Here it is."

Angie looked down at some kind of meat in a red sauce. After her experience with the cactus, she wasn't about to take any chances. "What is it?"

"It's another secret family recipe. Arizona stew."

Angie was aware of the others watching her. She knew why these were secret recipes—no one else wanted them. "What kind of stew?"

"Rabbit," LaVerne said. "Right from this area."

"Rabbit?" Clarissa said, shocked. "I don't eat rabbit!"

"But it's gourmet rabbit," LaVerne explained. "For the cookout."

"Oh, all right." Clarissa took the spoon, scooped up a piece with meat and tasted. "It has an aftertaste." Her mouth wrinkled. "Something very . . . different."

The others all leaned closer.

"That's what makes it special." LaVerne stood tall. "An Arizona treat. Horned toad. Dried, salted, then shredded. Just half a toad gives a lot of flavor. Want me to serve it to your guests?"

Angie gasped.

Dolores chuckled.

Clarissa looked horror-stricken. Trying to keep some semblance of dignity, she hurried from the room.

LaVerne's jaw dropped, her brow furrowed, and she looked quizzically at the astounded people still around her. "Do you think that's a 'no'?"

Chapter 28

"Those ostriches are a good metaphor," Teresa said when Angie opened the door to the bungalow later that afternoon. "Have I been hiding my head in the sand, too, not seeing what's around me?"

Angie looked over the birds. All were females, and none had found a mate to share a life with. Of course, smelling like rotten eggs and being champion kick-boxers usually scares males off . . .

Here, though, there simply weren't any males for them.

Teresa's metaphor might be more accurate than she first thought. "Come in." Angie opened the door wide.

"My mother didn't want me to come here," Teresa said. She wore jeans and a black T-shirt, no makeup, and her hair was pulled back in a low ponytail. Her face looked tired and haggard, as if she hadn't slept well for days. "She's still nervous about Joey and Clarissa. I think she's wrong."

Angie had to admit she was nervous as well. "If

your mother is right, isn't this the most unsafe place for you to be?"

"Yes . . . if she's right. But I've known Joey for years. I don't believe he's a killer. He's a poor, pathetic fellow whose father turned against him for being weak. Hal never forgave him for siding with his mother when they divorced, or for leaving the ranch to live with her. Hal was right—Joey was weak, but despite what Hal thought, Joey actually loved and admired his father. He simply never admitted it, especially not around his mother, who's just a bitter old woman."

"I have to agree on the last part," Angie admitted. "Everything will change for the better if a will turns up."

Teresa drew in her breath before continuing. "That's why I'm here. I remember a hiding spot Hal had. It was usually empty, but I want to check it out. I haven't been inside Hal's house since I left it five years ago. I never even realized that I'd left a couple of dresses behind! That whole part of my life is a blur."

"A hiding spot?" Angie's eyes widened.

Teresa couldn't help but smile. "Don't get your hopes up. It's probably as empty as ever, but at this point, I've got to see it for myself."

They were hurrying across the plaza when Lionel popped up. "Well, look who's back," he said, eyeing Teresa.

"Hello, Lionel." Teresa's expression looked like she'd rather step on him than have a conversation.

"You hoping to find someone to give you work?" he asked with a smirk. "Guess I'm the one who hires and fires around here these days.

Leastways, until Saturday, when the estate is divvied up."

"I don't want work." She glanced at Angie, and then said, "I'm looking for Joey. Have you seen him?"

"He took off an hour or so ago. Clarissa was riding him real good. He's probably at the Stagecoach Saloon."

"Poor guy," Teresa said.

"Poor?" Lionel snorted. "Not likely. Want me to tell him you were looking for him? I'm sure he'll be real happy to hear it."

"That's fine."

"We'll be in the common room," Angie added, linking her arm with Teresa's and moving away from Lionel. "If Joey returns soon, I'm sure he'll join us."

"It'll be a cold day in hell afore he'd miss happy hour," Lionel said, then smirked and continued toward his trailer.

They walked on, feeling Lionel's eyes watching them.

From the common room, Angie and Teresa waited until Lionel disappeared in his trailer, then they hurried to the hacienda.

The front door was visible from the plaza, so they went to the back. The doorjamb had been repaired, and the door locked, but Teresa's old key worked. Angie quickly realized this wasn't the sort of area where people thought to change their locks.

As Teresa wandered through the house, Angie couldn't imagine what it must have been like for her knowing she'd once been married to the owner of all this, and that if their marriage had been done openly, it all might have gone to her.

Teresa visibly paled at the bloodstained kitchen floor. When she saw the torn up floorboards, she murmured that her mother might be correct—there could be danger here.

She headed up to the bedroom, and blanched at the sight of drawers opened and clothes on the floor. She lifted one of her dresses from the floor, then threw it back down. "Clarissa saw this?"

"I'm sure she did," Angie said, looking at the strange heap and shaking her head.

"She had to have realized it was mine. I wonder if Joey noticed it."

"I don't know," Angie said, wondering why Teresa cared.

Teresa went into the room Hal had used as an office and went straight to his desk. She opened a drawer, removed the papers from it, and then lifted out a secret bottom. Angie gawked in surprise.

There was nothing in the drawer except some Mexican pesos in high denominations, and a small carved black stone.

"Oh, no," Teresa murmured as she picked up the small object.

"What is it?" Angie asked. "It looks like a charm."

Teresa shook her head. "It's an amulet. Mexican. Foolish old man!"

Angie realized it had to be the same as the one Paavo had found at Ned's. "Is that the symbol of the coyotes? The people who transport illegals across the border?"

"You know about them?" Teresa was surprised. She put the amulet in her pocket and restored the drawer the way it had been. "It answers a question for me."

"Has it been there long, do you think?" Angie asked.

"It wasn't there five years ago. I looked in here a couple of times, to see if he was hiding anything that would give me a clue as to what was troubling him, but it was always empty."

"So the money and amulet were only left there after he returned this winter?" Angie asked.

"Most likely, especially since he'd been in Mexico."

"Paavo found a coyote charm at Ned's house."

All the color left Teresa's face. "Ned's? No, impossible. He wouldn't get mixed up in that." She shook her head.

"Do you have a key to Ned's place, or know where he kept a spare one hidden?" Angie asked suddenly.

"Yes, but—"

"Then, let's go. I want you to see the amulet he has, to make sure it's not one of these." Angie thought they should pick up Paavo on the way, as well. Teresa might know more than she thought, and Paavo needed to hear about it. "I think it's a clue as to who killed him and Hal—a big clue."

Teresa looked nervous. "I suspect you're right."

"We'll go, then?" Angie asked.

"Yes."

"Let's pick up Paavo as we go through town," Angie added.

"No," Teresa said. Her next words made Angie suddenly uneasy. "There's a back way to the lake that's a lot faster."

The road was rutted and unpaved. It followed Ghost Hollow Creek to the Colorado River, by-passing the town. Also, from that road, a person could veer north into the foothills and high desert plains. The land was all but untouched by humans, except for a few fire roads and old Indian trails.

Teresa was driving her Ford pickup, a big 350 four-by-four. As they rode through the silence, Teresa told Angie stories of her life after Hal disappeared, and how Ned started coming around more and more. She soon realized that his feelings for her were much more than friendship, and it troubled her.

She tried hard to ignore him but—

A sound, much like a backfire, caused the women to jump and turn in their seats.

"What—" Angie began, as Teresa sped up.

"Someone just shot at us," Teresa yelled.

"Shot at us?" Angie cried. She clutched the dashboard. "Maybe it's a mistake. Maybe you had a blowout."

Another shot sounded as the ping of a bullet hit the roof. Teresa drove off the road toward the creek. "That's no blowout," Teresa said.

"Hurry! Can't this truck go any faster?" Angie cried. A rear tire exploded, making the truck jostle and jerk.

Teresa floored the gas pedal, but the truck was straining badly.

"Who's doing this?" Angie cried. "How do we stop them?"

"I wish I knew."

Reaching the brush along the bank of the creek, the truck continued forward only a few feet before the land dropped precipitously. The truck died in a tangle of shrubbery and vines. "Run," Teresa shouted.

"Run?" Angie could barely get the word out. "You're kidding me, right?"

But Teresa had already opened the driver's side door, leaped to the ground, and headed toward the creek.

"This can't be happening," Angie murmured, as she waited a moment before she forced herself from the passenger side, clutching her purse against her chest as if it might protect her from a bullet. Dropping low, she scurried, stumbled, and slid down the bank, then half crawled after Teresa. "Don't leave!"

"Come on!" Teresa ran along the bank.

With her heartbeat so loud it was drumming in her ears, Angie eventually found her footing and followed Teresa.

Breathless, they both soon stopped, crouching together behind some scrub. "We've got to find a place to hide," Teresa said, panting.

Angie was also taking deep breaths. "Can we make it back to the hacienda?"

"It's about seven, eight miles," Teresa answered, breathless.

"What about the lake?"

"About ten."

"You're right," Angie said. "Let's find a place to hide."

They crept deeper into the thicket.

Teresa paused and looked around. "I recognize this area."

"You do?"

"Remember, I lived and worked at the hacienda for years. I know the land." Teresa headed east. "This way."

At a bend in the creek, she found a grooved area, not exactly a cave, more like a hollow just a couple of feet deep. They crawled behind the brush and huddled inside, facing outward to search for any sign of danger. They waited, hoping against hope that their pursuer wouldn't find them.

As they waited, Angie realized what sixth sense had made her take her purse. Her cell phone was in it.

Chapter 29

Paavo hung up the phone.

He was in Merry Belle's office and had just finished speaking with the handwriting expert he'd often gone to for help in San Francisco. For a preliminary reaction, he had faxed the man a copy of the note that had been put in his pocket. It had been written on newsprint— some white space on the weekly *Jackpot Press Democrat*.

The fact that the writing was done in a childish block print could mean the writer was young or poorly educated, but it more likely meant that he or she had watched a TV show or movie which stated that block printing was the easiest way to disguise one's handwriting. The expert didn't think reviewing the original rather than a fax would do much good, and went on to lament the popularity of shows that gave away such valuable information and made police work ever more difficult.

Paavo thanked the expert and turned back to Merry Belle. He hated that he'd reached another dead end.

That had been the same result the day before. Agent Cragin managed to break into Hal's computer, only to discover that nothing important was on it. The only thing of interest, in fact, was that Hal had used "4clarissa" as his password. It gave Paavo pause that even after so many years, it was Clarissa's name that Hal had chosen. All in all, it seemed rather sad.

He and the FBI agents searched the computer's documents for a will. They found a generic form, but none of the blanks had been filled in.

They also read through old e-mails, trying to find any indication of why Hal might have taken off, or why he might have been killed. What they found was typical of older people—he had scarcely used his new, high-powered technology.

Paavo didn't know if it was because this case was cleaner than most or because he was in this unknown territory with none of the usual forensic and crime lab information, but all he was doing was growing increasingly frustrated at the lack of evidence and detail he had to work with. It seemed it wasn't a case that would be solved by forensics, but by understanding the emotions of the people involved. There were two layers—one, what everyone was saying and doing, and the other, what they were feeling. He had gathered about as much as he could of the first. He would have welcomed some straight talk about the second.

His cell phone rang. It was Lupe Flores. She was with Doc. The two were worried about Teresa, who had gone to see Angie earlier in the day. Lupe tried Teresa and Angie's cell phones, but neither worked, and no one answered the guest ranch number.

"I left Angie at the cabin," Paavo said. "I'll go see what's going on."

For a long while, Angie all but held her breath to be sure she made absolutely no noise. When her nose began to tickle from the nearby sage, she almost panicked. Fortunately, the tickle went away.

After an hour of silence, though, boredom began to set in. She took her cell phone from her handbag and tried to make a call. There was no service. So much for being clever.

"Why is it," Angie whispered, "that there's phone service at the cave where Hal's body was, and none out here?"

"There's service at the caves?" Teresa asked.

"Yes. I don't get it."

"Me neither—unless someone put equipment out there—boosters or receptors or whatever. Why would anyone do that?"

"Makes no sense to me," Angie said.

Teresa looked thoughtful, but didn't say anything more.

Minutes slowly ticked by, an hour seeming like an eternity, until Angie couldn't take it any longer. "What do you think about making a run for it?" she whispered.

"Run where?" Teresa glanced at her. "We don't know where the shooter is, if he's given up, or is sitting out there waiting for us to move. He can be anywhere between here and the hacienda, just waiting for us to return."

Angie recognized the logic of that, much as she didn't like it. "Okay, let's think about this. Whoever is after us has got to be someone from the guest ranch. They're the only ones who saw us leave, right? All we know is it's not Clarissa. She's no shooter."

"But she is," Teresa countered. "She used to enjoy skeet shooting. Hal told me she was good at it. I can see her thinking of me as nothing more than a clay pigeon! Also, she could easily have paid someone—a stranger, or someone in town who wanted money. Maybe someone who wants to leave here so badly that he'd do anything at all to get enough money to go."

Angie had the eerie feeling that Teresa was, in a sense, describing herself.

"Do you want to take the chance of leaving this hiding place while it's daylight?" Teresa asked.

"No," Angie admitted, cautiously eyeing her companion. "It's not worth the risk. If whoever wants us dead is still out there waiting, with this wide-open desert, we wouldn't have a chance. Night can't come soon enough."

Paavo rushed into the bungalow to see if Angie had left him a note. The door was unlocked, which wasn't like her. Growing up in a city, she never left anything unlocked if she could help it.

There was no note in the bungalow, but it felt different—violated—as if someone else had been there. When he looked around, however, he saw nothing amiss.

The cookhouse was empty, as was the common room.

On his way to the office he spotted Junior leaving the stables. He was wiping grit from his face, as if he'd just gotten back from a ride. Paavo called to him.

A rebellious sneer flickered across the man's features. He skulked closer. "You want me for something?"

"I heard Teresa came here to meet Angie. Have you seen either one this afternoon?"

"Hell, no," Junior said. "I been out on the range with those stupid, ugly, smelly, filthier than dirt birds."

Paavo eyed him sharply. "Come with me."

He rapped on the trailer door. Lionel stuck his head out. "Oh . . ." he gulped at Paavo's fierce expression, then came out. "Something wrong?"

"I'm looking for Teresa Flores and Angie," Paavo said.

"Uh . . . Teresa?" Lionel acted as if he never heard of her.

"She was here."

"Oh?"

"Listen, Lionel, I know you don't miss a thing that happens on this ranch, so what did you see?"

Lionel glanced at Junior, then said, "Oh, *that* Teresa. Didn't you see her, Junior?"

"I was feeding the ostriches," Junior mumbled, "and not paying much attention."

"Did you talk to her?" Paavo asked.

"No." Junior stared at the ground. "I was kind of . . ."

Embarrassed, Paavo thought, to show his daughter that all he'd done with his life was to become an ostrich feeder. Paavo turned to Lionel. "Did you talk to her, Lionel?"

"She was looking for Joey," he said.

"Joey!" Junior roared.

"That's all I know. Then, Buster showed up."

"What was Buster doing here?" Paavo asked.

"Said he was looking for Miss Angie. I told him she might be in the common room with Teresa, but apparently he couldn't find her there. In fact, there goes Buster now. I wonder where he's been all this time."

Paavo turned to see Buster's old Jeep pulling out from behind the workhouses. At the same time, Joey darted out from the common room and hurried across the plaza toward his bungalow.

Lionel waved. "Joey! Come on over!"

"Me? Why?" Joey asked.

"Have you seen Angie or Teresa?" Paavo asked. At Joey's confused expression, he added, "They were together, here, early this afternoon. No one's seen them for hours, apparently. Did you?"

"No. I was taking a walk, trying to clear my head," Joey said. "Teresa's missing?"

"Were you just talking to Buster?" Paavo asked.

"Buster?" He looked around nervously. "No. I'd rather not have anything to do with him. Is he here?"

Lionel suddenly found his tongue. "Come to think of it, I saw a truck that may have been Teresa's leave the ranch earlier."

"Back to town?" Paavo asked.

"No. It went the other way," Lionel said, scratching his chin stubble. "Out the back road toward the lake."

"If they broke down on that back road, no wonder no one has heard from them," Joey exclaimed. "I'll get a truck and look for them. It's four-wheel drive territory."

"I'll call the sheriff," Lionel said.

"Tell her to search the main road. Joey and I will take the back road to the lake," Paavo said, then to Joey, "we'll use both our vehicles. We can cover more territory that way."

"I'm sure they're all right," Joey offered. "Teresa knows the desert."

"I hope so," Paavo said, although with a killer around here, it wasn't the desert that worried him.

This had to have been one of the longest days of Angie's life. Not even the occasional rustle of a leaf broke the absolute stillness. In fact, there were no leaves, just prickly desert scrub and cactus. There was no wind. Not even a stray animal or bird.

Angie thought she'd lived a hundred years before night fell.

Most desert creatures had the sense to stay sheltered during the day. They came out at night.

The night was dark now. Beyond dark. Pitch-black.

Owls hooted. Coyotes howled, and sounded very, very near. Angie couldn't help but wonder what else was out there.

Quietly, the two women talked.

Angie told Teresa about her family and growing up in San Francisco as the fifth daughter of a wealthy shoe-store owner and real estate investor. Teresa told her about growing up in Jackpot, the only daughter of a woman who worked hundred-hour weeks in her restaurant.

Teresa had vowed her life would be better. Maybe that was part of Hal's attraction. Around the time Hal left, Maritza's health began to deteriorate, and Lupe needed Teresa to help her with both the restaurant and her grandmother. She felt stuck.

Angie understood how, given that, she couldn't just up and leave. As they talked, they found a lot in common—love of family, respect for their parents' toils, and wondering if they could ever do anything with their own lives to make a difference.

Now, hungry and thirsty, they decided to make a move.

Stiff and sore, crouching low, they made their way back to the truck, listening for footsteps or any indication that whoever had been stalking them was still around. They heard nothing.

The truck held food and water. Teresa had explained how, in the desert, it was important to keep some provisions—especially water—with you at all times. If a car broke down out here, it was so desolate it could be many hours before you were found. Much of the year, the temperature would be too hot to try to walk for aid; and without water, you wouldn't survive long in 130-degree weather.

That day, the temperature hadn't risen much above ninety. It might be "dry" desert heat, but for a San Francisco girl, it was still plenty hot.

Scouring the darkness to make sure no one had found the truck and was waiting to ambush them, they stealthily approached. Teresa reached behind the passenger seat and pulled out a small knapsack.

The two sat on the ground, and Teresa took out three water bottles. They shared one, saving the others for their long walk back to the guest ranch—or wherever cell service would work again.

Angie's real hope, though, was with Paavo. Once he returned to the bungalow and discovered she wasn't there, he would come looking for her.

He'd find her. Wouldn't he?

Earlier, as the sun dipped low in the sky and vultures circled over her head, she had wondered what they knew that she didn't. She wondered no more.

"What food do you have?" she asked.

Teresa sorted through the loot. Matches. Fire starter cubes. Flashlight. Knife. Can opener. One can of chili beans and another of Vienna sausages.

"That's it?" Angie said, trying to keep the disappointment out of her voice. She wasn't a fan of Vienna sausages—the meat in them was always a little too soft to suit her, and what was that gelatinous stuff they sat in?

"It's precooked and nourishing," Teresa said, waving a can as temptation. "We don't dare build a fire."

"You're right," Angie conceded. "And we'll eat no more than half. We'll save the rest for later."

Teresa opened both cans and set them on flat rocks. She lifted out a sausage, as did Angie.

Dejection settled like a shroud as Angie stared at her makeshift dinner. She hadn't eaten since breakfast. The front of her stomach was touching the back, and all she could think about was how much she wished she were with Paavo instead of stuck out here with a strange woman and a crazy killer with a rifle.

She dipped her sausage into the can of chili beans and balanced a bean on it. "Beanie," she murmured with a deep sigh as she morosely chewed the bean. Just before she bit into the sausage, she added, "Weenie."

It was all she could do not to cry.

With a sigh, she ate more cold chili.

It made LaVerne's food look good.

Both she and Teresa tried to take tiny nibbles and eat slowly so the food would last. It didn't work. In seconds they'd each devoured three sausages.

"Let's hope Paavo gets here soon," Angie said.

"Stiff upper lip," Teresa said encouragingly. "We can do it."

They skulked closer to the road, both anxious to be on their way back, despite their intent to wait.

Light flashed in the distance. Angie gripped Teresa's arm and pointed.

It was a set of headlights, and a second set followed not far behind. It was the first set, though, that intrigued Angie. High and wide like on a truck or SUV, it wasn't a "normal" headlight set, but Xenon hyper-whites. The only car she'd seen in Jackpot with those headlights was the Mercedes she and Paavo had rented.

She grabbed the knapsack, rummaging madly through it until she found the flashlight, and ran toward the road.

"What are you doing?" Teresa tried to grab and stop her, but missed.

"It's Paavo," Angie called, still running.

"Wait! You've got to be sure."

"I am sure." She frantically waved the flashlight toward the vehicles. They sped on.

She yelled, brandishing the light while fighting despair that help, so near, had eluded them.

Suddenly, the lead car slowed, then made a U-turn and stopped. The second car did the same.

Doors slammed.

Angie stood as if glued to the spot, praying she'd been right.

Fear that she'd made a deadly mistake kept her quiet until Paavo called her name.

"I'm here!" she shouted, relief and joy propelling her forward.

He met her halfway. "Are you all right?" he asked, holding her tight.

"Yes." She nestled against him. He felt so good, so warm and secure, that she nearly cried. "We were shot at—and Teresa's truck tire blew out and we ended up in some brush, nearly off the bank and into the creek."

Joey hurried toward Teresa. "Someone shot at you?" Joey asked. He hugged her, and for a moment she let him, but then pulled away and folded her arms as if she were cold.

"Did you see anything? Any sign to tell who it was?" Paavo asked.

"We couldn't see anyone," Teresa replied, moving toward them. Joey stood back and watched her go.

"We were trying to go to Ned's," Angie said. "We should still do it so Teresa can see the amulet he had. She found one hidden in Hal's office."

"In his office?" Paavo asked, then peered into the darkness. "Let's get out of here. We need to talk."

Chapter 30

Paavo, Angie, and Teresa piled into the SUV, while Joey went off on his own to call for a tow truck to take care of Teresa's vehicle.

Teresa listened with growing sadness as Paavo explained to her that the obsidian carving was no longer at Ned's home, and that the FBI agents had confirmed Hal's involvement with the coyote smugglers.

"Everything makes more sense now," Teresa said bitterly.

"What do you mean?" Paavo asked.

"When Hal brought the ostriches to his ranch, I asked him how he was going to handle them." Teresa folded her hands. "If he was going to breed, raise, and sell, or slaughter them, he'd need help. It wasn't the sort of thing people in town would be interested in, I was sure. He said he knew how to get all the help necessary. I didn't understand at the time, but now I think I do. He got the ostriches cheap, and would use free labor to raise them. Free, smuggled-in labor. Caves are often used as hiding places by illegals. Caves like on Hal's land. The fact that cell phone service was available out there makes sense now, doesn't it? He must have put receptors, or boosters, or some kind of relay system out there. The whole thing was another of Hal's schemes to make money."

Paavo started the SUV and headed toward the ranch.

"If that's what the cave would be used for, why was Hal's body put in it after he was murdered?" Angie asked. "That doesn't make sense to me."

"It was a message—telling the coyotes the area was no longer a safe haven," Teresa said. "That would explain why one day we had a lot of illegals, men mostly, and very poor, hanging around, but then they all disappeared."

"Who would want to give a warning like that?" Angie asked. "Ned? He also had an amulet, but if that's the case, it means he was Hal's killer."

"Ned would never kill anyone," Teresa insisted.

"Ned could have figured out Hal's connection," Paavo said. "He would have wondered about the ostriches, the way you did, Teresa. If he found the amulet somewhere, it might have told him who left the message for the coyotes. And whoever left that message is the one who killed Hal."

"Ned was trying to find out who wanted to hurt me, and it led him directly to Hal's killer." Teresa blinked back tears. "As I said, it's all my fault."

"It's not, Teresa." Angie squeezed her hand. "You had no idea any of this was going on."

"I want to go home," Teresa said. "I'm tired of hiding at Doc's house. Tomorrow after the cookout, Hal's estate will be distributed to Joey and

Clarissa. I can only pray that will end the madness all around here."

"Only if the killings have been about the inheritance," Paavo countered. "And whether they were or not, a killer's out there who must be caught. One more night at Doc's isn't a bad idea for you."

After Paavo and Angie brought Teresa to Doc's, they headed for Merritt's Café.

Paavo called Merry Belle from the car. He needed to give her the latest information. She was in a particularly bad mood when Paavo called, not only because she'd been asleep, but because she couldn't find Buster. He wasn't at the station, and hadn't been since early afternoon.

LaVerne, on the other hand, was delighted to see Angie and Paavo enter the diner. She practically sang the words, "I'll bring you something extra special."

"No!" Angie shouted. "I want something off your regular menu. Something basic, like chicken potpie. Wait, on second thought, I don't want to eat bird." Visions of ostriches came to her. Would she ever be able to eat fowl again? "Let's make that pot roast."

"Pot roast?" LaVerne looked stricken. "But you're a gourmet cook. Gourmets don't eat pot roast! I've got something extra special in the freezer. It'll heat up real fast. It's a thick turtle soup—made from Arizona turtles. Or tortoises. I never can remember which is which. But anyway, you'll love it. Not as much as my prairie dog souf-flé, but those stupid Feds followed when I left the diner with my shotgun, so I couldn't get any this morning."

"So you know that the fishermen are Feds?" Angie asked.

"Of course!" LaVerne said with a huff. "They first came around when Hal showed up with his ostriches. Then, they came back when his body was found. What else could they be? Probably, they're connected with Homeland Security because of the sudden increase in the number of illegals that came through here for a while."

"You knew about the illegals as well?" Paavo asked.

"I've got eyes, ears, and a brain, don't I?" LaVerne said, indignantly. "I've been reading about it in a few 'special' publications I get, plus my shortwave radio. Forget talk radio—shortwave is where you get the real story!"

"Why didn't you say anything earlier?" Angie asked.

"I did! To you." LaVerne looked affronted.

"But you said there were terrorists involved," Angie pointed out.

"Well?"

Angie stared at LaVerne. It all sounded remarkably far-fetched. She was surprised that Paavo offered no objections. Maybe the world was far-fetched these days.

LaVerne frowned in dismay at them both. "I'll bring you my turtle soup." With that, she turned and walked away.

"No, you won't!" Angie shrieked, standing. LaVerne gawked at her. "I don't want your turtle soup. I don't want any of your so-called gourmet foods! You're as much a gourmet as Roseanne Barr is anorexic! I'm hungry, I'm tired, I'm sick of the way everybody gives us only half-truths, but all of you know exactly what's going on. You're wasting my vacation!" As LaVerne backed toward the kitchen, Angie marched after her. "All I've eaten since breakfast is beanie-weenies. I want real food! No turtles, no prairie dogs, no javelina, and definitely no toads! I want something I can eat and enjoy!"

LaVerne flattened herself against the door to the kitchen, mouth agape. Suddenly, her face crumpled. "That is the meanest thing anyone's ever said to me! Not even Clarissa was so cruel when she didn't like my rabbit stew. You're just jealous of my cooking, that's all!" She took off her bifocals to wipe sudden tears. "I know others around here don't appreciate it, but I expected you would! Pardon me for being so wrong. I'll go get your boring pot roast!"

It was late when Angie and Paavo returned to the guest ranch. All was quiet, but Angie knew the next day would bring workmen, cooks, and chaos as the big cookout finally happened.

Instead of going inside, they stopped on the porch of their bungalow, and turned to face the night and the plaza.

"I can't help but feel," Paavo said, his thumbs hooked to his pockets as he surveyed the surroundings, "that all our questions about these deaths will come to a close tomorrow, and that, if we're lucky, the pieces will finally fall into place."

"I take it you don't think the solution has to do with Hal's inheritance," she said, hooking his arm with hers and leaning close, "or with settling the estate."

"No. That's only a small part of it—if anything at all. If whoever killed Hal was interested in the inheritance, why hide Hal's body? They'd have made it look like an accident or suicide and collected. Something else is going on, something we're overlooking."

"The illegals?"

"They're gone."

"They were here when Hal died," Angie pointed out. "One of those coyote smugglers could have done it."

"It's possible, sure, but why? Hal was helping them. No, it's something else. After Hal married Teresa, his paranoia grew until he was sure his life was in danger and he ran from the country. Then there were, apparently, attacks on Teresa as well. And now she can't find any proof of her marriage."

"That would mean it all began five years ago with the marriage," Angie said, "which ties in with the inheritance—which brings us right back to Joey and Clarissa."

"We're missing something, Angie," Paavo said. "But we'll find it. Hopefully, tomorrow."

"And the day after that," she murmured, "if things are settled here, we'll be going back home. I wish we'd had more time to simply enjoy this area." Angie rested her head against his shoulder.

"I'm surprised at how much I've remembered,"

Paavo said, wrapping an arm around her. "Good memories about Doc, Joaquin . . . Ned. Even as a boy I loved the desert on nights like this. The quiet, the peace."

Stars seemed so close she felt as if she could reach up and touch them. After the dinginess and sadness of the town, the guest ranch was like a different world. The plaza sparkled nearly white in the moonlight. No wonder Hal built this home as a sanctuary. It would, in fact, make a wonderful destination-wedding site. Not hers, though. She knew too much about the town and it held too many sad memories for that.

"Despite everything," she said, draping her arm around his waist, "I have to admit that this area is lovely. I can see why you enjoyed coming here as a boy."

His voice was little more than a whisper as he said, "I wish I'd realized, as a boy, how kind these people were to me, how open and friendly."

"You couldn't tell?" She glanced up at him, surprised.

His gaze seemed to turn inward. "I didn't let myself know. I was a tough little kid, and did all I could to shut people out, to not let them get close."

"You did it to protect yourself from more loss," she said, holding him closer. "I can understand it. At least, you've grown older and wiser. You can see it now."

"It isn't that I've grown wiser." Blue eyes caught hers. "It's that the barrier was broken down."

"Broken down? What do you mean?"

"You, Angie." One finger lightly brushed her

cheek. "You're the one—with your warm heart, and crazy ways. Without you, that little boy would still be outside, looking in."

She smiled at him, her big detective who could fight hardened criminals, but was just a big softie when it came to love. His admitting as much brought tears to her eyes. "If that's the case," she whispered, lifting her face to his, "I'm glad."

Chapter 31

 Merry Belle walked into her office the
next morning. It was quiet, which was
good. She didn't see Buster—and that
wasn't.

Last night when she joined Paavo and Angie at
Merritt's and then ate a plate of pot roast—she
never could pass up a good meal—Paavo filled her
in on the evening's events.

Between having eaten two dinners and the fact
that some loony with a gun had bushwhacked
Teresa Flores and Paavo's little girlfriend, Merry
Belle hadn't slept a wink all night. Not to mention
the exposure of Hal Edwards's illegal activities.
She'd long suspected Hal's ties to the illegals,
given the way a bunch descended on the town
when he returned and then—*poof!*—he disappeared, and so did they.

Somehow, she had to find Hal and Ned's killer
or killers so the Frisco cop and the Feds would
leave, and the town could go back to being the
sleepy little haven she loved and protected.

"Where the hell is Buster?" Merry Belle demanded from the night deputy sleepily sitting at the front desk where Buster should have been.

"Don't know. He hasn't called in."

As the sheriff poured herself a cup of coffee, she frowned. "You call his place?"

"Couple times. Either he ain't home or just don't want to answer."

"He phones in, you make sure he talks to me," Merry Belle said as she marched into her office, slamming the door behind her. She sat at her desk and glanced up at the picture of the governor on the opposite wall. As a little pick-me-up, she took a Mr. Goodbar from a drawer and chomped into it.

The telephone rang.

"Buster, you mealymouthed—oh—" It wasn't him. It was the crime lab in Phoenix calling with some results.

Merry Belle gulped down the mouthful of chocolate as she listened, then shared a smile with the governor. The blood on the kitchen floor in the hacienda had been Hal Edwards's, and the heel protector was definitely from Joey's boots. Now, if only she could find a way to tie those two facts together.

Joey had to be the killer. Good-bye, Joey Edwards! Patricide should be worth the death penalty, minimum.

Still . . . she wished she didn't have this nagging feeling of uncertainty. Paavo clearly had his doubts and Merry Belle was uneasier than she cared to admit. She had the evidence, though. What more did she need?

* * *

A little after seven that morning, Angie's mini-alarm woke her. There was already activity outside in the plaza area. She got out of bed, and with as little noise as possible prepared for the day, trying not to wake Paavo.

Outside the bungalow were a half-dozen men Angie had never seen before working to pitch an enormous tent in front of the hacienda. Others rushed about with hammers and wood.

The ostriches had the sense to stay out of their way. She didn't blame them.

As she crossed the plaza to the cookhouse, Lionel spotted her. He bent over an ice chest, pulled a beer from it, and raced her way.

"This is gonna be something," he said. Angie reeled from the blast of early morning beer breath. "Gonna give Hal a real send-off," Lionel went on excitedly. "And maybe it's the last time I gotta put up with Clarissa and her brat."

"Why would you think that? Won't Joey get the property?"

"Not if the sheriff arrests him for killing Hal," he said with a smirk. "I'm thinking she just wants to wait until after she's done eating her fill. When do you think she'll do it?"

"That's up to her—if she thinks she has enough evidence," Angie replied.

"Hell, what more does she need? She's got the heel protector," Lionel insisted. "Now we can really celebrate."

Angie was surprised to find that Paavo's doubts about Joey's guilt had crept into her thoughts as well. "It takes time to build a case."

"Moon Bottom Hermann damn well better not take too long! Doc's gonna be here this evening to divvy up Hal's estate," Lionel whined. "Hal's killer shouldn't get his money. It should go to a relative who loved him. Like me!"

Yeah, right. She wanted to say everything should go to Hal's widow, Teresa—if only there was proof of the marriage somewhere—but this wasn't the time and it wasn't her place to bring it up. Instead, she backed away. "I have to get to the cookhouse, Lionel, and prepare my contribution to the feast."

Lionel seemed lost in thought a moment, then jerked in reaction to her words. "Yeah, okay. Might be Joey's last good meal for a spell—if the sheriff does what's right. Maybe Clarissa's, too."

"You must really hate them." Angie was fascinated by the malice that filled Lionel's face.

"Me? I don't hate nobody," Lionel declared, then grinned. "I just can't stand them."

"I really have to start cooking." Angie walked away. Despite his denials, she was sure he hated them with the force of too many years of resentment.

"Lemme know if you need anything."

"I will, Lionel."

Paavo was surprised at how late he had slept, and by how quiet Angie could be when she wanted to. It had taken Merry Belle's call to wake him. She had phoned to say she was on the way to Yuma to get a certified copy of the confidential marriage record or find out exactly why none existed. The ducks were lining up, he thought.

As he sat in the living room, aware of all the activity outside the bungalow, and grateful for the coffee Angie had made, he was more certain than ever that today would be the day when there would be resolution to the mystery of Hal Edwards's death. Hal's death had led to Ned's—of that he was certain—and Paavo felt as if he was waiting for the proverbial other shoe to drop.

He looked at his watch. It was almost ten. He'd had trouble getting to sleep last night, thinking about these cases. Whenever he had insomnia in San Francisco, he would still wake early the next morning. Was it the weather out here, the quiet, or despite everything was he simply more at peace with himself than he'd been in a long, long time?

The door opened. "Hello, sleepyhead," Angie said as she swept in. His heart did a little rumba, as always, just seeing her. "I brought you some breakfast. A mushroom and cheese omelet, home-fried potatoes, perfect bacon, and toast with marmalade."

"Looks great," Paavo said as Angie put the plate on the coffee table. "I think I'll keep you."

"Not if you say things like that."

"I don't want to overdo it with praise."

"Yes, you do."

Paavo agreed. Between bites, he filled Angie in on Merry Belle's errand. Although Merry Belle was eager to confront Joey Edwards, Paavo wasn't yet satisfied with this case. Ironically, he'd felt more confident in other cases he'd had with weaker evidence. Attempts to frame an innocent person had crossed his path before.

"But Joey's got to be the one behind this," Angie

said. "I know I thought Joey couldn't be a killer, but now I'm convinced he did it."

"Let's wait and see. The whole town knew Joey was at the guest ranch last winter, and knew his relationship with Hal. Anyone could have planted something of his in the cave."

"That's too clever by half," Angie said. "You wait and see, Inspector. I'm with Merry Belle on this one."

Outside, they heard the sounds of people arriving. It was going to be a busy, festive day.

Merry Belle reached Yuma in no better mood than when she left Jackpot. Buster had finally phoned in, hungover and morose about his job and his life. He sounded oddly guilty and kept apologizing as if he expected to be blamed for something. He received a sobering tongue-lashing. Merry Belle's always low reserve of patience was bone dry as far as Buster was concerned.

The ride through the desert had been tedious and hot, and when she entered the Yuma records office she immediately froze the lone clerk behind the counter with an I'm-taking-no-bureaucratic-bullshit stare. The clerk, a tall lanky man with thinning brown hair, gulped as he eyed her uniform and fierce look.

"May I help you?" he croaked.

"I need to see the confidential marriage records for five years back. Now."

"But they're confidential," he said.

"No shit." Merry Belle cast him a withering glare.

"I m-mean . . . they're sealed," the clerk stammered.

"That's two things you've told me I already know. Get me the damn records."

"I . . . I . . ."

"I'm the sheriff of Jackpot and this is part of a murder investigation."

"Jackpot?"

"That's right. What of it?"

"The sheriff was here a week or two back and demanded to see the records. I showed him."

"I'm the damned sheriff, bub. Here"—she flashed her identification—"satisfied?"

"I'm confused, uh, Sheriff Hermann."

"Me too, fellah. So, why don't you describe this so-called sheriff."

"Well . . . he wore a badge, and even flashed an I.D. And, uh, he was tall, I remember, and his hair was pretty long. Dirty blond and kind of scraggly."

Merry Belle's squinty eyes narrowed even more. "What color eyes?"

"Uh . . . I don't know. They were mostly blood-shot."

Merry Belle drew in her breath. "Was he skinny?"

"Hmm, yes, I'd say so. His uniform was way too big for him. I figured he'd lost weight or something."

"Damn that Junior!" she murmured, then louder. "He's going to lose a lot more than weight before I finish with him!"

The clerk blanched.

How could he have gotten a uniform and

badge? she wondered. Then, she knew. "Did you notice anything special about the uniform?"

"No . . . I don't . . . uh, wait—yes! It had maroon piping along the pocket flaps, collar, and down the front near the buttons. In fact, it even had a checkered handkerchief in a pocket. Very elegant! It surprised me."

Merry Belle was ready to chew the counter. She was going to kill them both with her bare hands. "Okay, enough of that," she said. "I'll take care of the impersonator. Right now, I want to see those records. This is a murder case."

The clerk shook his head. "This is all too irregular."

"Irregular, my ass! You're obstructing justice," Merry Belle yelled as she leaned toward the cowering clerk. One hand hovered near her mace canister.

He crumpled like a cheap lawn chair. "Come around," he sputtered, "and follow me."

The clerk motioned Merry Belle behind the counter and led her across the work area into a large, brightly lit room filled with ceiling-high shelves.

"The confidential marriage records are all in one book in this locked cabinet," the clerk explained as he fumbled for his keys. "There are very few of them. It's something that's rarely used anymore. For years, nobody cared. And now, a fake sheriff, a distraught young woman, and a real sheriff all want to see them. It makes me curious as to why."

"Tough!" she said.

In a few moments he placed a ledger-style book

on a nearby table. "This is the book I gave the sheriff." At her glare, he amended it. "I mean, to the impersonator."

Merry Belle grunted and began turning pages in the book. She frowned and started flipping pages back and forth, stopping to run her finger along the inner spine. Her shoulders sagged and she sighed. "Looks to me like there's a page missing."

"That's impossible," the clerk protested.

"See for yourself."

The clerk hovered over the book examining it, a look of pained outrage on his face. Again and again, he ran his fingers over the pages as if willing the missing page to reappear. "I don't believe this."

"It's gone and I think we've both got an idea who took it," Merry Belle said glumly. "Was that guy left alone with the book?"

The now pallid clerk searched his memory, eyes closed and hands clasped as if in prayer. "Yes, I remember. I had to take a call. I had been expecting a call from my supervisor. I left you alone . . . I mean the other sheriff."

"He's not a sheriff!" Merry Belle was beyond rage and stood in fuming silence as the clerk explained that there were no other copies of the record either on microfilm or computer scanned. She nodded as he rambled on about when and how and by whom records were scheduled to be preserved.

Boredom competed with fury as the clerk lectured on records policy, procedure, and preservation. Unable to stomach any further bureaucratic minutia, she snorted and marched out of the archive toward the exit.

All she could think of was that she needed to get back to Jackpot as soon as possible and confront both Buster and Junior. Why would Junior want to take away proof of his daughter's marriage to Hal Edwards? It didn't make sense to her.

She turned toward the door, but the clerk jumped in front of her and continued explaining why none of this was his fault, and that he was an innocent employee just doing his job.

She began to huff and puff as he talked, distress giving way to all-consuming wrath. Finally, she told him if he didn't stop talking, she was going to have to shoot.

Chapter 32

All Angie's enjoyment at working in the controlled chaos of a busy kitchen fizzled when LaVerne Merritt entered.

Normally, Angie liked the pace of action and the chatter with other cooks as she worked. The cookhouse bustled even more than usual with several young Mexican women Dolores had hired to help. They dashed about, following Dolores's instructions to the nth degree.

Angie and Dolores had been taking a great interest in each other's preparations. Dolores was busy cooking vast quantities of barbecue sauce for the meat, a cauldron of chili, baked beans, ham hocks, mashed and boiled potatoes, plus dips, a huge green salad, potato salad, cakes, cookies, and pies. She even made her own tortillas and bread. It all smelled quite wonderful, and Angie had the suspicion she would be eating more of Dolores's cookout fare than her own.

"Something smells like it's burning." LaVerne's nose was high in the air as she put two large shopping bags on the counter.

Angie and Dolores made no comment. The kitchen helpers bent low over their respective workstations.

"What you cooking today?" Dolores asked.

"Since *some* people have told me they don't like my special recipes, I've changed my plans." LaVerne pressed her lips to thin slivers. "Why knock myself out trying to catch gecko if nobody will appreciate it? Besides, Clarissa phoned and said I was to cook only simple food. I have excellent recipes for macaroni and cheese, tuna noodle casserole, deviled eggs, and succotash. That's what I'll prepare."

"Sounds yummy," Angie said with a smirk. LaVerne gave her a withering glare.

LaVerne took over the largest cutting board in the room and unpacked her supplies. She looked hurt.

"Look, I'm sorry for last evening," Angie said. "It was rude of me."

"Rude? Crass is more like it!" LaVerne harrumphed, and adjusted her bifocals. "Don't worry. I know jealousy when I hear it."

"Jealousy?" Angie bit her lip. She wasn't going to argue. She continued to work.

LaVerne glanced smugly her way, then put on a pot of water for the elbow macaroni. As she began to remove the shells from two dozen hard-boiled eggs, she glanced at the pureed butternut squash Angie was scooping from the blender. "What's that? It looks like baby puke! Or worse."

"It's going to be a squash timbale—a custard."

LaVerne snorted. "Squash? That's so boring!"

"Not the way I make it!" Angie reached for some paprika.

"It won't stand up at all to my deviled eggs." She began to slice the eggs in half and scoop the yolks into a bowl. "And what's that other thing? Mashed beans? Why is all your food ground up? Do you think people in Jackpot don't have teeth?"

Angie's eyes narrowed. She pulled some cloves off a head of garlic. "It's called dal."

"That's not what I'd call it." LaVerne smirked.

"The best thing about today," Dolores said, "is that all the bickering around the hacienda should end."

Yeah, right, Angie thought, with a glower at LaVerne.

"Of course, if Lionel gets kicked off," LaVerne said, as she took bottles of dry thyme and parsley from Angie's workspace and sprinkled some onto her eggs, "he might bump off Clarissa and Joey and then you wouldn't have to worry about them, either." She chuckled wickedly. "I'm hearing rumors, though, that there was something between Hal and Teresa. I can't imagine that's the case. No one could have kept such a thing a secret!"

"I could," Dolores murmured.

Both Angie and LaVerne faced her. She looked up, as if surprised that they'd heard. "Well, why not?" she asked indignantly. "It made my boss look very foolish. An old man like that—he should have been ashamed!"

"I wonder if Lionel knew about it as well," LaVerne mused. "If so, he might have worried that Hal would write her in and him out of his will."

Angie took her spices back.

"Lionel didn't know," Dolores said, her face contorted with disgust.

"Well, you found out!" LaVerne said. "Are you so much more clever than Lionel?"

"I cleaned Mr. Edwards's house—changed his sheets. There wasn't much he could hide from me." Dolores's words were quietly spoken and she turned away. Still, Dolores's irritation at LaVerne came through to Angie even though she was busy guarding her coriander and cumin.

"Don't be so sure about Lionel. He doesn't miss much." LaVerne wouldn't let the conversation drop, despite the shell game she was playing with Angie's sea salt.

"You're saying he's not as dumb as he seems?" Angie asked, grabbing the salt once she finally spotted where LaVerne had hidden it. She was slicing the salmon into thin slabs. Afterward, she'd cover a slab with curled leeks, roll it up like a pinwheel, add cracked black pepper, and cut it into individual portions to be sautéed.

"Dumb?" LaVerne grimaced. Her macaroni was cooked, and she was mixing it with mild cheddar cheese. "He's not dumb at all. Dumb is people who think they're great cooks and don't even have a job."

"I beg your pardon!" Angie put down her knife.

"Well, you never talk about a job," LaVerne said. "Most good chefs I've ever heard of do something with their ability."

"I've had lots of jobs!" Angie cried.

"And obviously lost them all."

Angie seethed. "You have your nerve criticizing

my talent! With the ingredients you use in your so-called 'special' dishes, you're lucky you haven't killed anybody!"

"I take great care with my cooking!"

"If that's the case, talk about a major waste of time!" Angie glared at LaVerne. She picked up a knife, and continued slicing the salmon.

LaVerne glared back so fiercely her weak eyelid no longer drooped. She pushed her sleeves up past her elbows, grabbed a huge wooden spoon, and began stirring her concoction. "I can't understand why anyone would be making fish at a barbecue!"

"Clarissa wanted it," Angie said. "And my seared cracked black pepper salmon roulade with cucumber sauce is prized by many."

LaVerne rolled her eyes. "This is cattle country. It figures you and Clarissa would get it wrong. Birds of a feather."

Angie decided to ignore her. "I learned recently," she said to Dolores as she began to work on the stuffing, "that Hal might have been involved in helping illegals across the border."

The kitchen suddenly turned absolutely silent. Dolores froze. The kitchen helpers stopped chopping, mixing, and stirring the various dishes. Making no comment, Dolores quietly picked up a knife and began to chop more celery. The young women warily went back to work.

"If being involved with illegals is what killed him," LaVerne chirped up, "a whole lot of Arizona's population would be dead." She caught Angie's eye and held it firmly as she whispered, "You-don't-want-to-talk-about-illegals-here."

Angie got the message. She glanced from Dolores to the kitchen helpers who quietly continued their cooking duties.

Eventually, Angie started to breathe again.

She and LaVerne, eyeing each other from time to time, turned their concentration to their dishes.

As Angie worked with professional alacrity, knives clattered, spices flew, and bowls clanked. LaVerne did the same, struggling to work even faster than Angie.

Angie noticed, and began to stir and mix her ingredients at breakneck speed. LaVerne did all she could to keep up.

They tussled over the Kitchenaid mixer, swiped spices, sniped at smells, tastes, and the other's lack of perfection when mincing, slicing, and chopping. Accusations flew.

"Too foreign."

"Too plebeian."

"Too much garlic."

"Too much butter."

"Too hot."

"Too bland."

In the end, as Angie slumped in a chair, exhausted, she was sure the gunfight at the OK Corral had nothing on them.

Merry Belle had roared out of Yuma in a blind fury, her mind coming up with a thousand ways for Buster and Junior's slow, painful deaths. She considered feeding them feet-first through a wood chipper, but rejected it as too humane. Looking down at the speedometer, she realized that she was close to setting a land speed record for a

Hummer and slowed down. She wasn't about to let the two off the hook by killing herself.

Ahead, lonely and dilapidated in the desolate desert landscape, was a gas station with an attached diner. Merry Belle pulled over and strode inside. The look on her face plunged its occupants into an uneasy silence. She felt better after a couple of bacon cheeseburgers, an order of fries, and a vanilla milk shake ordered "for the road." Self-discipline restrained her from the pie. She did have to leave some room for the cookout.

To the great relief of the diner's patrons and staff, she soon trudged back to the Hummer. There, she raised Buster on the car radio.

She greeted him with, "You're dead meat!"

"I already told you I'm sorry! I know I did a bad thing." He sounded on the verge of blubbering. "But I was just curious and then I nearly got caught and ran, and then got to drinking and didn't hear the alarm and—"

"Quit jabbering! I've been to Yuma. You let Junior wear your uniform!"

After a long pause, Buster said, "I didn't catch that. I got interference on the radio." He began tapping the mouthpiece hard, causing great bursts of sound to pop against Merry Belle's eardrums.

"I'm going to interfere with your life expectancy," she roared. "Cut that out! You know damned well what I said."

"Junior didn't do nothing wrong," he whined. "The wimpy clerk must've told you a bunch of lies."

"Damn it, Buster, you're dumber than dumb,"

Merry Belle yelled. "If Junior didn't tell you, then how'd you know the clerk's wimpy?"

There was a sullen silence.

"You there, Buster?"

"Yes, Aunt Merry Belle," he replied meekly.

"Don't call me that! You're disowned!"

"But I told you I was sorry," Buster cried.

"Listen up. I'm more than halfway home. I better see your sorry face in my office when I get back. And you better have some answers. Don't you even try to lie! You're too dumb."

More silence.

"You heard me."

"Yes, ma'am."

"You be there. And what was that you said about nearly getting caught?"

Buster croaked, "Ten-four," and hung up.

"Ten-four, my ass!" Merry Belle slammed the handset down and in a cloud of dust and gravel sped away from the diner.

Buster stared, confused, at the radiophone.

It seemed Aunt Merry Belle only cared that he'd helped Junior. She didn't seem to mind at all that he'd broken into Angie's bungalow to study how her clothes were put together.

He'd been so engrossed in the way darts had been added, seams finished, and hems unevenly stitched, so that they fell in a more interesting flow than if they'd been sewn straight, that he'd been startled when he looked out the window and saw Paavo's SUV parked. He was so worried about being caught, his hand slipped as he was shutting a drawer and the clasp on his wristwatch snagged an Emilio Pucci scarf. Then, when he pulled it out, the expensive scarf tore. He didn't know what to do, so he grabbed it, stuffed it in his pocket, and ran like the dickens.

Maybe he should have simply confessed.

But nobody in Jackpot understood his interest in clothes design, and he knew better than to try to explain. They'd call him weird, or gay, or both. The unfortunate thing was that he was also realistic enough to know that nothing would ever come of this enthusiasm. As much as he might want to be the next Joseph Abboud or Yves St. Laurent, deep in his heart he knew he not only lacked the money for classes and the brains for study, but—truth be told—the talent and imagination as well. So, Jackpot's deputy he'd remain.

And his secret passion would stay just that. A secret.

All that aside, it seemed Junior was what had upset his aunt. Buster hadn't seen any harm in lending a friend his uniform. He was surprised more people didn't want to borrow it. Its maroon trim made it pretty. He'd been honored when Junior had asked.

Maybe that was his calling—to design great uniforms! He should look into it, matter of fact. He knew more about law enforcement uniforms than most designers, that was for sure.

Now, though, unless he was mistaken, Junior had done something that was going to cause him trouble.

The more he thought about it, the more nervous he became, and the more certain that he didn't want to face Merry Belle alone.

Finally, shaking and desperate for help, he reached for his cell phone.

By the time Angie stepped out of the cookhouse, people from town were crowded onto the plaza.

The workmen had completely transformed it. Long serving tables were arranged inside a large tent. A smaller tent served as a makeshift bar with a table laden with liquor bottles and glassware, and beer in ice-filled washtubs. A small combo of fiddlers and guitarists played jaunty tunes. Flags, banners, and balloons were attached to any available space on the hacienda's veranda pillars. Propped up on the veranda was a large, sepia-toned portrait of Hal Edwards as a handsome, smiling young man, casually leaning back against a barn, one leg bent and his foot on the wood.

It reminded Angie of the dream she'd had when she first arrived, before she'd come to know the town and so many of its people. Looking at the poster, at the joy and promise in it, she couldn't help but feel sorrow at the way it had all turned out, both for Hal and those whose lives he'd touched.

Was it his fault that Clarissa had loved someone else and was all but forced into marriage with him by parents who prized Hal's money more than their daughter's feelings? Or that the young woman he'd turned to in his unhappiness simply wanted a way out of a dreary life?

The twists and turns life takes, Angie realized as she gazed at the poster, were completely unpredictable. Despite all the planning and care one might do, surprises could still turn up and bite you.

Beyond the two tents and near the far corner of the hacienda, a barbecue pit had been dug. Smoke rose from the glowing embers beneath the turning spits on which huge sides of beef and three pigs slowly rotated. An enormous, florid, and toothless man with the filthiest apron Angie had ever seen danced around with a bucket and hand mop slopping a cooking sauce onto the meat. On a large table near the pit were rows of skewered chicken parts and plump sausages.

The whole scene was a vegetarian's worst nightmare.

Angie saw that Doc had arrived and was in animated conversation with Paavo. She was glad to see Doc looking much better than when she last saw him. The man had gone through a terrible ordeal but was holding up remarkably well. She walked up and gave him a hug. "I'm so glad you decided to come here today," she said with a smile.

"I never was one to stay in bed, my head under the covers, lamenting things that can't be undone." Doc gave her a stern look. "I was just telling Paavo that something's got me on edge today. He says he's feeling the same way."

"I know." A shiver went down her back. "I hope it has nothing to do with the cookout, though. Everyone here has worked hard on it. Even LaVerne."

"Uh-oh," both Doc and Paavo said at the same time. After a momentary chuckle, Doc asked, "Is the chuck wagon ready to roll?"

"Not yet," Angie replied. "Lionel has to hitch up the horses. The meat is still cooking, so we've got plenty of time. Have you seen him or Clarissa?" She looked around the plaza.

"No," Paavo said. "I haven't seen Joey either."

"If we're lucky, neither of them will show up today," Doc said. "They'd do nothing but ruin a good party."

"Are Lupe and Teresa coming?"

Doc shook his head and a worried frown passed over his face. "They're staying near the hospital."

"I see," Angie said. She was sorry that, the way things stood, nothing could develop between Doc and Lupe. In her opinion, that was wrong—they deserved happiness together. At the same time, she understood Lupe's position. Life wasn't always fair.

"Even though not much food is out here yet," she added in a forcibly jovial tone, "they've put out the beer. I'll bet you could go for some, right Doc?"

The faraway look in his eyes had Angie considering that he, too, had been thinking about Lupe. But then he gave her a sudden smile. "Music to my ears."

The black truck skidded to a stop in front of Junior's old and battered truck and RV trailer.

"Thanks for coming so fast," Junior said, climbing out of the trailer onto the dirt road.

"So Merry Belle's a problem." The driver got out of the truck.

"Yeah, but we can handle her." Junior swaggered closer. "I think we should go now to see Teresa. I'll talk to her. Tell her it's all up to me, like we planned."

"No." The voice was firm. Something about it made Junior's blood run cold.

"What do you mean?" he asked.

"Get inside your truck, behind the wheel."

Junior's eyes grew wide and round at the gun pointed at him. "Inside? I don't get it." Junior hesitated only a second, then climbed onto the driver's seat. "What's this about? You and me are together in this."

"Are we?"

Junior held his hands out, pleading. "What are you doing? I've got all the proof of Teresa's marriage—the church and civil records—just like we need. I'm her father. If she wants to inherit Hal's property, she has to agree to give me half or I keep the proof and she gets nothing! You'll get your share. That's our deal. You and me—partners, right? In everything. I'll give you a bigger percentage if that's what you want. Or . . . or maybe we could split it three ways with Teresa. What does she know about money? She's just a kid, happy to work with her mother. You and me—we appreciate the fine things in life. We'll each take a third, right? Without me—and you—Teresa gets nothing. She has no proof, right?"

"Junior, you make me sick."

His face fell, and he stared as if he couldn't believe his own ears. "What are you saying? It's our plan. It's a good plan. We're going to be rich."

"Wrong."

Fear and uncertainty made Junior's voice crack as realization flashed across his bloodshot eyes. He gripped the steering wheel, looking for the truck's keys, but they were deep in the pocket of his Wranglers. "What do you want?"

Silence.

"You used me, didn't you?"

More silence.

"You set people up! You killed Hal and Ned! And Teresa . . . my God! I understand now. Everything. I understand everything." Junior's face paled, his voice turned quiet, as if figuring it all out was slightly miraculous to him.

"Congratulations."

A gunshot sounded, and Junior would never figure out anything again.

Chapter 33

With a woeful Buster beside her, Merry Belle drove along the narrow road where Junior Whitney had parked his trailer. She could hardly wait to get her hands on him.

The sheriff came close to achieving warp speed as she held her foot steady on the accelerator. *I'm going to kill myself driving like this*, she warned herself again. Despite the high speed, she felt like she had driven for hours before spotting her objective. Merry Belle slammed on the brakes, kicking up dust and fishtailing to a stop. She jumped from the Hummer shouting for Junior to come out and face her like a man.

As the swirling dust cloud settled, she saw an outline slumped over the steering wheel of the truck.

She raced over and pushed Junior back against the seat. His chest was covered with blood, his eyes opened but sightless, his expression both frightened and bewildered. She touched his neck, hoping against hope to find a pulse. There was none.

Merry Belle gently closed his eyes.

Buster stumbled into the brush and threw up.

Angie watched as Lionel led a couple of horses toward the chuck wagon. For some reason, the process began making her more and more nervous.

Paavo's cell phone rang. Angie and Doc listened in shock to Paavo's side of the conversation. He was grim when he disconnected.

"Junior's dead," he said flatly. "Shot. I'm meeting the sheriff."

"It's all coming to a head," Doc said in a barely audible voice, "just as I thought it would."

"I'm coming with you," Angie said.

"No." Paavo answered with a finality that left no room for argument.

"Let's take my car," Doc said. "I've got all my gear in it. I am the assistant coroner, after all. I'll . . . I'll do the certification, then call Lupe."

They walked across the plaza to the parking lot. Doc got behind the wheel of his car.

Paavo paused by the passenger door and looked apologetically at Angie. "I'm sorry I'll miss your big entry on the chuck wagon."

"I'm sure it'll be quite boring," she said, her heart heavy that death had once again come to this town.

"Be careful," he warned.

"It's a chuck wagon—what could go wrong?" She tried to smile, but failed. "You're the one who'd better be careful. There's a killer out there, Paavo."

They kissed and Paavo got in the car.

As Doc's Cadillac pulled away, Angie felt afraid. Not only for Paavo, but for all of them.

She walked back to the plaza and the lively celebration. *I'll keep this to myself*, she thought. *Let the living have their fun.*

Lionel was waving at her like a demented maestro. "Where you been?" he called. "It's time." He ushered her to the chuck wagon.

Angie looked at the two horses hitched to it. One, Chloe, looked sweet and gentle. The other was Bucky. She didn't dare go near him. His teeth looked awfully big, her fingers awfully small, and she didn't like the way he stared at her as if she offended him.

"All right, Miss Angie. Time to set yourselves up front and ride the wagon over," Lionel said with a grand flourish of his battered Stetson.

"Let LaVerne and Dolores get up there first," Angie said.

Dolores laughed, nudging her forward. "LaVerne doesn't do stuff like this, and I'm just a hired hand."

"I can't do it alone!" Angie stared up at the chuck wagon's seat. It was high above the ground. Her legs didn't want to move.

"Get up there, girl," Dolores said. "You're our guest of honor. Go on, before the food gets cold!"

"But I don't know how to drive a chuck wagon!" Angie said, her voice tiny.

"You just pull back on the reins to slow them down, and say *'whoa'* when you want them to stop," Lionel said.

Dolores leaned forward and whispered to her,

"Don't worry—me and Lionel lead the horses, but no one's supposed to know that."

"But still—"

Propelled by Dolores, Angie found herself sitting on the bench seat with the reins in her hands. Bucky turned his head back toward her with another nasty look. "I don't know about this," Angie murmured, trying to hide her unease.

Dolores chuckled. Angie looked for Lionel and saw him near his trailer. So much for counting on his help! Bucky turned once again and cast a malevolent stare at her. What was with that darn horse? You'd think she'd taken away his feed bucket.

"Time to roll!" Dolores said, taking the reins and walking Bucky forward. The chuck wagon lurched and swayed. Angie almost let out a shriek as she felt the ancient wood strain and creak. Eventually, the contraption began to roll forward.

Although her imagination saw it as something akin to a chariot race, the chuck wagon moved slowly. They reached the corner of the hacienda, and to her surprise and utter relief, Dolores led the horses so that they turned smoothly onto the plaza. A cheer went up from the crowd, Bucky's ears stretched flat. He snorted and tried to surge forward. Angie pulled back on the reins, holding them so tight her fingers cramped, but he settled down before Angie went into cardiac arrest.

Cheering and applauding, the crowd watched the chuck wagon approach the tents. Angie knew she had to get the look of utter terror off her face and scanned the crowd for support. Clarissa and Joey were on the veranda looking glum and bored.

She found Doc's old friend Joaquin nodding at her. Angie almost managed to smile back.

As they reached the tent where she was supposed to stop, she looked for Dolores and Lionel to help her.

Neither was nearby. Nearly spinning like a top in the wagon seat, she searched the crowd trying to find them. Where were they? What had happened to them?

Suddenly, the tent was right beside her. Bucky continued on, almost past it. She had to do something.

"*Whoa*," she cried, and pulled back on the reins. Nothing happened. The horses continued forward.

"*Whoa, whoa*," she yelled louder, half standing as she pulled back hard on the reins. "Please! Please stop!"

To her shock, Bucky and Chloe stopped in perfect position. *Amazing*, Angie thought, nearly numb with relief. *Maybe I am a real cowgirl after all.* Her grin was a mixture of euphoria and stunned incredulity.

As people applauded, she stood and waved at the crowd, feeling very good about herself. Why had she been scared? How silly of her. Too bad Paavo had missed her grand entrance.

Suddenly, there was a ruckus from the far side of the hacienda. Startled, she looked over her shoulder to see a cloud of dust billowing into the sky. At the same time she heard a strange and ominous pounding.

"What—"

The word wasn't out of her mouth when her voice choked. She let out a shriek.

Of horror.

The entire flock of ostriches was running toward the plaza like a seven-foot-tall tidal wave. "Oh, oh!" she cried, unable to even form words. People began screaming and running, while she tried to decide if she was better off leaping from the chuck wagon and running as well, or staying on it and hoping the ostriches went around her.

She didn't need to make the decision.

"I always said he should rot in hell for the way he treated Lupe and Teresa," Doc muttered as he looked at Junior's body. "Maybe now he is."

As Doc proceeded with the examination for his coroner's report, Paavo walked over to the sheriff and Buster. There was worry and upset on Buster's face, anger on the sheriff's, but also a deep weariness.

"Any ideas?" he asked.

"He wasn't much, Paavo," Merry Belle said in a low voice, "but I knew him my whole life. He was pretty nice sometimes when he was a boy, but it all went to hell in a bottle of Jim Beam. What a waste. The town failed him."

"People fail themselves," Paavo said.

"Perhaps."

They took one last look at the body. "Buster," Merry Belle said, "you going to tell us about it?"

"I don't know, I told you!" Buster was near tears. "Junior gave me money to borrow my uniform. That's all. If you paid more than minimum wage, I wouldn't have to do such things!"

"If you worked more than the minimum, I might think about it!" she yelled.

Paavo had them both calm down and tell him what was going on.

Spooked by the charging birds and the shaking of the earth, Bucky reared up and rocketed forward with Chloe sharing the sudden panic. The reins flew from Angie's hands and she somersaulted backward over the bench seat to land on the wagon flatbed.

While ostriches bounced like pinballs off tents and tables they ran into and knocked over, the two horses plowed straight through the crowd, pulling the chuck wagon—and Angie—with them.

Angie held on to whatever part of the wagon she could as she crawled forward trying to reach the seat and retake the reins. She watched townspeople scatter as pots, plates, dishes, and trays flew from the chuck wagon, spraying everyone and everything in its path. Her carefully prepared scrolled disks of salmon spun from the wagon like flying fish Frisbees, landing on people's hair and clothes. And sticking.

One of Dolores's pork roasts jettisoned from a plate with such force it knocked a man over; macaroni and cheese speckled others from head to foot.

Deviled eggs shot out over the plaza like Ping-Pong balls from a toy bazooka.

Even the ostriches were showered with corn, chili, and Angie's fancy dal. A banana cream pie hit the cowlicked bird smack in the face. She halted, momentarily stunned.

The chuck wagon lurched and swayed, knocking Angie back onto its bed. Punch washed over her, followed by bread and rolls. An entire tuna-noodle casserole splattered over her, the ingredients all but gluing themselves to her hair and clothes like giant leeches. The bean pot, which fortunately had been secured, spewed red beans like a volcano, turning the bed of the chuck wagon into a gooey, slithery swamp.

Everything, including Angie, went airborne as the wagon bounced over bumps and ruts. As it swayed and shimmied, she tried to scramble to her feet, but slipped and slid, and didn't get anywhere.

To her amazement, she spotted Joaquin on horseback, racing through zigzagging ostriches toward her. Miraculously, he soon reached the thundering Bucky and Chloe and used his skill as a horseman to somehow make them turn back toward the plaza. Angie skittered sideways as the circling wagon tilted on two wheels. She covered her head, sure the cart was going to flip over. In an endless flash of time, more varieties of salad rained down on her. Corn bread bounced off her head, ham hocks pelted her, and another violent tilt of the wagon caused her to land facedown in a puddle of salsa. Sputtering, she somehow managed to sit up again.

The wagon righted itself, and next thing Angie knew, Joaquin had grabbed the horse's bridle and was shouting, *"Whoa."*

What a blessed word! she thought, her heart pounding with relief.

The two frightened horses came to a sudden halt in a cloud of dust. Equally abruptly, the wagon stopped. Angie and everything she was sitting in lurched and sloshed forward, then—in demonstration that for every action there is an equal and opposite reaction—momentum tossed her and the food like a whiplash toward the back of the wagon.

"Noooooo," she cried, scrambling to grab hold of something, anything, to save herself. Her fingers could find nothing solid. Feet-first, she smacked into the chuck box. It hit the tailboard, causing the old wood to split like tissue paper.

The chuck box flew off the rear of the wagon onto the plaza.

And, riding atop a tidal wave of churned food like a kid on a water slide, Angie shot out after it.

Chapter 34

Lying on the ground, eyes shut, Angie's first thought was that this absolutely hadn't happened to her.

"Is she okay?"

"Did you see her fly?"

"What a set of lungs!"

"Never heard nothin' screech like that li'l gal."

She opened her eyes to see the ostrich with the cowlick silhouetted against the harsh sun and staring down at her.

With a groan, she struggled to sit up. Joey knelt at her side. Joaquin stood beside him while others, including LaVerne, hovered near.

Clarissa looked like she'd laughed for the first time in years.

"Can you move your legs, Angie?" Joey asked. "Now your arms. Okay. How's your head? It hurt?" He looked around. "Where's Doc Griggs? He should be here."

"I'm okay." Angie blinked a couple of times and shoved away the ostrich who was trying to peck at her hair. She wiped congealed slop off her face, hands, and arms, but her hair was so full of gelatinous goop it was sticking up and out, spiked Goth-style.

"Let me see her," Dr. Westlake said, working his way through the crowd. As he introduced himself to Angie, she stood up, to everyone's relief. She'd finally met Dr. Griggs's replacement.

"I'm fine," she repeated after he studied her pupils and declared her all right. "Thanks to Joaquin." She gave him a hug, careful to not smear him with food. "My hero."

He blushed.

At her feet, the old chuck box lay on its side, the ancient wood split, and the bottom fell off and lay several feet away. Stuck up inside the back of the box, as if it had been pushed behind a drawer, was some paper. Angie reached for it. It crackled with age and dryness.

"What's that?" she said. "It looks like a letter."

"A letter?" Joey asked.

Angie saw that it was two pages, written in a flowery European script. She unfolded it and read,

Dear Jim,

I regret that it became incumbent upon me to leave without saying goodbye. I thank you for all the help you gave to Miss Lune and me.

I entrust to you the journal of recipes I developed with great care in the course of my westward sojourn, and with it, a letter. Please send them both to my nephew, Oscar Tschirky, in care of the

*Waldorf Hotel, NYC, NY. A dollar is enclosed,
which should cover the cost of postage.*

> *Thank you,
> Wm. V. Beerstraeden*

She peered up into the chuck box. Unfortunately, both the dollar and the journal were gone, which gave Angie a good idea about this "Jim" character. She turned to the second letter.

My Dear Oscar,

*I am sending you my journal. I hope you enjoy the
recipes I've created entirely with native fare. I
have no need for them, and I'm sure they will benefit you in your new endeavor.*

    *Do not worry about me, Oscar, although this is
the last time you shall hear from me. God has provided extremely well for me in a most wonderful
and unexpected fashion. Because of it, however, I
must disappear and can never be found. Accompanying me is a most kind and virtuous woman
named Miss Daisy Lane. She has consented to become my wife. I have never expected such happiness in this life.*

    I wish you great success in your career.

> *Your most loving uncle,
> Wm. V. Beerstraeden*

"God has provided extremely well . . ." Angie reread the words. Was Beerstraeden referring to the Dalton money? Did he and the not-so-virtuous Daisy Lane end up with it?

What else could he have been talking about?

Joey took the letters from her and read them. "The money's gone," he whispered, obviously reaching the same conclusion as Angie.

"Yes." She had to agree. When the attack was made on Hoot Dalton and his money—whether by the stagecoach drivers or outsiders—Beerstraeden and Daisy must have grabbed the money and run. Eventually, they must have joined up with a cattle drive heading out of the desert, perhaps with Beerstraeden helping the cook. That could explain how his letter got stuffed into the back of a chuck box.

"There's no treasure?" LaVerne asked.

"No treasure," she replied. Around her, Angie heard the others' disappointed murmur. No one really thought they'd find the Dalton treasure, yet up to this point, the hope had been there, the dream of riches alive in every one of them. She understood what they were feeling. Up to this point she'd hoped to find the cookbook and, with it, imagined the fame it might bring her. Now, her dreams, as well as everyone else's, were gone.

Hopes and dreams. They were so often the key—the reason for so much good in life, and sometimes for so much that went badly.

As food dripped off her, she looked around at the people discussing the letters, and realized then what she'd been dealing with all week—hopes and dreams.

Hal Edwards had hoped Clarissa would love

him. Clarissa had hoped for happiness in wealth, since she'd given up love for money. Teresa had hoped to leave town. Doc hoped Lupe would be with him one day. Lionel hoped to find peace in a bottle. And Joey, poor Joey, hoped for self-worth.

All around her, Jackpot was filled with people who came here looking for something more in life. And when such desires were shattered, the disappointment was fierce.

The pile of clothes on the floor in Hal's bedroom should have been an immediate clue. Now she knew why their being there had struck her as so odd. That wasn't the sort of thing a person did when searching for a will . . . that was the sort of thing done because of anger, jealousy, and loss . . . when there was no more hope.

Angie looked around. She saw Lionel standing near his trailer, LaVerne picking up food and tossing it in garbage bags, Clarissa still staring at her and chuckling.

How had she missed it?

She began to walk toward the cookhouse. Joey followed.

"Joseph!" Clarissa called, commanding her son to her side.

Joey ignored her and continued on with Angie. "Are you all right?" he asked. "What's wrong?"

"I've got to find Dolores," Angie said. Quiet Dolores, who'd practically brought Hal back to life, never married, and stayed in the background loyal and loving.

The cookhouse was empty, the food and equipment left unattended.

They hurried to the cabin where the help stayed. Joey showed Angie to Dolores's room. It was empty, as well. Everything was neat. Too neat. She was gone.

Joaquin appeared in the doorway, breathing heavily as if he'd run to the room. "I found out which way she headed, Angie." He'd obviously followed her thoughts about Dolores. "Some little boys saw her leave in her truck. They said she had a rifle and some other things with her. She drove out the back road."

"Toward the lake?" Angie asked.

"Or into the foothills," Joey said. "If you're thinking what I am, it's an area where a person could hide out forever."

Angie ran to her bungalow, leaving a trail of tuna, noodles, chili beans, and butternut squash in her wake. There, she thrust the Beerstraeden letters into a drawer, grabbed the car keys and her cell phone, and ran out to the SUV.

"Lionel has to be behind this," Doc said as Paavo and Merry Belle examined the body and the surrounding area for clues. They gave Buster the job of guarding the area, and not touching a thing. "I don't see who else could have gotten Junior to do such a thing."

"Does Lionel have the brains to pull this off?" Paavo asked as he and Merry Belle cordoned off the area with fresh tire tracks right in front of Junior's trailer. "Or the cruelty? Despite everything, it seems he truly did love his uncle, and he'd been friends with Ned—and Junior. No, I don't think it was Lionel. We need to think of who could have gotten Junior to do something like this. Who could convince him?"

"Joey?" Merry Belle suggested, rubbing her aching back. Searching for clues and securing crime scenes was hard work. "He'd want to hide the proof that Teresa was married to Hal."

"But Junior couldn't stand Joey or Clarissa. I don't see either of them working with the other," Paavo reminded them.

He walked over to Doc, and Merry Belle joined them.

"Junior might not have been a good father," Doc said, "but in his way, he did love his daughter. If she had a chance to inherit Hal's estate, I don't think he'd work against her to give it to Joey."

"The same reasoning would rule out Clarissa," Paavo added.

Buster had been listening, and called out, "Junior didn't like any of them out at the ranch, except maybe Dolores." He smirked. "They had a thing going, in fact."

"Dolores?" Doc looked appalled. "I didn't think she'd give him the time of day!"

"Didn't she live at the ranch for years taking care of Hal?" Paavo asked.

"She doted on Hal," Merry Belle said. "Nursed him through his sickness, took care of his physical therapy. You name it, she did it."

The three looked at each other as the same thought struck.

Buster was confused. "Why are you all silent all of a sudden?"

Doc spoke first. "Hal wanted to keep his marriage to Teresa a secret. We all assumed it was because of Clarissa, but that never made a lot of sense. What if it was because of Dolores? Because he feared her jealousy? But she found out. That's why his life was in danger—and why he left. Maybe he couldn't handle the guilt over the way he'd treated her, and since he was unbalanced anyway, it was enough to push him over the edge."

Disgust darkened Merry Belle's round face. "He should have understood her better."

"When he came back," Doc theorized, "I wonder if Dolores thought he'd returned for her. But when one of the first things he did was try to get back Teresa, Dolores couldn't take it. She killed him."

"She probably knew Hal was helping illegals come into the country," Paavo added. "She's strong enough to have moved Hal's body to the caves. It was a good hiding place and would warn the coyotes the area was no longer safe. In Ned's line of work, he'd know a lot of people—legally here and not. As he learned of the attacks on Teresa, he started looking into them. He must have come across something—the amulet, most likely—that scared Dolores, that told her he was on to her. Somehow, she lured him to the caves and killed him."

"I could see Junior letting her use him," Doc said. "She got him to do her dirty work, break into the church and my office, looking for a will or any evidence about Teresa's marriage. She must have convinced him that it would be to Teresa's benefit—or to his."

"Hold on, you all," Merry Belle said. "You can't

go blaming Dolores when I've got proof that Joey's the killer! I've got the heel rand. I don't believe Dolores would try to pin the crime on Joey."

"She didn't," Paavo said. "Lionel did. It was an action of opportunity, that's all. He didn't know about Hal's marriage. He thought Joey stood in the way of his inheritance. If Joey was locked up for Hal's death, Joey couldn't inherit, and Lionel was next in line. He probably found the heel rand on the ranch and was waiting for an opportunity to use it. The day he went out to the caves with Angie gave it to him. He brought the heel rand with him and then supposedly 'found' it. He's also the one who put the note in my pocket. But that's all he did."

"Lionel often said that all he ever wanted was for life to go on as it had the five years Hal was away," Buster added. "He liked being boss."

"Let's get back to the cookout," Paavo said. "We need to ask Dolores a few questions."

Chapter 35

Dolores made her way through the narrow trails that led to the foothills. Much as she would have liked to try to brazen this out, to continue to be unseen and unnoticed as she had most of her life, she was afraid that this time she couldn't pull it off. She'd been so shaken and upset by Junior's call that Merry Belle was onto him, she hadn't thought clearly, and had used a gun that could be traced back to her.

Also, the visitors troubled her. Paavo Smith was a real cop, not someone who didn't want to make waves like Sheriff Hermann. And where the people in town paid no attention to Dolores, Angie Amalfi wasn't that way. Angie noticed things. Noticed *her.* That was why she'd tried to scare them into leaving. It hadn't worked.

Dolores was afraid to take the chance of staying put. She'd created an opportunity—it had been easy to stampede the ostriches by shouting and waving a red tablecloth at them like some toreador. When everyone's attention was on the chaos, she threw a few things into her truck and ran.

Now, she began to speed.

Calm down, she told herself. It would take a long time before the people at the ranch put everything together, and she'd have a good head start. The disruption she'd created at the cookout should keep people too busy to miss her for hours. No one ever thought about her until there was work to be done.

Once they did miss her, they'd figure she headed for the Mexican border. Let them think that. She just had to get into the hills, the high desert, and she could hide out there a month or two before turning south.

It wasn't the first time she'd been on the run; not the first time she'd had to live in the desert, relying on her skill at hunting and foraging for sustenance. She'd been only twelve years old when she crossed into this country with her uncle and cousins. She could do it again.

Thinking about them, about the uncle and two cousins who were dead now, about all she'd been through in this country, and about Hal Edwards, a great sorrow filled her.

Tears clouded her vision.

The evil she'd done was all Hal's fault. How could he have treated her as he did? After the way she'd stayed at his side when everyone else, even his own wife, abandoned him; the way she'd nursed him back to good health after his stroke; the way she'd worked to make him strong again. She'd loved him, taken him to her bed, given him everything she could.

Once he was healthy again, she wasn't good enough for him. He wanted her back in the kitchen.

And now . . .

She wiped the tears that kept falling and falling.

She had to get away. She couldn't let them catch her. The state would kill her; take her life, like she took Hal's. And Ned's. And Junior's. And possibly even Maritza's, a good woman who never did harm to anyone.

"Damn you, Hal!" she cried, her foot pressing down even harder on the gas pedal. "I hate you!"

The road curved sharply around the hillside. She swung the wheel hard as she tried to wipe away the tears that were blinding her. Her vision cleared just in time to see there, in the middle of the road, a large boulder.

The grass ground out an agonized shriek as Angie drove her SUV away from the parking area. Joey was with her, riding shotgun.

The ostrich with the cowlick stood by the side of the road, its eyes wide with surprise and curiosity as she zipped by.

Angie sped into the desert. She had to find Dolores. Most likely, Dolores wouldn't think she was being followed and might not go too fast.

As she somehow managed to keep control of the SUV, she pulled out her phone. Nearing the cave area, she had enough cell phone service to call Paavo. The phone kept cutting out, but he understood well enough to tell her to go back.

"I'll be careful," she said just as the cell failed completely. She doubted he heard her.

* * *

"There's a whole maze of old trails, some fire roads, and dry creek beds Dolores could drive through," Merry Belle said. She'd left Buster in charge of the crime scene, Doc with him, while she drove the Hummer. Paavo was at her side. "If Dolores gets far enough and starts hoofing it, she can hide out for years. She knows the desert, knows how to survive in it."

"I only hope Angie doesn't catch up to her," Paavo said grimly, hands clenched.

"You told her not to go after Dolores," Merry Belle reminded him.

"Yes." Paavo's response came through gritted teeth.

"Don't worry," Merry Belle said with sudden insight. "We'll probably find Angie stuck off the road. Anybody who doesn't know those trails won't get very far."

"I hope you're right."

Merry Belle got on the radio to request aerial backup from the State Police as they sped past the hacienda and onto the back road.

"Turn there," Joey yelled, "or you'll end up on the road to the lake. I don't think that's where she's going."

"Agreed." Angie made the sharp turn, and found herself on a narrow fire road. The higher the dirt trail went into the foothills, the more twisted and winding it became, the surface rougher and more treacherous. The constant bounces and jolts made her already banged-up body ache even more.

She tried to call Paavo to tell him the road she'd taken, but the signal was gone.

"I'm never leaving home again!" she muttered as she pressed forward.

"And miss all this fun?" Joey asked. "You're doing fine."

The SUV rental skidded as she careened around an unexpectedly sharp bend. Before her, Dolores's black pickup jutted onto the roadway. It had crashed into a boulder, leaving the hood crumpled. The driver's side door hung open.

Angie stomped hard on the brakes. The SUV went into a spin. As the back end skidded on the rocky road, the side swiped against the truck with a grinding whir. Finally, the SUV bounced off the roadway and the engine died.

"I guess I spoke a little too soon," Joey grumbled, rubbing his head where it had bumped the windshield. He'd put on his seat belt as soon as Angie had begun driving, so he hadn't hit too hard.

When Angie realized she was still in one piece, she stared with horror at the black truck, certain that Dolores was going to leap out of it with guns blazing.

She didn't.

Joey reached over and tugged at Angie's shoulder. She immediately realized the wisdom of his action, and quickly bent down the same way. The two of them cowered behind the dash.

"Where do you think Dolores might be?" she whispered. "She's not in the pickup, so she must have gone off on foot. She could be far . . . or she could be watching us this very moment."

"I don't know," Joey whispered back. "She must

have been hurt in that crash. She might be lying across the seat, or dead. I don't like this."

"But the door's open. I think she got out."

"That's likely, too," Joey said, not exactly helpfully.

"Do you think she'd hurt us?" Angie's voice was tiny. "To me, she seemed like such a nice lady."

"Hurt us? Are you kidding? She's only killed three people that we know of—including my father!" Joey cried, sounding very nervous. "Of course she'd hurt us!"

Enough said. Angie turned the ignition key. When the engine refused to turn over, she pumped the gas pedal. Still nothing. She kept trying.

"Stop," Joey whispered. "You're flooding the engine. It won't help."

"Paavo and the sheriff shouldn't be far behind," she said. "If Dolores is gone, we can simply sit here and wait."

"You don't know how fast the sheriff drives," Joey said. "If her big Hummer zips around the blind curve too fast, it could flatten this car with us in it. We should try to walk down the road to meet them."

"Okay." She pushed the door open when a shot rang out. The bullet tore a wide hole in the windshield and the rest of the glass spidered. The console between the driver's and passenger's seats splintered from the bullet's impact.

Angie gave a yelp, pulled her door shut and locked it, then crawled completely under the dashboard.

Joey was already down there.

"Maybe that wasn't such a good idea," Joey said.

"At least we found out where Dolores is," Angie added, trying to stay positive even as she peeked up at the cracked windshield and the ruined console.

"Get out of that car! I need it." The voice was shrill and quaking, and came from high above and off the road.

"Don't listen to her," Joey whimpered.

"I'll give you one minute to think it over and get out. Then, I'm coming down. I don't want to kill you, Angie! But I need your car."

Angie reached up to try the ignition key again, but before doing so, whispered to Joey, "What do you think she'll do if she finds out the engine is stalled?" Angie asked.

"Probably kill us," Joey answered glumly.

Angie pulled her hand back, fast. At Joey's words, her breathing turned ragged, her stomach plummeted, and all her positive thinking switched to negative. Thoughts of Paavo came to her, of the beautiful wedding they'd never have, and her eyes filled with tears. Why had she been so ridiculous about the ceremony and the locale? Who cared how extra-special it was? It was a wedding, for pity's sake, not a royal inauguration!

Then she heard the roar of a fast approaching vehicle.

"Oh, my God!" Joey covered his head. "It's Merry Belle!"

Angie screamed.

The impact could have been heard in seven counties. Or so it seemed to the two inside the sheriff's

Hummer. When Paavo had gotten his breath back from the jolt of his safety belt, he saw that the Hummer hadn't crushed the SUV as he imagined. It was a fender-bender, true, but at least the SUV didn't resemble an accordion.

It had been a complete shock to round the bend, Merry Belle going at bat-out-of-hell speed, and to see both the pickup and SUV right in front of them.

Merry Belle braked, all the while roaring profanities. By some miracle, she had managed to stop in time.

Angie's head popped up from inside the SUV just long enough to catch Paavo's eye. A French-manicured fingernail pointed toward the hills. Then she ducked again.

Rifle in hand, before Paavo could say a word, Merry Belle sprung open her door. "I'll show her!"

"No, wait!" Paavo tried to grab her, but she jumped out and ran for the cover of Dolores's pickup. She wasn't fast enough. A shot fired from above. Merry Belle dropped instantly to the ground, clutching her leg.

"She shot me! I don't believe it. I've actually been wounded in the line of duty!" She was more in rage than pain, and dragged herself to the cover of the truck. "Now I'm really mad."

More shots rained down on the window of the Hummer. The bulletproof glass dimpled but held. Paavo, lying flat, called to Merry Belle, "How badly are you hit?"

"Leg wound. Lots of blood," Merry Belle gasped. "But I'll live to see Dolores pay for this."

"Stay put." Paavo repositioned himself on the front seat and pushed open the passenger door. It was no more than a foot away from the driver's door of the SUV.

Looking out, he had a clear view of the SUV's shattered windshield. "Angie, are you all right?"

A muffled voice yelled back, "Yes."

He breathed again with relief. "Don't stick your head up again," he shouted. "Just listen. I want you to open the driver's door—kick it open—if you can."

He waited. At last Angie's door swung open until it met and overlapped with his. Angie looked up from under the dash, a wild grin on her face. Behind her, he saw Joey's head pop up. "Maybe I will have my wedding after all," she said.

"Not if we stay pinned down like this," Paavo warned. "Dolores is panicked right now. You can't trust that she'll be at all rational. Remember that."

Angie's face fell even as she nodded, and for the first time, Paavo noticed the strange bits of . . . something . . . plastered to her hair and clothes. "You sure you're not hurt?"

"Only my pride."

Joey cried out, "Just get us out of this!"

Dolores fired again. Shots bounced off the windshield of the Hummer and into the hood of the SUV.

"Angie, listen to me. I want you two to come into the Hummer. It's safer, and the windshield's bulletproof. The doors will provide you some cover, but you're going to have to move faster than you've ever moved before."

"It's so far!" She looked so scared he wondered if she could move at all. "You mean it?"

"I've never been more serious."

* * *

Dolores felt woozy. Every part of her body ached from the earlier crash of her truck, but especially her neck and head, which had seemed to bounce like a tennis ball between the windshield and the back of the seat. It had been all she could do to drag herself from the truck. She knew she'd be found if she stayed on the road, and so had worked her way up the hill. Overland—that was the way to safety.

It had been hard going. Every step jarred her, and her neck felt as if it were on fire. She was halfway up the hill, halfway to safety, when she heard a car engine.

She thought she'd caught a break when she saw Angie in the driver's seat, Joey with her.

If only they'd listened to her, gotten out of the SUV and walked away, she would have let them go.

Wouldn't she?

Or was it too late for that?

Then the Hummer showed up with the sheriff and a real cop.

Her head ached; she couldn't think. She couldn't walk very far; she needed Angie's car so she could go away. That's all she wanted; to go away; to forget about all this.

Why didn't everyone simply leave her alone?

Angie moved about on her seat and took a deep breath. She sprang out feet-first, hit the ground, caught her balance, took a step, and dived into the Hummer. As Paavo pulled her in, shots hit the open doors, causing them to swing shut.

Paavo and Joey pushed them open again, and Joey followed Angie's lead.

Bullets slammed into the glass. Frostlike, webbed lines spread over the windshield, but it held.

Paavo faced Joey. "We can reach Merry Belle by going out the driver's door. I'll go first, then provide cover while you follow. Angie, you stay here and keep your head down."

"That's all?" she asked.

"That's enough. You ready, Joey?"

He gulped and nodded.

Using the door for some cover, Paavo fired toward the hill as he and Joey scrambled out of the Hummer and ducked behind the pickup.

"Glad to see you all," Merry Belle said. She was pale, and her trousers were heavily bloodstained. Her belt was wrapped as a makeshift tourniquet on her thigh. "Don't sweat it, Paavo. I've got the bleeding under control," she said, sweat glistening on her face. "I also watch *ER* on TV."

"Can I do anything?" Angie called.

"No!" the others called back.

"Oh," she murmured.

Facing Joey and Merry Belle, Paavo said, "The way we're pinned down, we have to look up into the sun to keep track of Dolores, and it's not going to work. I've got to get up there and get around behind her."

"How?" Merry Belle asked. "We *are* pinned down,"

"I'll draw her fire. We'll do some play-acting. Angie can help. You know the drill, M.B.?"

She smiled like a Cheshire cat. "Got it."

"Can't we wait for help?" Joey mumbled.

"We don't have the luxury," Paavo said. "She's

desperate and will probably make a move soon. If I'm up there with her, it should at least guarantee a standoff until help arrives."

"He's right, Joey," Merry Belle said, handing him her revolver. "Follow my lead. I don't think Dolores will shoot back right away—she'll probably be ducking."

Joey paled at the gun in his hand.

"Angie." Paavo gave a loud whisper. "Merry Belle will cue you in."

"Cue me?" Angie asked, confused.

Paavo helped Merry Belle position herself to lean against the truck. "Do your thing, San Francisco," she said.

"On the count of three," Paavo said, "start shooting."

He tucked the Beretta in his waistband and positioned himself like a sprinter.

"One . . . two . . . *three*!"

With a groan, Merry Belle raised herself up. Joey rose with her and both opened fire as Paavo ran. The noise was deafening.

Paavo dashed toward the rocks as shots rained from above. He clutched at his chest and went down. His body rolled to the shelter of the rocks.

"Paavo!" Angie screamed, horrified. She couldn't move for a moment, then began to scramble out of the Hummer.

"Stop!" Merry Belle commanded, then dropped her voice. "Your man's acting," she hissed.

Behind shelter, Paavo gave a thumbs-up. Angie gaped, feeling all but faint. His plan slowly sunk in, yet there was blood on his upper left arm. That was no act. He pointed at his arm, and gave another thumbs-up.

"You can act, too," Merry Belle said. "Start yelling and crying."

It took Angie a moment to catch her breath. "Paavo, Paavo!"

His smile blinded her, and as relief coursed through her blood, she got into it even more. "Oh God! I'll come to you, my darling!"

Merry Belle picked up her cue and yelled, "Stay down! He's dead, dammit! Dead!"

"Noooo!" Angie let out a scream that might have had distant wolves howling.

Dolores opened fire again, peppering the hood and roof of the pickup. Merry Belle fired back. Joey tried to join her, but he was so pale and shaking so hard, he dropped the revolver.

"Go away!" Dolores shrieked. "I'll kill you all if I have to!"

"Give up, Dolores," Merry Belle yelled. "You can't get away from us."

"Oh, Paavo," Angie wailed, really loud. "Oh, my love! My life! Dead! *Dead!*"

Merry Belle gaped at her with an expression that said her stomach was turning nauseous. Joey looked at her with something akin to revulsion.

Angie grimaced. No one appreciated her acting.

Meanwhile, Paavo had begun working his way up the rocks.

Dolores's most recent shots had given away her position.

* * *

"I'm sorry, Angie!" Dolores called. She wondered what they were up to, and if the cop was really dead. "I didn't want to do it, but it couldn't be helped. Please—put your guns down and back away from the Hummer. All I want is to go away. I'll never bother you again."

"You'll give us as much chance as you gave Junior," Merry Belle snarled.

"I didn't want to hurt him," Dolores complained. "But I had no choice."

"Like you had no choice about Ned . . . or Hal?"

"Ned figured it out. He asked questions of people I didn't think he knew. He came to me, asking about Hal. Somehow, he figured it out."

"How did you get him to go with you to the caves?"

"I didn't force him there." Dolores was crying. How she hated to think about any of that. "All I did was to tell him I had found Hal's will, that it gave everything to Teresa. I said I'd hidden it near the caves, and would give it to him if he'd let me go. He believed me. He didn't know . . ."

All was quiet for a moment, then Angie called out, "Didn't know *what*? What do you mean?"

Dolores didn't want to talk any more. Her head hurt, she was tired. If only she could leave . . .

"Tell me!" Angie demanded, until Dolores couldn't stand to listen to her a moment longer.

"*He didn't know me!* No one really saw me most of the time," she cried. "Not even Hal. He used me, let me work for him, love him—and he never even saw me. I might live beneath the shadows because of the way I entered this country, but I still have feelings, hopes, dreams, just like everyone else. I—and others like me—we come and go, through people's homes, businesses, gardens— and no one really sees us. Am I invisible? I thought Hal could see me, with his heart as well as his eyes. Perhaps he did, once. But then he turned away, became blind. He married Teresa. It should have been me!"

Angie again glanced over at Merry Belle. She was sitting back against the truck, breathing hard. Loss of blood and pain had gotten to her, and for that reason, Angie had lowered the driver's side window and took over distracting Dolores with questions. "If you really loved Hal, you wouldn't have killed him!"

"I did love him," she shrieked. "But he left me for that young nothing after I spent my life caring for him! How could he—what's the word?— forsake me for her? How could he do it?"

Angie had no answer, but she knew she had to keep Dolores talking to help mask the sound of Paavo sneaking near.

But suddenly, she saw her ostrich friend walk up to the Hummer and begin to peck at the door. The foolish bird had followed her all the way up here! It was going to end up fricasseed if it didn't watch out. "Go away!" she whispered.

The ostrich stuck its head against the passenger's side window and one big black eye peered inside at Angie. "You'll get yourself killed!" Angie hissed. "Now, go home! Run!"

The bird just stared at her.

Angie called to Dolores, "You wanted to kill Teresa, too, didn't you?"

"No! I'm a good person, not a killer! Maybe at first I wished she was dead—I was angry, hurt. But it didn't work, and then, I lost my desire. I felt bad, but after a time, everything went back to the way it had been when Hal was in Mexico. All I wanted to do was to go on with my life. Then, his body was found."

"That made you try to kill Teresa again?" Merry Belle called, her voice weak.

"I still didn't want to, but I also didn't want to see her as the owner of all Hal's things—to profit from his death when she was the cause of it! That wouldn't be fair! I got Junior to steal the proof of her marriage. That's all. But then, Ned asked questions, and Junior wanted to give the proofs to Teresa, and everything went bad. It wasn't my fault!"

"Why did you hurt Maritza?" Angie asked.

The ostrich went around to the back of the Hummer, apparently fascinated by the red taillights.

"I watched her walk to the restaurant alone. I followed, and asked her what she was doing. She just looked at me, and I could see it in her eyes. She knew. She got scared, then said, 'You loved him.' And I had to stop her!"

"Give up, Dolores!" Merry Belle called. "Come down here."

At that, Dolores shot at Merry Belle again. The bullet bounced off the rocks.

The ostrich ran, but soon returned and began to peck at the side-view mirror on the rented Mercedes. "Go away!" Angie said, trying to shoo it from harm.

Merry Belle returned fire, but as she felt in her

pockets for rifle bullets, she found she'd used the last one.

Joey handed her back her service revolver.

She just stared at it.

"Shoot!" he cried.

Dolores shouted again. "The sun is behind me. You'll never see me coming. I need the Hummer! Give up."

"Your story is horrible!" Angie yelled, needing to make noise, hoping Paavo had time to climb up behind Dolores by now. "You make excuses, but you're just a hateful, jealous woman. No wonder Hal dumped you!"

"I thought you were my friend!" Dolores shrieked. "You're going to make it easy for me to kill you!"

"Why are you just sitting there?" Joey said to Merry Belle, nearly in tears. "Paavo needs you to shoot!"

"It only has blanks," Merry Belle wailed. "I didn't want to carry live bullets around Jackpot with me! What if someone got hurt?"

"Blanks?" he repeated.

"Blanks," she said morosely. "Until today, with this rifle, I've never shot a gun with real bullets anywhere except a shooting range."

"Oh . . . my . . . God!"

He took the gun from her. "If I have to, I'll use it. At least it makes a lot of noise."

"She could kill you!" Merry Belle said.

As Joey and Merry Belle quivered with dismay, Angie knew that if Dolores wasn't distracted, she might notice Paavo.

Desperate to find a stray bullet or two—maybe even a little gun—Angie rummaged through the backseat of the Hummer, then the glove compartment. It was stuffed tight with papers, junk food wrappers, and heaven only knew what else. Merry Belle seemed pretty careless about everything else, why would she be any different with guns and ammo?

She pulled everything out of the glove compartment. Something had to be there to help.

In the very back, under everything else, was a black strip of some kind. She pulled it out. It was a lace garter.

What in the world? She held it up. It was big—so big it probably could have fit around both her thighs at once. So big it probably fit Merry Belle . . .

Merry Belle and a black lace garter? She pushed away the torturous image from her mind.

The ostrich continued to peck at the mirror.

Angie looked from the ostrich, up to where Dolores was hiding. And as she did, a plan formed.

Glancing at the ostrich, she reached up to remove an earring.

She wasn't wearing any! She hadn't put any on that morning, mostly because she didn't want to be bothered by the birds while she worked on the cookout.

Her heart sank. So much for her great idea.

But then, another thought came to her.

A horrifying, ghastly, appalling thought . . .

Still, she needed to create a distraction, and that should do it.

The only bright, shiny thing the ostriches loved

that Angie absolutely had refused to remove was—
her heart nearly stopped at the thought and she
clasped her fingers over it—her engagement ring.

How could she even think . . . ? But Paavo was
up there . . .

She tested the garter belt. It had a lot of stretch
left in it. It should work.

Practically holding her breath at the all-but sac-
rilegious act, she took off her engagement ring
and waggled it so that the sun caught the facets of
the beautiful Siberian diamond. The diamond she
loved more than any she'd ever seen anywhere,
anytime . . .

Intrigued, the ostrich did an about-face and
headed toward her.

As the ostrich watched, Angie stretched the
garter belt between her thumb and forefinger,
then placed the ring against it and pulled back like
a slingshot.

Quickly moving her hands through the Hummer's open window, she aimed upward, in the direction where Dolores hid, pulled back as hard as
she could on the elastic, and let go.

The ring flew high in the air, up, up, she
watched her most precious possession fly,
sparkling in the sunlight, until it landed on rocks
just behind Dolores. Angie cringed as it bounced
and scraped against the rough ground.

The ostrich let out a raucous squawk and clambered up the hill, its little useless wings flapping,
its heavy legs pumping.

"What the hell!" Dolores stood up as the bird
neared, aiming her rifle at the beast.

Before she fired, Paavo stood up behind her,

shouted her name, and told her to drop the gun. Instead of obeying, Dolores spun around, facing him.

The ostrich didn't stop, but ran right into her. Dolores flipped head over heels in one direction, her rifle in the other.

Then, as Angie watched, the worst possible thing happened.

The ostrich found her ring.

And ate it.

Chapter 36

Angie sat in Jackpot's medical clinic waiting room, Joey beside her. Paavo had gone into an office with Doc, who had insisted on personally cleaning and dressing the gunshot wound.

Half the town, it seemed, was milling about. Word had spread quickly about Junior's murder, Dolores's shocking confessions, and the shootout. Sheriff Merry Belle Hermann, who was also in the clinic being treated, was lauded as a hero, her re-election guaranteed for many years to come.

Angie rubbed the empty spot on her ring finger.

"We'll get it back," Joey promised, seeing her forlorn expression.

She turned to Joey. "You can give the ostrich ipecac or something to make her throw up, right?"

He looked abashed. "I'm afraid that won't work. Ostriches swallow sand and stones to help them digest food since they have no teeth. Their stomachs are tough. Your ring is staying at the guest ranch a while longer."

"Oh, no! What am I going to do?" Angie wailed.

323

"Don't worry," Joey had said with a wide grin. "Everything will come out all right in the end."

The worst day of her life had just gotten a whole lot worse.

"We'll clean it up real good for you," Joey continued, "sterilize it and everything. No one will ever know."

"I'll know," Angie said mournfully.

Just then, Lupe and Teresa found her and Joey. "My mother woke up this afternoon," Lupe said to them both, "right after Doc contacted me at the hospital and told me about Dolores. First he called and told me about Junior, then later, about Dolores. I could hardly believe either call, and yet, it's almost as if some evil that had dwelt in this town has been lifted. My mother's going to be all right. Her mind, everything about her is much better than the doctors expected."

"Thank goodness," Angie said.

"We heard you helped as well, Joey," Lupe said, facing him without her usual hatred. "Thank you."

"I did nothing," Joey replied, looking abashed by Lupe's words. He also appeared surprisingly composed, even likable. Angie wondered if being away from Clarissa was what did it.

"I'm sorry I ever suspected you," Angie confessed to him.

"I'm sorry, too, that you could have thought so poorly of me," he said quietly. "I can understand it, though. Murder does terrible things, and not only to the victim. Ned was a friend, and frankly, I suspected him of killing my father."

"You did?" Teresa asked.

"I'm sorry." He scooted over to give the Flores

women room on the bench. Teresa sat beside him.
"Did you suspect me as well?" he asked.

"I never did, Joey."

He looked at her, swallowed hard a couple of
times, then simply whispered, "Thank you."

"I should have known it was Dolores," LaVerne
announced, joining them and wiping the dust
from her bifocals. She was slightly breathless from
dashing over to the clinic to get all the latest information, and zeroed in on the little group. "That
woman would never talk much at all to me. There
was definitely something wrong with her."

"Was the cookout ruined?" Angie asked.

"Ruined?" LaVerne gave her a big smile. "It was
bigger and better than ever! Only a small portion
of what Dolores and I cooked was on the chuck
wagon you practically destroyed. Later, the entire
town showed up to find out all they could about
the shootout. They especially liked my macaroni
and cheese." LaVerne's eyebrows arched. "Too
bad all *your* food was ruined."

Angie had had it with her. "Just why did you
come here, LaVerne?" she snapped.

LaVerne squared her shoulders. "Actually, I
came to show you something. Those old letters
got me thinking. The recipe journal—maybe it
wasn't written by one of my ancestors, after all. In
fact, my great grandfather's name was Jim—the
name of the man who received the letters." She
handed Angie an ancient leather-bound volume.
"Will you look at it? Is it worth a lot of money? Am
I going to be rich?"

"Oh, my God!" Angie whispered as she looked
at the book in her hands. Could it be? LaVerne had

put plastic wrap on the cover to protect it. Angie's heart began to beat a little faster. The book's pages were brown with age, but it opened easily. She turned to the frontispiece.

It read "Recipes Developed on My Travels West" and was signed Willem van Beerstraeden. "This is it!" she cried. "The missing journal!"

She turned the page. The first recipe was for "Gila Monster Egg Surprise."

Her face fell, and she knew she didn't want to learn what the surprise might be. Actually, the surprise would be that anyone would think— ever—of eating Gila monster eggs.

She quickly turned more pages, her heart dropping more and more as she read. "Fried Porcupine Quill Crunchies," "Kangaroo Rat Bisque," and at least thirty ways to fry, sauté, broil, stew, boil, or grill rattlesnakes and its varieties, such as sidewinders and diamondbacks.

All in all, Angie thought, the recipes LaVerne had chosen to cook weren't half bad compared to what else was in there. She gave a deep sigh. "I think I now know what Oscar Tschirky meant when he said he didn't want the recipes to fall into the wrong hands, and that he wanted to retrieve it for the family's name and honor."

LaVerne's eyes widened. "He meant we're going to be rich, didn't he?"

Angie shook her head. "I think he wanted it so no one else would see it."

"What?" LaVerne shrieked. "No!"

"These recipes are horrible! No one should eat this stuff. Half the animals are poisonous, the other half endangered. You shouldn't even be

cooking from this book. No wonder van Beerstraeden gave away his recipes. If he learned anything at all from Oscar, he knew how bad a cook
he was."

"These recipes are awful?" LaVerne asked
glumly. "I thought gourmet food was supposed to
taste that way. Damn! I surely would have liked to
become rich."

Angie stared, equally doleful, at the book. "And
I surely would have liked to have been the one to
discover how Oscar of the Waldorf came up with
his famous recipes. Maybe he really did develop
them himself."

"It's too bad," LaVerne said with a heavy sigh.

"Yes, it is." Angie tried to give the book back to
LaVerne, who refused to take it, and promptly
left.

Angie felt Paavo's hand on her shoulder. She
looked up to see him standing behind her. He'd
heard everything and now seemed to be struggling not to crack even the tiniest of smiles.

"It's not so bad, Angie," he said, patting her.

"Not bad at all, except that my engagement
ring is somewhere I don't want to think about,
my fiancé has been shot, I spent hours and hours
chasing a recipe book by a chef who has no idea
about good food, and the worst cook on the
planet had more people liking her food than
mine! Sometimes I feel I must live under a very
black cloud."

Maritza was still groggy when Paavo and Doc
walked into her hospital room. Doc had asked
Paavo to take her statement about what happened

that day at the restaurant. Merry Belle wanted to take it, Doc said, but she was crankier and more obnoxious than ever with that leg wound.

Maritza spoke slowly, and explained that something had made her go to the restaurant. Once she was there, though, she couldn't remember what it was. To her surprise, Dolores entered, and that was the last she knew.

It was good enough. Paavo and Doc were ready to leave when Maritza said, "When I sleep, though, then it come to me."

They stopped.

"I see Mr. Edwards—Hal. I know it's a dream, but it seem so real. He come and remind me of the day he see me at the restaurant. I'm in my chair. He give me an envelope and say to hold it for him. That I will keep it safe. He trust me. I put it in a drawer of the chest under the picture of Our Lady. I know she will not let anything happen to it until Mr. Edwards want it back."

"What was in the envelope?" Paavo asked.

"Mr. Edwards doesn't tell me. But I think it's important. If not, why does he come into my dream?"

Lupe easily found the sealed envelope Maritza had spoken of. She handed it to Doc.

Teresa, Angie, Paavo, and Joey were also there to watch as Doc took out the papers and read through them.

"Although I suspect it'll be challenged"—Doc glanced at Joey—"this appears to be a properly executed, witnessed, sealed, and notarized copy of the last will and testament of Hal Edwards, dated January of this year in Bisbee, Arizona."

"What does it say?" Angie asked eagerly.

Doc read the will aloud. In it, Hal requested that his cattle ranch be sold. Of the proceeds, half would go to Jackpot's medical clinic and half to the library.

To Dolores Huerta, who had been loyal to him for years and stayed with him through his stroke and rehabilitation, he gave the sum of two hundred fifty thousand dollars.

"She won't be collecting that," Angie said.

Doc continued. "To my cousin, Lionel, his trailer and twenty-five thousand dollars in cash. To my ex-wife, Clarissa Edwards, the knowledge that if only you'd loved me the way I loved you, I would have given you the world. To our son Joseph Edwards"—Doc cleared his throat and eyed Joey before going on—"the recognition that I failed you as a father, but, Joey, you failed me as a son."

Joey's face fell, then he nodded and bowed his head.

"And finally, to my wife, Teresa Flores, a.k.a. Teresa Flores Edwards, I bequeath the remainder of all my worldly goods, including the Ghost Hollow Guest Ranch, stocks, bonds, and bank accounts. See list attached."

Doc held out the long list, then placed the will on Maritza's chair.

Everyone stared at it in silence.

Chapter 37

The next afternoon, Angie and Paavo stopped at the Stagecoach Saloon on their way out of town to say good-bye to Doc and others who had gathered there to wish them well. Since their SUV had been destroyed, Joey let them use his Lexus for the drive to the airport. He'd retrieve it sometime soon. He planned to return to Los Angeles long enough to pack up his things.

He was moving to Jackpot, to the Ghost Hollow Guest Ranch, and was going to be its new manager. He'd offered his services to Teresa, and she'd gladly accepted them. Lionel didn't have the energy or brains to make it the kind of resort it should be—a first-class one, and a possible destination-wedding site as well.

As Joey had explained the evening before to his appalled mother, he'd always liked both the hacienda and Teresa. Liked, not loved, he emphasized. Teresa had always been kind to him—kinder than anyone else, in fact. He didn't want to fight the will. He had no reason to. And for the first time in his life he put his foot down and told Clarissa that if she tried to fight it, he'd do all he could to oppose her.

Sheriff Merry Belle Hermann was at the saloon as well. She leaned against a crutch, Buster beside her. She recounted time and again the "Shootout at Ghost Hollow Ridge," as she called it—a day that would live in infamy, at least in her own mind.

Buster took Angie aside and apologized about her Emilio Pucci scarf, offering to buy her a new one. She told him to forget it, she had plenty of others. She also promised to send him a bunch of her favorite high-fashion catalogues and brochures so he could order clothes to his heart's content—perhaps best done using a post office box in another town. He was thrilled.

Doris Flynn's appearance saved Angie the need for a trip to the library. She handed Willem van Beerstraeden's letters and recipe journal to the librarian. Doris clutched them to her heart, and promised to give the materials a prominent place in a glass case in her new library annex with a plaque thanking Angelina Amalfi for her generous historical gift. It might even bring a few more tourists to Jackpot.

Whether that happened or not, the whole town believed Angie deserved the plaque simply for convincing LaVerne to stop cooking her "old family recipes."

Angie invited Teresa to come to San Francisco for a visit. Teresa agreed. She planned to spend a year or more traveling. There was much she had to sort out in her mind, and much sorrow to forget. It was time for her to get to know who Teresa Flores Edwards was, and what she valued in her life.

To Angie's surprise—and Teresa's own—she added that after the year ended, she'd very likely be happy to come back to Jackpot. She'd kept her heart wrapped up in a protective shell all these years, and she couldn't help but suspect that to work her way out of it, the best place was home.

Angie suspected she was right.

Doc and Lupe were together, arms around each other's waists, beaming, and looking for all the world like young lovers. Angie was glad to see it.

Soon, the time came for her and Paavo to leave, to make the long drive to Palm Springs and then the plane ride back to San Francisco.

Angie felt strangely melancholy about saying good-bye to so many new friends. She had a special hug for Doc.

Doc told her that she and Paavo were good for each other, and she told him that the same went for him and Lupe.

Lupe took Paavo's hands. "Don't stay away so long, next time."

"I won't," he promised and gave her a warm embrace.

He then turned to Doc and held him a long moment as thoughts of the friend who wasn't there hit them hard. Both were a little misty-eyed when they parted.

Merry Belle stood near the front door, ready to rush—or hobble—outside if need be to protect Jackpot.

Paavo said good-bye to her with a handshake, but at the last moment, leaned forward and kissed her on the cheek. Merry Belle blushed twenty shades of red, then gave him an affectionate tap on the chest that nearly sent him through the saloon window.

With smiles and grins, and more than a little sadness, Angie and Paavo left.

As they passed Merritt's Café, both stuck an arm out the window and waved at LaVerne, who was watching, her nose pressed to the glass and a coffeepot in hand.

Just past town at one point where the creek neared the highway, Angie found herself studying the horizon.

"Beautiful, isn't it?" Paavo asked.

"Yes," she replied. The more she'd come to know the desert, the more she appreciated it. She, who was a city girl through and through, was surprised at the beauty she'd found in lonesome stretches of land broken up only by a cactus or some low-lying scrub, at the horses, the cattle, and even the hard-working people in the sleepy Western town.

"I never did get to go fishing," Paavo said. "And I used to enjoy it as a kid. I enjoyed it a lot, in fact."

"We'll do it someday," she promised.

"I wonder what's going to happen to Ned's business," Paavo said quietly. "If it'll be put up for sale?"

Her head swiveled toward him at warp speed. "For sale?" Her throat felt like it was closing.

"You don't think you'd be happy working on boats and gutting fish for your husband?"

She was speechless.

"Don't worry, Angie. Not now. But..." He

looked out at the empty vistas and smiled wistfully. "Maybe someday."

She eased herself against the passenger seat. She'd hoped that from this vacation she'd learn more about Paavo, and she certainly had.

Now she just had to figure out their destination-wedding site. Wherever it might be, she knew that it'd have nothing whatsoever to do with the Old West, cowboys, horses . . . and especially not ostriches.

From the Kitchen
of Angelina Amalfi

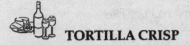 **TORTILLA CRISP**

1 large flour tortilla
1 cup shredded cheddar cheese
1 can whole chili peppers cut into strips
1 clove minced garlic
salt to taste
canola oil or lard

Preheat oven to 400°F. Grease a cookie sheet with canola oil or, for more authenticity, lard. Place the tortilla on it, then cover it with cheese, pepper, garlic, and salt. Bake at 400° until the cheese is melted and slightly bubbling.

MARITZA'S PORK STEW

3 pounds lean boneless pork country ribs
1 teaspoon oil
1 can black beans
1 large chopped onion
2 poblano chili peppers, seeded and chopped
2 Anaheim chili peppers, seeded and chopped
3–4 cloves garlic, chopped
juice of one lime
1 can tomato sauce (8 ounces)
1 teaspoon oregano
1 minced jalapeño pepper
salt to taste
cooked rice
sour cream
salsa

Preheat oven to 325°F. Heat oil in an ovenproof pot and brown the country ribs in it.

Next, add the beans, onion, chili peppers (note: you can substitute one can of chopped chilis if you can't find fresh ones), garlic, lime, tomato sauce, oregano, jalapeño, and salt. Add enough water to cover the ribs. Cover the pot and move it into a 325° oven and cook 1½ to 2 hours, until the meat is tender and breaks apart with a fork. Add more water if needed. Remove any excess pork fat that rises to the surface before serving.

Serve over white rice. Top with sour cream and your favorite salsa.

BOURBON PECAN CHOCOLATE PIE

1 cup coarsely chopped pecans
4 eggs
½ cup light corn syrup
¼ cup honey
⅓ cup sugar
⅓ cup packed light brown sugar
6 tablespoons unsalted butter, melted
3 tablespoons bourbon
1 tablespoon vanilla
1 tablespoon all-purpose flour
pinch ground nutmeg
pinch ground cinnamon
8 ounces bittersweet chocolate
pastry for 1 pie crust

Heat oven to 350°F. Toast the pecans in a small skillet over medium-high heat, stirring often until they are evenly toasted and crisp, about 4 minutes. (Note: you can substitute walnuts, or use half pecans and half walnuts.) Set aside to cool.

In a bowl, add eggs, corn syrup, honey, sugar, brown sugar, butter, bourbon, vanilla, flour, nutmeg, and cinnamon. Whisk or blend until mixture is smooth.

Break chocolate into ½-inch-square chunks. Stir chocolate and nuts into mix.

Pour into uncooked pie crust and bake at 350° until set, 40 to 50 minutes. (A cake tester or toothpick inserted into center should come out clean.) Serve slightly warm or at room temperature.

Enter the Delicious World of
Joanne Pence's Angie Amalfi Series

From the kitchen to the deck of a cruise ship, Joanne Pence's mysteries are always a delight. Starring career-challenged Angie Amalfi and her handsome homicide-detective boyfriend Paavo Smith, Joanne Pence serves up a mystery feast complete with humor, a dead body or two, and delicious recipes.

Enjoy the pages that follow, which give a glimpse into Angie and Paavo's world.

For sassy and single food writer Angie Amalfi, life's a banquet—until the man who's been contributing unusual recipes for her food column is found dead. But in SOMETHING'S COOKING, *Angie is hardly one to simper in fear—so instead she simmers over the delectable homicide detective assigned to the case.*

A while passed before she looked up again. When she did, she saw a dark-haired man standing in the doorway to her apartment, surveying the scene. Tall and broad shouldered, his stance was aloof and forceful as he made a cold assessment of all that he saw.

If you're going to gawk, she thought, come in with the rest of the busybodies.

He looked directly at her, and her grip tightened on the chair. His expression was hard, his pale blue eyes icy. He was a stranger, of that she was certain. His wasn't the type of face or demeanor she'd easily forget. And someone, it seemed, had just sent her a bomb. Who? Why? What if this stranger. . .

340

In TOO MANY COOKS, *Angie's talked her way into a job on a pompous, third-rate chef's radio call-in show. But when a successful and much envied restaurateur is poisoned, Angie finds the case far more interesting than trying to make her pretentious boss sound good.*

Angie glanced up from the monitor. She'd been debating whether or not to try to take the next call, if and when one came in, when her attention was caught by the caller's strange voice. It was oddly muffled. Angie couldn't tell if the caller was a man or a woman.

"I didn't catch your name," Henry said.

"Pat."

Angie's eyebrows rose. A neuter-sounding Pat? What was this, a *Saturday Night Live* routine?

"Well, Pat, what can I do for you?"

"I was concerned about the restaurant killer in your city."

Henry's eye caught Angie's. "Thank you. I'm sure the police will capture the person responsible in no time."

"I'm glad you think so, because—you're next."

Henry jumped up and slapped the disconnect button. "And now," he said, his voice quivering, "a word from our sponsor."

Angie Amalfi's latest job, developing the menu for a new inn, sounds enticing—especially since it means spending a week in scenic northern California with her homicide-detective boyfriend. But once she arrives at the soon-to-be-opened Hill Haven Inn, she's not so sure anymore. In COOKING UP TROUBLE, *the added ingredients of an ominous threat, a missing person, and a woman making eyes at her man, leave Angie convinced that the only recipe in this inn's kitchen is one for disaster.*

She placed her hand over his large strong one, scarcely able to believe that they were here, in this strange yet lovely room, alone. "But I am real, Paavo."

"Are you?" He bent to kiss her lightly, his eyes intent, his hand moving from her chin to the back of her head to intertwine with the curls of her hair. The mystical aura of the room, the patter of the rain, the solitude of the setting stole over him and made him think of things he didn't want to ponder—things like being together with Angie forever, like never being alone again. He tried to mentally break the spell. He needed time—cold, logical time. "There's no way a woman like you should be in my life," he said finally. "Sometimes I think you can't be any more real than the Sempler ghosts. That I'll close my eyes and you'll disappear. Or that I'm just imagining you."

"Inspector," she said, returning his kiss with one that seared, "there's no way you could imagine me."

Cold logic melted in the midst of her fire, and all his careful resolve went with it. His heart filled, and the solemnity of his expression broke. "I know," he said softly, "and that's the best part."

As his lips met hers, a bolt of lightning lit their room for just a moment. Then a scream filled the darkness.

Food columnist Angie Amalfi has it all. But in COOKING MOST DEADLY, *while she's wondering if it's time to cut the wedding cake with her boyfriend, Paavo, he becomes obsessed with a grisly homicide that has claimed two female victims.*

"You've got to keep City Hall out of this case. As far as the press knows, she was a typist. Nothing more. Mumble when you say where she worked." Lieutenant Hollins got up from behind his desk, walked around to the front of it, and leaned against the edge. Paavo and Yosh sat facing him. They'd just completed briefing him on the Tiffany Rogers investigation. Hollins made it a point not to get involved in his men's investigations unless political heat was turned on. In this case, the heat was on high.

"Her friends and coworkers are at City Hall, and there's a good chance the guy she's been seeing is there as well," Paavo said.

"It's our only lead, Chief," Yosh added. "So far, the CSI unit can't even find a suspicious fingerprint to lift. The crime scene is clean as a whistle. She always met her boyfriend away from her apartment. We aren't sure where yet. We've got a few leads we're still checking."

"So you've got nothing except for a dead woman lying in her own blood on the floor of her own living room!" Hollins added.

In COOK'S NIGHT OUT, *Angie has decided to make her culinary name by creating the perfect chocolate confection:* angelinas. *Donating her delicious rejects to a local mission, Angie soon finds that the mission harbors more than the needy, and to save not only her life, but Paavo's as well, she's going to have to discover the truth faster than you can beat egg whites to a peak.*

Angelina Amalfi flung open the window over the kitchen sink. After two days of cooking with chocolate, the mouthwatering, luscious, inviting smell of it made her sick.

That was the price one must pay, she supposed, to become a famous chocolatier.

She found an old fan in the closet, put it on the kitchen table, and turned the dial to high. The comforting aroma of home cooking wafting out from a kitchen was one thing, but the smell of Willy Wonka's chocolate factory was quite another.

She'd been trying out intricate, elegant recipes for chocolate candies, searching for the perfect confection on which to build a business to call her own. Her kitchen was filled with truffles, nut bouchées, exotic fudges, and butter creams.

So far, she'd divulged her business plans only to Paavo, the man for whom she had plans of a very different nature. She was going to have to let someone

345

else know soon, though, or she wouldn't have any room left in the kitchen to cook. She didn't want to start eating the calorie-oozing, waistline-expanding chocolates out of sheer enjoyment—her taste tests were another thing altogether and totally justifiable, she reasoned—and throwing the chocolates away had to be sinful.

Angie Amalfi's long-awaited vacation with her detective boyfriend has all the ingredients of a romantic getaway—a sail to Acapulco aboard a freighter, no crowds, no Homicide Department worries, and a red bikini. But in COOKS OVERBOARD, *it isn't long before Angie's* Love Boat *fantasies are headed for stormy seas—the cook tries to jump off the ship, Paavo is acting mighty strange, and someone's added murder to the menu . . .*

Paavo became aware, in a semi-asleep state, that the storm was much worse than anyone had expected it would be. The best thing to do was to try to sleep through it, to ignore the roar of the sea, the banging of rain against the windows, the almost human cry of the wind through the ship.

He reached out to Angie. She wasn't there. She must have gotten up to use the bathroom. Maybe her getting up was what had awakened him. He rolled over to go back to sleep.

When he awoke again, the sun was peeking over the horizon. He turned over to check on Angie, but she still wasn't beside him. Was she up already? That wasn't like her. He remembered a terrible storm last night. He sat up, suddenly wide awake. Where was Angie?

Angie Amalfi has a way with food and people, but her newest business idea is turning out to be shakier than a fruit-filled gelatin mold. In A COOK IN TIME, her first—and only—clients for "Fantasy Dinners" are none other than a group of UFO chasers and government conspiracy fanatics. But when it seems that the group has a hidden agenda greater than anything on the X-Files, Angie's determined to find out the truth before it takes her out of this world—for good.

The nude body was that of a male Caucasian, early forties or so, about 5'10", 160 pounds. The skin was an opaque white. Lips, nose, and ears had been removed, and the entire area from approximately the pubis to the sigmoid colon had been cored out, leaving a clean, bloodless cavity. No postmortem lividity appeared on the part of the body pressed against the ground. The whole thing had a tidy, almost surreal appearance. No blood spattered the area. No blood was anywhere; apparently, not even in the victim. A gutted, empty shell.

The man's hair was neatly razor-cut; his hands were free of calluses or stains, the skin soft, the nails manicured; his toenails were short and square-cut, and his feet without bunions or other effects of ill-fitting shoes. In short, all signs of a comfortable life. Until now.

Between her latest "sure-fire" foray into the food industry—video restaurant reviews—and her concern over Paavo's depressed state, Angie's plate is full to overflowing. Paavo has never come to terms with the fact that his mother abandoned him when he was four, leaving behind only a mysterious present. But when the token disappears in TO CATCH A COOK, Angie discovers a lethal goulash of intrigue, betrayal, and mayhem that may spell disaster for her and Paavo.

The bedroom had also been torn apart and the mattress slashed. This was far, far more frightening than what had happened to her own apartment. There was anger here, perhaps hatred.

"What is going on?" she cried. "Why would anyone destroy your things?"

"It looks like a search, followed by frustration."

As she wandered through the little house, she realized he was right. It wasn't random destruction as she had first thought, but where the search of her apartment had appeared slow and meticulous, here it was hurried and frenzied.

"Hercules!" he called. "Herc? Come on, boy, are you all right?"

For once Angie's newest culinary venture, "Comical Cakes," seems to be a roaring success! But in BELL, COOK, AND CANDLE, *there's nothing funny about her boyfriend Paavo's latest case—a series of baffling murders that may be rooted in satanic ritual. And it gets harder to focus on pastry alone when strange "accidents" and desecrations to her baked creations begin occurring with frightening regularity—leaving Angie to wonder whether she may end up as devil's food of a different kind.*

Angie was beside herself. She'd been called to go to a house to discuss baking cakes for a party of twenty, and yet no one was there when she arrived. This was the second time that had happened to her. Was someone playing tricks, or were people really so careless as to make appointments and then not keep them?

She really didn't have time for this. But at least she was getting smart. She'd brought a cake with her that had to be delivered to a horse's birthday party not far from her appointment. She never thought she'd be baking cakes for a horse, but Heidi was being boarded some forty miles outside the city, and the owner visited her on weekends only. That was why the owner wanted a Comical Cake of the mare.

Angie couldn't imagine eating something that looked

like a beloved pet or animal. She was meeting real ding-a-lings in this line of work.

Still muttering to herself about the thoughtlessness of the public, she got into her new car. A vaguely familiar yet disquieting smell hit her. A stain smeared the bottom of the cake box. She peered closer. The smell was stronger, and the bottom of the box was wet.

She opened the driver's side door, ready to jump out of the car as her hand slowly reached for the box top. Thoughts of flies and toads pounded her. What now?

She flipped back the lid and shrank away from it.

Nothing moved. Nothing jumped out.

Poor Heidi was now a bright-red color, but it wasn't frosting. The familiar smell was blood, and it had been poured on her cake. Shifting the box, she saw that it had seeped through onto the leather seat and was dripping to the floor mat.

*In IF COOKS COULD KILL, Angie Amalfi's culinary
adventures always seem to fall flat, so now she's decided to cook up something different: love. But her
earnest attempts at matchmaking don't go so well—
her friend Connie is stood up by a no-show jock. Now
Connie's fallen for a tarnished loner, and soon finds
herself in the middle of a murder investigation, thanks
to her association with her new crush. Angie's determined to find the real killer, but when the trail leads
her into the kitchen of her favorite restaurant, she
fears she's about to discover a family recipe that
dishes out disaster . . . and murder!*

"Here's some salad and bread, Miss Connie," Earl said. "I don't t'ink you need to
starve just 'cause some jerk-off is late
showin' up for your date."

"Thanks, Earl," she murmured. "But right now, I'm
not even hungry." Okay, it was a lie, but she was too
humiliated to eat.

"It's on da house." He left a green salad with Roque-
fort dressing, Connie's favorite, and walked away. The
aroma of the French bread wafted up to her. She
touched it. Warm. Firm crust. Soft center. Perfect for
spreading butter which, unfortunately, was loaded with
empty, straight-to-the-hips calories . . .

She checked her watch again. 7:30. Why bother with
a guy who couldn't tell time? She kicked off her shoes

and took a big bite of buttered, crusty bread. Heaven!

Just then, like magic, the restaurant's front door opened and a man alone entered. Connie's breath caught, causing her to nearly choke on the bread. She swallowed it in a scarcely chewed lump.

It quickly became obvious that the man who walked in was no football player.

Angie hates to leave the side of her hunky fiancé, Paavo, but in TWO COOKS A-KILLING, she gets an offer she can't refuse. She'll be preparing the banquet for her favorite soap opera's reunion special, on the estate where the show was originally filmed! But when a corpse turns up in the mansion's cellar, and Angie starts snooping around to investigate a past on-set death, she discovers that real-life events may be even more theatrical than the soap's on-screen drama.

Now the cast was being reassembled for a ten-year reunion show, a Christmas reunion, and she, Angelina Rosaria Maria Amalfi, had been asked to be a part of it.

A major part, if she said so herself. She was so anxious to get to Eagle Crest, it was all she could do to stick to the speed limit.

Her father had phoned the day before. He'd gotten a call from his old friend Dr. Waterfield: the woman who was to prepare the important centerpiece meal of the show had broken her leg. Dr. Waterfield wanted to know if Angie could handle it.

Could she ever!

Against her instinct, Angie agrees to let her control-freak mother plan her engagement party—she's just too busy to do it herself. And in COURTING DISASTER, Angie's even more swamped when murder enters the picture. Now she must follow the trail of a mysterious pregnant kitchen helper at a nearby Greek eatery—a woman who her friendly neighbor Stan is infatuated with. And when a second murder enters the picture, and Angie gets a little too close to the action, it looks like Angie's poor fiancé Paavo may end up celebrating solo, after the untimely d.o.a. of his hapless fiancée!

Stan headed for the water, enjoying the dark, chilled air that so well matched his mood. A number of boats were moored, all rocking slightly from the tide. His peaceful solitude was broken, however, by the sound of raised but muffled voices.

His waiter berated a woman who sat on a rough-hewn, backless wooden bench at the water's edge. His face was hard, his expression intense, and she was shaking her head, not looking at him, but staring out at the water as if it hurt to hear his words. Her feet were propped up on a railroad tie. A hooded rain parka, the cheap kind that was basically a sheet of heavy green plastic worn by slipping it over the head, covered her hair. The way she sat scrunched on the bench, the parka draped her body like a tent.

The waiter bent close, grabbed her shoulder, and said something straight into her face. She turned her head away from him and the hood slipped down. The waiter then straightened and strode away. She reached out her hand toward him, but he didn't turn back. She raised her chin, apparently struggling to hold her emotions in check.

PERENNIAL DARK ALLEY

Men from Boys: A short story collection featuring some of the true masters of crime fiction, including Dennis Lehane, Lawrence Block, and Michael Connelly.
0-06-076285-3

Fender Benders: From **Bill Fitzhugh** comes the story of three people planning on making a "killing" on Nashville's music row.
0-06-081523-X

Cross Dressing: It'll take nothing short of a miracle to get Dan Steele, counterfeit cleric, out of a sinfully funny jam in this wickedly good tale from **Bill Fitzhugh.**
0-06-081524-8

The Fix: Debut crime novelist **Anthony Lee** tells the story of a young gangster who finds himself caught between honor and necessity.
0-06-059534-5

The Pearl Diver: From **Sujata Massey**, antiques dealer and sometime sleuth Rei Shimura travels to Washington D.C. in search of her missing cousin.
0-06-059790-9

The Blood Price: In this novel by **Jonathan Evans**, international trekker Paul Wood must navigate through the world of international people smugglers.
0-06-078236-6

The Reunion: A group of extremely disfunctional teenagers in a psychiatric hospital are forced to reconnect when two of them die unexpectedly in this thriller by **Sue Walker**.
0-06-083265-7

PERENNIAL
DARK
ALLEY
An Imprint of HarperCollins*Publishers*
www.harpercollins.com

Visit www.AuthorTracker.com for exclusive information on you favorite HarperCollins authors.

DKA 1105